DRAGON RAIN

VONNIE WINSLOW CRIST

MOCHA MEMOIRS PRESS

Rock Hill, SC

ISBN: 978-1-7371320-1-1

Copyright© 2021 Vonnie Winslow Crist

Cover Art by Maya Presiler

Editor: Alexandra Christian

Proofreader: Rie Sheridan Rose/Nicole Givens Kurtz

Publisher: Mocha Memoirs Press

"Weathermaker" ©2010 Vonnie Winslow Crist. *Dragon's Lure.*

"Beneath the Cherry Blossoms" ©2020 Vonnie Winslow Crist. *Castles and Kimono.*

"Princess Rina's Execution Day" ©2020 Vonnie Winslow Crist. *Witches, Warriors, and Wyverns.*

"The Hearth Dragon" ©2019 Vonnie Winslow Crist. *Coffins & Dragons.*

"Dragonflies" ©2021 Vonnie Winslow Crist.

"Motherhood" ©2019 Vonnie Winslow Crist. *Curse of the Gods: A Greek Myth Anthology.*

"Balancing the Scales" ©2019 Vonnie Winslow Crist. *Samhain Secrets.*

"Riches" ©2020 Vonnie Winslow Crist. *Villains.*

"Wolfbane" ©2019 Vonnie Winslow Crist. *FrostFire Worlds.*

"Kindness" ©2019 Vonnie Winslow Crist. *Of Kami & Yokai: A Japanese Myth Anthology.*

"Bloodguiltless" ©2019 Vonnie Winslow Crist. *Outpost of Beyond.*

"Bayou" ©2021 Vonnie Winslow Crist. *Arcane.*

"Dragonskin" ©2020 Vonnie Winslow Crist. *Faerie.*

PRAISE FOR DRAGON RAIN AND VONNIE WINSLOW CRIST

"A delightful set of dragon tales that kept me reading right through to the end! " – Debbie Mumford, bestselling author of *Sorcha's Children series, The White Dragon and the Red* and other books

"Vonnie Winslow Crist is a chameleon of a writer—as a reader, you never know where her tales will take you—yet there's always one thing you can count on: top-notch storytelling." – Richard Chizmar, *New York Times* bestselling author of *Gwendy's Button Box Trilogy, The Girl on the Porch,* and other books

"Immerse yourself in *Dragon Rain,* eighteen enchanting fantasy stories penned by a master weaver of magical tales. Vonnie Winslow Crists's imagination gives new life to dragon legends from across the breadth and history of our world, and of others. Shape-shifting, telepathic fire-breathers, her mystic serpentine creatures teach lessons, reward kindness, and punish cruelty. Here also be wyverns, wyrms, drakes, and water dragons, so beware. You might well be swept away by *Dragon Rain.*" – Steven R. Southard, dragon enthusiast and author of *What Man Hath Wrought* series

"An enchanting collection of stories, sure to please every dracophile." – G. Scott Huggins, award-winning author of *Responsibility of the Crown, All Things Huge and Hideous,* and other books

BOOKS BY VONNIE WINSLOW CRIST

The Chronicles of Lifthrasir

The Enchanted Dagger

Beyond the Sheercliffs

Novelette

Murder on Marawa Prime

Story Collections

Dragon Rain

Beneath Raven's Wing

Owl Light

The Greener Forest

Children's

Leprechaun Cake & Other Tales

Poetry Collections River of Stars

River of Stars

Essential Fables

OTHER MOCHA MEMOIRS FANTASY TITLES

The Soul Cages by Nicole Givens Kurtz

Forest of Bones by Crymsyn Hart

Hollow Men by Todd Sullivan

Mutiny on the Moonbeam by Rie Sheridan Rose

Fantastic Fittings by C. M. Ries

Kill Three Birds by Nicole Givens Kurtz

For Ernie, Tim & Dawn, Phil & Kristin,
Nathaniel & Gabriel, Melissa & Aria,
and
all those who believe in dragons.

"If you are out
on a bring-the-dog-in night
when even the moon
has hidden her face
and dragon's breath
billows over the land—

take a few steps
into the blinding smoke
and reach out—
you might stroke slick scales;
stare—
you might see flashing eyes.

But don't step, don't reach, don't look,
unless you want to believe
in dragons."
—Vonnie Winslow Crist, *River of Stars*

TABLE OF CONTENTS

WEATHERMAKER

May glanced over her shoulder at the closed door. She tipped her head in the direction of the heat vent and listened for the muffled sound of her parents' voices. She smiled. They were still downstairs in the kitchen. Confident she wouldn't be bothered, May stretched out on her stomach and squirmed under Papa Chang's bed.

The space under the box-spring was only about twelve inches high, so May was thankful her ancestors had been slender and small-boned. Even at age twenty, she was still able to easily fit under the bed. She clicked on a small flashlight and stuck it between her teeth, which freed her hands to search for the loose floorboard. She slid her palms along the dusty oak floor and crawled toward the head of the bed. May sneezed twice, dropping the light both times.

Frustrated, she took the flashlight out of her mouth and shined it on the floor.

"Where are you?" she muttered as she ran a fingernail along the joint where one piece of flooring abutted another. She sighed. There was no hint of a secret compartment. She ran a fingernail around a second board. Nothing. She sneezed again. The flashlight dimmed slightly.

"I know you're..." Before May could finish her sentence, she felt the third floorboard from the wall lift slightly as her fingernails traced its edge.

"Yes!" May pried the board up, reached inside the small wooden compartment attached to the side of a support beam. She didn't know if Papa Chang had built the secret box above the first-floor ceiling and below his bedroom's floorboards, but as a child she'd seen him tuck a book, swaddled in red fabric, into it several times.

"Why do you hide the book?" May had inquired the first time she'd caught her grandfather concealing the silk-wrapped bundle.

"Because it's magical," Papa Chang had answered with a wink.

"Can I read it, too?" she'd begged.

"Not yet." Papa Chang had patted her head. "It's written in Chinese, though I've made some notes in English. When it's your turn to take care of the dragon, then you may read it."

"But I help you, now," she'd reminded her grandfather.

"Yes, but that's not the same. When I'm no longer able to honor Lung, then you must do so."

Papa Chang had taken her hands in his, looked into her dark eyes, and added, "No one else in this family believes except for you and me, so it is up to us. When I am gone, the book is yours."

Then, he'd stood up and brushed the dust from his knees. "But tell no one about the book. Not your mother or father. Not your brother. Not even your friends. Promise me."

"I promise," May had declared, and she'd kept her word.

"And I'll keep my word tonight," she told Papa Chang's spirit as she shimmied out from under the bed.

Six months had passed since her grandfather's heart attack,

six months had gone by since anyone had visited the dragon, and their county had been six months without a drop of rain. May worried her shirking of dragon-duty was responsible for the drought. But certain the solution could be found in Papa Chang's book. She sat cross-legged and undid the wrappings.

Her fingers tingled when they touched its dark leather binding. The leather was ridged in a diamond-like pattern and softer than she'd thought it would be. When she opened the cover, she saw that the volume was indeed written in Chinese. The characters were small and exquisitely rendered in black ink. As she flipped through the pages, she spotted her grandfather's notes. May hoped the words she needed were translated.

She leaned against a bed post, turned back to the beginning, and began scanning the pages one by one. When she located Papa Chang's translations, she read them. Often, her grandfather had begun to translate a section, then stopped mid-sentence as if whatever he'd been looking for wasn't there. And much of what was in English seemed mundane. But every now and again there'd be something interesting: "Deaf dragons are *kiao-lung*. Dragons who can hear are *kioh-lung*." or "Dragons are fond of roasted swallows."

She'd leafed through nearly half of the book when she finally found what she was searching for: "Supplications and Deals with Dragons." The fourth translated supplication was the one she needed. May marked the page with a couple of loose red threads from the silk cloth, then stuck the book and flashlight into her waiting backpack.

After sneaking out of Papa Chang's old bedroom, May jogged down the stairs and strolled into the kitchen. Her father was reading the paper at the table and her mother was putting the finishing touches on a casserole for the next night's dinner. May went to the refrigerator, took out the milk, and poured a quart of the cold liquid into a glass jar.

Her father lowered the paper. "It's been months since your grandfather wasted milk on his imaginary dragon. Why are you bothering to go down to the pond tonight?"

"I promised I would."

"Well, you've certainly taken your time getting..."

"Shen," May's mother said in her doctor-in-charge voice. "I don't think there's any harm in May wasting a little milk once a month." She rubbed her forehead, then continued in a more normal tone. "If nothing else, the stray cats will appreciate it."

"Thanks, Mom."

May glanced at her mother. She noted Mom's lips were pressed tightly together. She supposed Mom missed her father, too, though neither of her parents had talked much about Papa Chang since the week after the funeral.

Her grandfather's ashes had barely been spread on the surface of Willow's Watch Pond when life for the rest of the family had returned to normal. Her brother had flown back to New York to continue his residency at one of the city's biggest hospitals. Dad had resumed teaching Anatomy and Physiology at the University. And Mom continued to work extra hours at the hospital whenever she got the chance.

I miss Papa Chang more than anyone else does, May thought as she stepped out the back door and hiked toward the pond. She hurried across the lawn. The night was full of lightning bugs blinking all around her and cicadas singing in the trees. They reminded May of the insects Papa Chang had taught her to paint.

May felt a tightening in her chest as she remembered their painting ritual. First, they'd pick a spot to paint. When the weather was agreeable, it was Willow's Watch Pond, and when it was cold or rainy, their home's glassed-in porch. Once they had set up their drawing-boards, her grandfather would drop some water on an inkstone, then grind an inkstick against the stone using a smooth circular motion. Before long, the ink would be ready. They'd each spread a piece of *xuan*, grass, or Moon Palace paper on the board in front of them and pick up their wolf-hair brushes. Of course, some days they'd use goat-hair brushes for leaves and petals.

"Balance your brush like this," her grandfather would say while holding his bamboo-handled brush between his second finger and his ring finger. "Steady it with your thumb."

Under Papa Chang's tutelage, May had learned the seven shades and five colors of black ink. She'd grown adept at varying the pressure and speed of her strokes. She'd also learned to use Chinese watercolors instead of Western varieties, because they amalgamated better with the paper. It wasn't long until her compositions and understanding of design caught the attention of her teachers. Enough so, in fact, she'd earned a scholarship to study art at a local college.

Her grandfather had been proud. Her father, mother, and brother had been horrified. Their family was a family of science.

Papa Chang had died before she could graduate from college, but May remained determined to become an artist. She'd focused on doing well in her classes, and the disapproving grunts and raised eyebrows of her parents weren't going to stop her from painting Siamese fighting fish, prawn, lotus blooms, bamboo, cranes, and dragons.

Dragons! May was so lost in thought she nearly missed the trail leading down to the small slate patio her grandfather had built near the edge of Willow's Watch Pond. As she stepped onto the proper path, she stumbled on a loose rock and nearly dropped the Mason jar of milk.

"Careful," she said to herself. It was a long hike to the house, and she didn't want to have to make it twice.

A few minutes later, May reached her grandfather's patio. She knelt, set down the jar of milk, and opened her knapsack. She took out a blue-chip enamelware bowl. It clinked as she placed it on the slate. She heard a splash from the pond. May chewed on her lower lip, scanned the watery green surface in front of her. There were dragonflies, water spiders, and the occasional venturous minnow visible, but no cow's ears or stag's horns.

She shrugged her shoulders. It had probably been nothing more than a frog spooked from its lily pad by her presence, though the dimming light made it difficult to see clearly for more than fifteen to twenty feet.

May picked up the quart jar of milk. Her hand shook ever so slightly as she unscrewed the metal lid, tipped the jar, and slowly poured the cool, white liquid into the enamelware vessel. She tried to forget vengeful mythical beasts and focus instead on filling the bowl. Though the milk sloshed back and forth and splashed a bit as the last drops dribbled in, none washed over the sides onto the slate. She exhaled slowly. Spilt milk showed disrespect.

May swallowed hard. Milk was only the first step in luring a dragon. She grabbed the slumped over knapsack she'd lugged down to the pond, rifled through its contents, and removed a stick of incense, an incense burner carved from a pinkish stone into the shape of a reclining dragon, and a book of matches. She lit the incense and set it beside the milk bowl.

The selection of the incense had been difficult. She'd never paid attention to which scent Papa Chang had used. When May had searched through her grandfather's wooden storage chest this afternoon, she'd found several kinds: cinnamon, sandalwood, patchouli, and ylang ylang. She'd decided on sandalwood.

"Lung," May called. "I ask for your help." She blew the thin line of drifting smoke in the direction of the water. "Lung," she repeated. "There's a drought, the plants are dying, and the earth turns to dust."

This was a bit of an exaggeration. Still, most of the county's farmers were filing for government aid. It was all over the news.

Their crops had failed or were so meager they could barely feed their own livestock. There was little surplus corn, oats, and hay to sell to dairy farms, stables, or homeowners who kept a grazing animal or two.

At the Big & Small Veterinary Clinic where she worked every afternoon after class, there'd been an increase in the clients who wanted to find new homes for their ponies and goats. When asked why, most responded that they couldn't afford to keep the pet any longer. There'd even been a client who'd posted a note on the clinic's bulletin board that read, "New owner needed for Mitzi, a tame and very lovable llama."

"Lung," she called for the third time. "Your pond has a spring, but many lakes, streams, ponds, and rivers are drying up."

If there was a dragon in Willow's Watch Pond, Lung was not its full name. But Lung was all May could remember. Papa Chang had known the full names of all kinds of dragons; May did not. She did recollect that all the dragon names her grandfather had used contained *Lung*.

A loud splash came from the shallows to her left. With her flashlight, she surveyed the shoreline and water surface. She spotted some cattails across the pond swaying, heard loud rustling from that direction, and then, the light reflected off of a pair of eyes.

"Jeeze!" she exclaimed, and immediately dropped the light. As she fumbled in the dark to retrieve it, May realized the glowing eyes still peered at her from between the cattails. Even without her hand-held light, they shimmered an orangish-gold— just the color she imagined a demon's eyes would be.

The clouds chose that moment to set free the full moon. Across Willow's Watch Pond, a dark head on a snakish neck lifted out of the water. The head resembled a camel's, the ears looked like those of a cow, the horns were like the branched antlers of a stag, and the gleaming eyes were surely those of a demon.

The creature swam nearer.

May sat motionless as the beast lifted one front leg and then the other from the water. When it partially crawled onto the slate patio, she heard clicking. She glanced down and saw four giant eagle claws on each foot. The creature was big, but not enormous. She guessed the part of its body she could see weighed five or six times as much as a full-grown horse.

"I have come," it stated in a voice like the cello section of a symphonic orchestra. In fact, though it moved its mouth, May wasn't certain the voice issued from the animal's throat. How could it? Nothing so beautifully musical could come from vocal chords alone. Surely, its melodious thoughts came directly from the creature's brain to hers.

May tried to speak but found she could not.

"You have called. I have appeared, Chang Yao's granddaughter."

The dragon—for that is what May knew it must be—tilted his head. As he did so, his profuse beard fell slightly to one side, and she could see the luminous sheen of a large pearl wedged between the skin folds beneath the dragon's chin.

Ah, she thought. *The dragon is most certainly male.*

"Lung?" she began in a voice barely above a whisper.

"It is not my name, but it will do."

"I would gladly call you by your name if I knew it," offered May.

The dragon snorted like a quick trumpet blast. "For now, I choose not to give you the power of my name. Lung will do. Of course," the dragon scratched a brow ridge with one of his claws. "When we know each other better, I might give you a different name to call me."

May lowered her eyes. "As you wish."

"You speak of a drought," Lung began. He ran his claws through his beard, and as he did so, May saw the soles of his feet were like those of a tiger. "This is something I can solve."

"Really?"

Lung lifted his brows.

"I mean, thank you." May didn't want to appear doubtful, but this all seemed too easy. Papa Chang had always preached: *If it seems too easy, there's a catch. If it seems too good to be true, it is!*

"But let us visit a while," Lung urged as he dipped one claw into the enamelware bowl and swirled the milk around. "I know you from your many journeys to the pond with your grandfather. I have even swum near you and your brother as you played in the pond."

May gasped. "That was you." She often recalled feeling something brush past her when she and Jimmy played tag or Marco Polo. She'd told her brother it felt like a small carp or even a water snake was rubbing against her skin. He'd laughed at her. Sometimes, she'd been caught off-guard by the touch of scales, and she'd screamed. Then, Jimmy had not only laughed, but teased her in front of his friends. As she'd gotten older, May had blamed the strange sensations on water plants and an over-active imagination.

"You frightened me. You made me the punchline of my brother's jokes."

The dragon's lips pulled back, and his teeth shown in the moonlight. May hoped he was smiling.

"But you were never in danger of drowning while in my pond. I would have transported you safely to shore had you ever had a problem swimming. And," Lung continued, "I would have even saved Jimmy and his rambunctious friends, if need be. Though in olden times..." The dragon seemed to reconsider. "But that doesn't matter nowadays."

"What about the olden times?"

Lung raised his right paw, tiger-pads up, and made a slight gesture. "The world was different then. A drowning victim seemed a suitable offering for a dragon's favors."

"What!"

"You know as well as I, sacrifices were made thousands of years ago to all sorts of creatures. Dragons were only one of them."

"Thousands of years ago? Just how old are you, Lung?"

"Ah, now there's a question. I was what appeared to be a rock on the seashore for a thousand years. One day, it was my time, and the rock split. But I was nothing but a small blue snake."

The dragon paused, stirred the milk again, then licked his dripping claw. "Mmm," he said in a hum of violas.

"Wait, I've brought you some other things to eat." May searched through her knapsack and found the two containers of yogurt and four low-fat skim milk mozzarella cheese sticks she'd grabbed at the last minute from the refrigerator.

"Here they are," she said and looked at the dragon. "Aah!" She managed to squelch a scream. Lung's face was inches from hers.

"Hmm," Lung remarked in a voice like an oboe as he watched her pull the foil cover from the yogurt containers. "I'd hoped for roasted swallows."

"I think you'll like this better." May held the yogurt out to the dragon.

Rather than take the proffered containers, Lung grinned, then licked the vanilla-flavored milk product from the plastic cups while May held them. Several times, his long, forked tongue swept across her skin. When it did, she shivered.

"First, you were a blue snake. What next?" May asked as she set aside the yogurt cups and struggled to tear the plastic off of the first cheese stick.

Lung lowered his eyelids slightly. "I squirmed between

pebbles to the ocean's salty waters, and by the end of five hundred years, I had the head of a carp."

"I can't imagine you with a fish head." May offered the first mozzarella stick to Lung. "It seems so..."

"Un-dragonly?" Lung skewered the cheese and brought it to his mouth. "Then, you wouldn't have liked my appearance for the next millennium as I grew into a fishy dragon." He finished chewing the cheese and licked his lips. "That really is quite good," he commented as he impaled the second cheese stick.

"But not as good as swallows."

Lung chuckled, and May thought of bass fiddles being plucked. "Close, Chang Yao's granddaughter. Close."

The dragon stuck out his front paw. May slid a cheese stick onto two of his claws. As she did, she felt his leathery paw-pads rub against her wrists. They felt warmer than the scaly skin on the upper part of his paws. She cleared her throat.

"From fishy you went to..."

"Anguine," replied the dragon as he finished off the cheese.

"Anguine?"

"A snake-like dragon. My face and tail elongated, my legs and beard grew. After another five hundred years, my horns sprouted. And now, the nubs of wings have appeared on my back."

"When you grow them, you'll be able to fly?"

The dragon laughed. It was a metallic sound—harsh, though not all together unpleasant. It reminded May of cymbals and pipes.

"I can fly now, even without wings."

"Then, why do you need wings?"

"I don't," answered Lung. "They're just part of the next stage of dragonhood." Lung's eyelids lowered again. "But we are not here to discuss the stages of dragonhood. We're here to discuss a lack of precipitation."

"Yes." May took a deep breath, brought her hands up in front of her, pressed her palms together, and bowed her head. Then, she withdrew her grandfather's book from the knapsack, opened it to the page marked by the silk threads.

By moonlight, she read Papa Chang's translation. "I call upon the benevolent nature of dragons. I remind you that your kind are the ancient ancestors of humankind. I revere you and your kind as tireless protectors of the earth and ask for your skills as Weathermaker to bring rain to this land."

In the silence that followed, May never took her eyes off of the dragon's face. Lung looked at the book, her face, the pearly moon, then back at the book. At last, the dragon spoke. "Did you show your grandfather's book to anyone else?"

There was something in Lung's tone that made May's heart pound. "The book was hidden in his room. He said it was to be mine after his..." The word caught on her tongue like a hair. "After his death." A sense of relief washed over May. She'd admitted out loud that Papa Chang was dead. "I've shown it to no one. It's in Chinese, but there are a few English translations. The Weathermaker Supplication was one of those."

The dragon extended his paw. She placed her grandfather's book in it. The faded brown book cover looked even older, dingier when held in Lung's beautiful azure paw. He rubbed a claw back and forth across its leather cover.

"It's covered with dragonskin," explained Lung. "The dragon was young—to her murderer she'd have appeared to be a snake. Still, the book is covered with dragonskin."

"I'm so sorry. I didn't know."

"No, you couldn't have known. This book was written before your grandfather's grandfather's grandfather was born. And its cover was crafted from dragonskin a half a world away." Lung sighed.

To May is sounded like the plaintive notes of a single violin. She wrinkled her nose at the faint scent of sulfur.

May reached out, touched Lung's front leg above the paw. "Did you know this dragon?"

Lung nodded. "She emerged from her rocky egg the same day as I." He caressed the book's cover again. "She swam in the salty waters with me and the other hatchlings."

"Lung, I didn't mean to upset you. I just..."

"I am not upset," the dragon responded in a mournful cello voice. "When the murderous fisherman tasted her dragonflesh, he realized his terrible mistake. Magically, his mind was sharper than a tiger's tooth. He could read and write, recite poetry, play music with ease, and understand the world around him, but he was ashamed of having slain a dragon."

May wiped away the tears that trickled from the corners of her eyes. She reached out, stroked the dragon's neck.

Lung made a rumbling sound like distant timpani, and then, he continued. "The dragonslayer did his best to honor his victim with poems, music, incantations, and solemn rituals. He authored a book that contained these things, covered it with the dragon's skin, and passed it secretly on to a grandchild. Thus, it has been for generations. That long-ago Chang swore that one member of his family would honor dragons until the end of time."

"Chang!" May frowned. "So my ancestor was the dragonslayer, and that's why Papa Chang faithfully came to the pond." She nodded. It all made sense to her. "I wish he'd told me. I didn't understand..."

"Just like you don't understand what the rest of the page from which you quoted says, since your grandfather wisely stopped translating whenever he thought the text was dangerous." Lung raised his muzzle so his demon eyes stared directly into her eyes. "But it matters not Chang Yao's granddaughter, you have begun the Weathermaker ritual, and I, a dragon of the Olden Lands, accept your offer."

"My offer?" The frown-lines between May's eyebrows deepened. "I don't know what you're talking about."

Lung smiled his dragonish smile. Though this time, May thought it looked more like a leer. And with greater speed and agility then she thought a creature his size could muster, Lung climbed up onto the patio, stood on his hind legs, and shape-shifted into a man.

She opened her mouth to shriek, but Lung pressed two fingers to her lips, and May found herself unable to utter a sound.

"It is in man form that I must answer your request," explained the dragon. "And it is in man form I will tell you what you could not read for yourself in this book, and what Chang Yao dared not translate."

Lung, now dressed in a Mandarin-collared white shirt and ultramarine pants and jacket, raised slightly the hand that held Papa Chang's old tome. "But you must agree not to scream."

May nodded, and Lung removed his fingers from her lips, though her skin tingled where he'd touched her. And it occurred to her, as the dragon continued to speak, that even in human-form, his voice retained its allure and musicality.

"I have waited alone in oceans, in rivers, in other ponds for this night. Beneath countless full moons I have been lured by incense, milk, roasted swallows, and lotus blooms. Those who summoned me asked for riches, long life, good health, strong children, and such. But you, May Chang, are the first to quote from the sacred dragon book the bride's words."

"Bride's words?" May's voice trembled. *What have I done?* she thought.

Lung slid the book into the pocket of his blue jacket. "The Weathermaker ritual concludes with the mating of two dragons in the clouds. The rain that follows is the blessing of their lovemaking."

"But I didn't know..."

"It doesn't matter. You are an adult. You began the ritual. I accepted your offer. Now, if you are willing to become my wife, we must both drink from the bridal bowl of milk." Lung raised the enamelware bowl to his lips, drank about half of its contents, and then, held the bowl to May's mouth.

As she parted her lips to ask the details of her supposed transformation, the dragon-man poured some of the milk into her mouth. She had a choice—spit out the liquid and refuse his proposal or allow it to trickle down her throat. May chose to swallow the milk. She felt light-headed and weak-kneed. Lung grasped her shoulders and looked deep into her eyes.

"You have summoned me with milk and incense by full moon's glow all your life. Did you never feel my presence as you lured me closer?"

May closed her eyes. The pond had been her favorite place in the world whether Papa Chang had been there or not. Sometimes, just for fun, she'd brought milk to the pond and left it next to the water's edge in an old pie tin. She opened her eyes, felt a rising breeze send her waist-length hair fluttering behind her like silken wings.

"Be my partner for a thousand years, maybe ten thousand for all we know. I have watched you, loved you since the first time Chang Yao carried you down to the pond. You and I can bring rain to this place, then sail to a bigger lake or river or even the deepest ocean."

"But my family will wonder what's become of me." May was certain they'd miss her, though her parents and brother would eventually return to their normal lives. Papa Chang had been an old man. It would be harder for them to lose a daughter and sister.

"And I'd miss them."

"You can speak with them in dreams and watch them from

below the surface of the water."

As she felt Lung's warm breath on her cheek, May recalled the dragon of *her* dreams. He'd thanked her for the milk and given her hints on how to paint better. Her dream dragon had instructed her to set aside the yellow grass paper and creamy xuan paper. Use only the pure white Moon Palace sheets, he'd told her in a voice as euphonious as a waterfall. It would seem, in the land of dreams, Lung had conversed with her for years.

With great effort, May stated, "But I am no dragon." It seemed to take an enormous amount of energy to speak. She was so tired her bones ached.

"And if you were?"

"I suppose if I were a dragon..." May continued to gaze into his demon eyes. She felt a terrible longing. This *was* her match. None of the boys at school, at college, at work, anywhere—none of them were for her. "I suppose if I were a dragon," she repeated, "I'd choose you for my mate."

"Done," responded Lung before he pressed his lips to hers, pulled her close, and swifter than lightning transformed back into dragon-shape.

May felt her face elongate, her ears grow, and her little fingers and ring fingers merge. Wrapped in Lung's embrace, she felt his tail twine with hers and his smooth-as-a-clam-shell belly rub against her own. Though her demon eyes were locked in a lovers' gaze with Lung's, she saw in her peripheral vision the clouds all around them.

"Stay with me, beloved," murmured Lung in her ear. "Let me give you my true name."

May exhaled a plume of smoke and smiled a dragonish smile as the wind curled around their joined forms. She saw the moon over her beloved's shoulder hide its face, giving them privacy for the final moments of their lovemaking.

And then, it rained.

BENEATH THE CHERRY BLOSSOMS

Hisa wished for love as she stood beneath a spread of Somei Yoshino cherry blossoms. The wisp of a late April breeze which sent pink petals sailing to the grass, paths, and red bridge arching over the blossom-covered water, also fluttered her ebony hair. Transient as youth, Hisa knew the delicately-scented blooms would be gone in a few days, though she supposed the weeping cherries nearer the castle would be in bloom a little longer. She breathed deeply. Such a subtle smell and fleeting loveliness must be savored while it was here. Once the crowd had thinned, Hisa strolled onto the brightly painted bridge which arched over Hirodaki Castle's moat. One of only twelve remaining castles from the Edo Period, Hirodaki's keep and grounds were a popular tourist and blossom-viewing site.

Pale hands gripping the railing, she surveyed a small flotilla of blue, white, and yellow rental boats passing under her. Some contained a single rower; others featured a pair of boaters. She closed her eyes and wished someone would invite her to share a rowboat.

As she walked back to land, Hisa studied the many *hanami* party-goers laughing and greeting each other. She wished someone would ask her to join one. But that was never the case. She lived alone. Worked alone. Slept alone.

Making herself appear smaller than she was by hunching her shoulders, Hisa eased past couples strolling hand-in-hand down the pathway. Careful not to step on the roots of an especially gnarled tree overhanging the moat, she knelt at the water's edge. As she knelt, seven tears fell from her eyes into the cool water.

Abruptly, the water parted, and a black, orange, and golden-scaled snout lifted from its surface. Had she not been so shocked, Hisa would've stood and scrambled away from the creature. Instead, she stayed as still as the castle while the beast reached one three-toed paw out and placed it on her knee.

Why do you cry? she heard in her head.

Hisa gazed into the flaming eyes of what she knew in her heart to be a dragon. "I long for love and companionship," she managed to say.

Hmm, replied the dragon while raising his eye ridge slightly and lifting his neck.

Though the moat was shaded, and cherry blossoms blanketed large swaths of the surface, the dragon's movement allowed Hisa to see he was large, serpentine, and wingless.

You have offered me your tears, began the water deity, *so I will bless you with wisdom and good fortune in all things—including love. But there is a price for my blessing.*

"What must I do to receive such a gift?" Hisa's pulse fluttered like a fritillary looking for nectar.

Return each April, said the dragon, *and make payment of seven heartfelt tears. Also today, I require a kiss to seal the bargain.*

"I promise," whispered Hisa, leaning closer to the dragon and placing her lips on his.

The water deity ran his claws gently through her hair. Then as

suddenly as he'd appeared, the dragon of Hirosaki Castle
vanished beneath the water.

"Careful!" called a man's voice from behind Hisa. "Leaning
over the water like that, you're going to fall in."

Hisa felt a hand firmly grasp her upper arm and pull her back
from the moat. When she turned to look at the man who
thought he was saving her, she gasped—for his was the face she
saw in her dreams every night.

"Sorry, I didn't mean to scare you," said the man, smiling
shyly. "Though saving her from drowning is an interesting way
to meet a pretty girl."

Hisa laughed. "I wasn't drowning. I wasn't even in the water."

The man tilted his head. "Well, not yet, but you never know.
By the way, I'm Kioshi, and you would be?"

"Hisa," she responded.

And as more than two-thousand-six-hundred cherry trees and
a submerged water deity watched, Kioshi took Hisa's hand,
helped her up the bank, then said, "I'm here alone. Any chance
you want to walk with me? Maybe share a rowboat?"

"I'd love to," Hisa replied as she gazed into his kind, brown
eyes.

In her thoughts, she thanked the dragon. Then, while still
holding Kioshi's hand, Hisa silently renewed her promise to visit
Hirosaki Castle each year for as long as she lived to shed seven
tears.

PRINCESS RINA'S EXECUTION DAY

"**I**f it had not been for the dragon, I would be queen of one of Lenatnahi's neighbors by now. Though *Her Royal Highness* of which realm, I am uncertain," said the princess.

The man in the black hood nodded.

"Ouch! Please, Honorable Executioner, do not tie the bindings so tightly around my wrists. I swear, I have no intention of running off."

The man took pity on his prisoner. He loosened the rope wrapped around the princess's arms—slightly.

"Ah, much better. Thank you for your kindness. While we wait, I'll tell you how I came to be on these gallows today."

After yawning, the executioner nodded and leaned against a wooden pillar.

"My father, Uniford the Magnificent, was negotiating with three countries at the time of my sacrifice. My hand in marriage was part of the deal between Lenatnahi and her chosen ally. Security and economics were the deciding factors in the negotiations, not my preference of husbands. In truth, none of the candidates were to my liking—a toothless old goat, a child, and a calculating widower whose previous wives had all met untimely, and I might add, suspicious ends. So you might say, the dragon was my best choice."

Not wanting to wait until the last minute to get things in order, the executioner bent down and picked up a bundle of heavy rope.

"Wait!" cried the young woman. "You need not put the noose around my neck yet. There is still time for that when the crowd has fully arrived."

He paused, then dropped the rope.

"In any case, the dragon, a golden-scaled beast with a taste for prized bulls and rams, first appeared on the Feast of Saint Marinus. Do you celebrate the Marinus Feast with rum cakes and small candies shaped like ships, and of course, the tossing of fish?"

The hooded man shook his head.

"A pity. The traditional festivities and menu remain a central part of the Feast of Saint Marinus in Lenatnahi's coastal cities—which is where the first dragon attacks occurred. But I digress. The enormous reptile arrived in Port Brigela with a nor'easter at his back. The storm howled, ice pellets tapped against windowpanes like the finger bones of dead pirates, and a fog settled over Port Brigela like a shroud."

The corners of the executioner's mouth turned down.

"No, no, nothing personal in the shroud reference. It is just part of the story."

Once she had assured him that no mockery was intended, the man seemed to relax.

"Where was I? Oh, yes. The city's population huddled in their homes hoping the dragon would move on without delay. Unfortunately for them, the beast needed sustenance, and so he visited one livestock yard after another consuming grazing animals until sating his hunger. When the dragon had filled his belly with Port Brigela's finest cattle, sheep, and goats, he lifted into the air with a dozen flaps of his mighty wings. As a farewell gesture, with a few blasts of his fiery breath, he set seventeen docked ships ablaze."

"Fire seems a terrible way to go," mumbled the executioner.

"Yes, you are quite right. I do prefer hanging to being burned at the stake. I suspect it is less torturous to have one's neck quickly snapped."

"True," he responded, then added, "so keep telling your tale."

"Of course, I will continue. I am pleased you are enjoying my tale of the events of these past few weeks—which leads me to the couriers arriving at all hours of the day and night carrying urgent messages from the coast. According to the stack of reports presented to my father, the dragon had ravaged six seaside cities before turning inland. His behavior remained the same: consumption of grazing animals followed by incineration of buildings, ships, wagons, whatever. After consulting with the court magician, astronomer, astrologer, and various other purported sage men, Uniford the Magnificent determined that I, a virgin of royal blood, must be sacrificed to the creature to appease his anger. Though in case I proved unacceptable to the dragon, Father rounded up fifty virgins as back-up offerings."

"Maybe he just wanted food, not a maiden," suggested the hooded man who'd become Princess Rina's audience of one.

"I agree! You would think they'd realize the creature was hungry, not angry. You, Honorable Executioner, are a wiser man than all of my father's councilors combined. But time is not my friend, so let me continue. Father had me brought before him on the raised dais of Adjudication Square."

"There?" asked the executioner as he pointed in front of them.

"Yes, right across the pave stones from these gallows. Dressed in a simple gown of white silk, I stood before not only his advisers and members of court, but all the citizens of Lenatnahi's capital city of Pearial who had gathered to witness my father's judgment. By the way, were you here that day?"

"No." The man cracked his knuckles while he listened to the story.

"No? It's a pity—with its billowy sleeves and gathered waist, my gown was really quite stunning. And, in this vast forum, my father praised my purity and devotion to duty. Then, without an ounce of compassion, he proclaimed me a sacred payment to the dragon—a sacrifice *he* willingly made for the good of the people of Lenatnahi."

The man shook his head and grunted.

"Can you believe it? *His* sacrifice!" Princess Rina sighed, then resumed speaking, "Upon my mother's conveniently-timed passing, when I was but eleven years of age, he turned my education and care over to nursemaids, ladies-in-waiting, tutors, and such. He saw me only once or twice a year on ceremonial occasions. I say *conveniently-timed passing*, because legendary beauty, Treacheena of the Hollows, was at that point of a marriageable age."

"Did you go to the wedding?" asked the executioner.

"Oh, yes. I *was* invited to Father's marriage to Queen Treacheena, mother of my half-brother, Artimus, Uniford the Magnificent's heir apparent. Did I mention Treacheena is only three years my senior?"

The black-hooded man shook his head.

"But let us return to the story. Before I could protest or make clear *who* was actually making the sacrifice, Father had me bound and taken to a remote cliff two hours' ride from Pearial. Once there, his soldiers chained me to a metal ring attached to a stone column whose circumference eclipsed fourteen feet and whose height was at least that of our castle walls. The column formed one corner of a temple of ancient construction, surely used in the past for sacrifices to werebeasts, ogres, creatures from bottomless caves, and the other monstrosities of our legends."

"Would you like me to get you a hood so you don't have to see the crowd staring at you while you die?" asked the executioner in a kind voice.

"No, thank you. I prefer not to wear a hood during the hanging. I want to observe the crowd until the last second, and I want my countrymen and countrywomen to remember my face. But enough of execution details, let me set the scene at the temple for you before the crowd grows too rambunctious."

"Continue," agreed the executioner.

"Five fire pits surrounded my column. The soldiers who took me to the temple, built, then lit, a towering bonfire in each pit. And though some among the rank and file glanced at me with shame in their eyes—none had the courage to question their orders. Certain of my fate, the soldiers left me so bound, and began their march back to Pearial. Therefore, no one remained to witness the dragon's arrival save me."

"Amazing you're still alive," said the executioner.

"I agree. It *is* amazing that I am here to share this story but let me tell you of the dragon. I heard the creature speaking in my mind before I saw him flying like a golden bird in the sea-blue sky."

"Speaking!" exclaimed the man.

"Yes, I said *speaking*! I was as shocked as you to hear his voice —a voice filled with self-assurance and compassion. 'Do not fear,' he said. 'I have no intention of eating you. I am here to rescue you from Uniford the Magnificent and your dreary life.' And even though I knew his talk of rescue might be a lie—I could think of no reason for trickery. Attached to the column, I was an easy meal, certainly unable to defend myself or run away. So, why deceive me?"

The man rubbed his chin. "How did he know Uniford sired you?"

"I, too, wondered how he knew my father's name. Then, the creature explained things to me. It seems he was driven onto our shore by the aforementioned nor'easter. Famished, the dragon satisfied his hunger and took the time to survey Lenatnahi and her neighbors. Upon overhearing discussions at a local tavern of my impending betrothal to one king or the other, he decided it behooved him to offer himself as my husband for a generous dowry of gold, silver, and precious stones."

The executioner laughed. "Oh, to be a fly on the side of the tavern."

"I know, wouldn't that have been a sight—a dragon curled up beneath the trees eavesdropping on a bunch of men and women deep in their cups."

The executioner laughed again. "Sorry for the snorting," he said.

The princess smiled. "I don't mind that you snort when you laugh. It is a far more natural display of laughter than the false twitterings of the men at court. But now, back to the story. You and I both know how fond dragons are of treasure—fond enough to become allies with Lenatnahi through marriage in order to acquire a considerable amount of it. And think of the advantages of such an alliance? Which of our enemies would be willing to attack Lenatnahi if they believed a formation of dragons could suddenly appear on the horizon? But again my thoughts wander."

The man bent down, picked up the thicker rope, but didn't loop it around the princess's neck.

"Using his claws with a speed and dexterity that belied their great size, the creature released me from my bindings. After sharing his name with me along with the exact amount of treasure required for a deal to be struck between his homeland, Longwei, and Lenatnahi, we spent the rest of the day and that night together discussing many things. The next morning, he allowed me to climb upon his back and flew me to within ten minutes walking time of the front gates of Pearial. Whereupon, I strolled into the city, up to the gates of the palace, and was escorted to Father's throne room. After telling Uniford the Magnificent the story I have shared with you, I was promptly called a traitor and liar who desired to save my own skin by condemning Lenatnahi to destruction by dragonfire. Though I begged my father to accept the dragon's offer, he and the court only laughed at me. Then, did my father condemn me to hang. Which is why, I stand before you now, Honorable Executioner."

"That's not really my name," said the man dressed in dark clothing.

"Of course I know that is not your true name—but what name would you have me call you before you pull the lever and I dance upon air with a noose around my neck? Sir Death? Learned Hangman? No, I think Honorable Executioner is a good enough name."

"It's time for the rope, princess," said the hooded man.

"I suppose you are right. It is time for the noose. Still, before the crowd noise and the shouts of the pie vendors drown out my voice, I would like to tell you the rest of the dragon's plan. Jinhai..."

"Jinhai?" repeated the executioner as he placed the noose around Princess Rina's neck.

"Yes, that is his name. Jinhai promised to rescue me again should my father not agree to his terms. Though, I suspect when the time is right, I will rescue myself. Which brings me to your family—are they here today?"

"No," answered the man.

"That is good," said the young woman. "I understand your

reluctance to have your offspring witness you at work. By the way, is it a family business?"

"Yes," said the man proudly. "There have been fifteen kinfolk before me who served the royals as executioner."

"Really? So you are the sixteenth in your family to be an executioner. I did not know it was such a legacy," said Princess Rina as she gave the man her most winning smile.

"I have had a longer conversation with you, Honorable Executioner, than most of my father's subjects. It is for that reason I hope you will be able to save yourself when Jinhai arrives. He is sure to be in a foul mood when he sees how his future wife and queen of Longwei is being treated and might in the ensuing pandemonium roast my supposed executioner."

"What about you?" The man took a small step back.

"Oh, not to worry. His aim is excellent, so I will be unharmed. And as I have explained, he is quite able to release my bindings."

"Then, I had better duck beneath the gallows if I see a dragon on the horizon," said the executioner with a half-smile.

"It would be wise," responded the princess. "With the gallows platform being constructed of stone, I think seeking shelter under it should prevent your untimely roasting. And I do not judge you, Honorable Executioner. I understand your situation. Don't we *all* wish to see our grandchildren."

The man took another small step back. "I do want to see my grandchildren." Then, he cocked his head. "Wait—you and the dragon can have a family?"

"You *are* quick-minded. Children and grandchildren do bring up an interesting question. One, I might add, which I asked of Jinhai. He assured me dragons can assume human shape when necessary. It is how they often woo their life-partners."

"Life-partners?" The man took another step back.

"Yes, life-partners. Dragons mate for life."

"For life?" Again, the executioner increased the distance between himself and the princess.

"I know. Who would have thought dragons remained faithful to one partner? Of course, it *is* a tit-for-tat situation. Once mated with a dragon, a human can assume dragon shape. It is much more convenient that way."

"Did you join with Jinhai?" asked the man in a voice tinged with fear.

"Why, Honorable Executioner, what an impertinent question! A princess does not share such details. Though it would be beneficial—extra claws to carry treasure, if you get my meaning," said Princess Rina as she lifted her chin for the rope to set more comfortably.

"Ah, I see Father and his entourage have arrived. And he has left Treacheena and Artimus behind. Splendid. Though you will note he's dragged the fifty virgins, chained together in pairs, along. Can you see Jinhai to the west, just over Screeling's Forest? He *is* magnificent."

The executioner hurried forward and lifted the rope from Princess Rina's slender neck.

"How kind of you to remove the noose."

"Let me free your hands as well," said the man in a shaky voice.

"You wish to unbind my hands, also? You *are* a gentleman, Honorable Executioner. I will remember this thoughtfulness when my husband arrives, and I assume my place at his side as his equal."

"Husband?" queried the hooded man as once again he stepped away from the princess.

"Why, yes. We said our vows and consummated our marriage at the old temple. It seems a priest is not a necessity at a dragon's wedding."

"Then, you can become a dragon at will," stated the executioner.

"I intend to transform upon Jinhai's arrival," explained the princess. "As you will soon see, my scales are not golden like my husband's—instead they are burnished copper with just a hint of teal."

"That sounds beautiful," said the executioner.

"Agreed. Quite a lovely coloration for a queen."

"Between your husband's arrival and your change, won't people be terrified? There are sure to be casualties," observed the man in the black hood.

"It saddens me to admit you *are* correct. There *will* be many injured spectators. Scattering in a panic at the arrival of a dragon, much less witnessing a second dragon suddenly appear, likely won't end well for a crowd."

The executioner pointed at the royal party and quipped, "Your father looks horrified at the sight of the dragon."

"Agreed. The expression on Uniford the Magnificent's face is priceless. I will remember it with pleasure as Prince Jinhai and I carry the bags of treasure across the ocean to Longwei. But in truth, I will think little of my father during the many centuries of my life."

"Centuries!" exclaimed the executioner.

"Oh, yes! It is a boon of assuming dragon shape. I could live a thousand years or more."

"While your father will be lucky to live out the day." The man laughed.

"Ah, your snorting laughter is rather endearing. I shall miss you," said the princess as her eye color changed to red and her skin took on a distinctive copper tint.

"You are changing," stated the executioner as he backed to the edge of the platform.

"Yes," answered the princess. "*Now* would be a good time to test the fireproof nature of this stone gallows. Fare thee well, Honorable Executioner. May you be blessed with years of good times with your children and grandchildren. And please check into the traditions of the Feast of Saint Marinus. I think your family would find them most delightful. Especially the tossing of fish."

Just prior to ducking under the gallows platform, the executioner shouted, "Princess, may you and your king also be blessed with many children and grandchildren."

"Why, thank you. I *do* intend to lay, hatch, then enjoy many clutches of wyrmlings and rule for a thousand years. But for now, I must grow scales, fangs, a tail, and wings, and join Jinhai in securing our treasure. And, of course, with great happiness and not a small amount of sarcasm, I shall instruct my foolish father to set free the virgins, *if* I let him live!" said Princess Rina as she continued to transform.

Moments later, when Princess Rina's claws and belly scales scraped against stone, the executioner peeked once more over the edge of the platform. An enormous copper dragon with just a hint of teal on the edges of her scales grinned at him.

"Time for a chat with the king," said the dragon who was Princess Rina, now Queen Rina of Longwei. She winked a scarlet eye, roared, spewed forth a massive fountain of fire, then lifted into the air with several flaps of her beautiful wings.

Quickly, the executioner crept below the platform, closed his eyes, covered his ears, and prayed he didn't feel dragonfire.

THE HEARTH DRAGON

When Luca Rannell entered the metal smith's work
area, Dolph Skarsgard barely looked up from his
anvil. "Sorry to hear about your grandfather's
death," Skarsgard said before he returned to hammering an
iron bar.

"Thank you," shouted Luca over the clamor. He cleared his
throat to hide the grief threatening to spill out in a tearful
episode. Poppi had died less than two weeks before. The wound
was still raw.

"At least, you had a casket at the ready," added the burly man
before plunging the red-hot metal hanger he had been shaping
into a barrel of water. The water hissed and bubbled.

Luca nodded. It went without saying Rannell's Cabinet and
Casket Makers would have a fine wooden coffin available for the
head of the business. The Rannell family had excelled in the
making of wooden chests, cabinets, coffins, tables, and storage
benches for more than eighty years. Now, the weight of
completing items for current contracts and soliciting new orders
fell to Luca—a heavy responsibility for an eighteen-year-old.

The smithy faced Luca, wiped his hands on the already dirty cloth apron he wore, reached out a meaty hand, and grabbed the young carpenter by the upper arm. "Now that you are in charge of the business," said Skarsgard, "you need to know how things work here."

Before he could protest, Luca found himself propelled down a narrow hallway and into a stone-walled room. A room which contained a chained dragon.

For a few seconds, Luca couldn't speak. He'd heard of dragons, even seen drawings of them, but he'd never expected to meet one. Even chained, the creature filled him with wonder. Attempting to slow his racing pulse, he took a deep breath. Luca regretted it immediately.

He covered his nose with one hand, while wiping away tears with the other. Between coughs, he managed to ask, "What *is* that smell?"

"It's the dragon, boy," laughed Skarsgard. "The foul beast produces the fire I use for my metal-shaping." He kicked the side of the dragon for emphasis.

The dragon flinched, but its restraints didn't allow the beast to move away from the smithy's boot. Luca thought he heard it groan.

"Feeding whatever scraps the bakers, butchers, and tavern cooks don't want to the animal is cheaper than hiring someone to go to the forest, cut down trees, chop the wood into manageable pieces, and drag the firewood into town. Plus, I save on hiring a boy to pump the bellows and clean out the ashes."

"But look at the dragon," said Luca as he saw the obviously underfed beast anchored in place by not only manacles around each leg, but by a heavy chain harness stretching from tail to neck. Saddened by the appearance of a magical animal from childhood tales, he felt certain if the huge creature's scales were scrubbed clean, it would be a beautiful blue-green.

Still surprised to be so close to a legendary creature, Luca coughed again. A quick glance told him the horrible stench burning his nose and throat did indeed emanate from the dragon. Unable to relieve itself elsewhere, the beast stood in its own filth.

"It's nothing but an animal. It has no feelings," replied the metal smith with another kick to the dragon's side. "Come on, let's go back up to my work hearth. You can tell me why you are here."

Certain he heard the dragon moan this time, Luca asked, "May I touch the dragon?" as he surveyed the condition of the animal.

There was little doubt the dragon had been cruelly treated since the beginning of its service to the metal smith. He could see the snug iron collar bolted around its neck had left nasty-looking scars. He imagined there were sores on its feet and belly from the excrement. Likely, there were raw places where the chains rubbed against its skin.

"Do as you like," Skarsgard called over his shoulder as he strode back up the passage to his hammer, anvil, and dragon fire forge.

"I am sorry," whispered Luca as he placed a palm against the dragon's side. He felt the creature's ribs protruding. "I know he's not feeding you enough food either, is he, boy?"

No, came the response in Luca's mind.

Luca gasped. He studied the side of the dragon's face. Beneath a prominent eye ridge, the animal stared at him with a faintly glowing, golden eye. "Do you talk to the smithy, too?" he inquired.

No, you are the first person since I was chained in place to hear me.

Luca frowned. His grandfather must have known about the dragon and had done nothing to help the beast. "How long have you been here?"

Thirty-two years—though it seems much longer, replied the creature, in what sounded, in Luca's mind, like a forlorn voice. *But I do not have the heart to last another thirty-two years—even if Skarsgard feeds me more food.*

"This is wrong," said Luca. Unsure what he could do about the situation, he knew he must do something. He realized his father must have known about the dragon, too, and frowned as he considered his family's complicity in the dragon's servitude.

"If you were freed, could you even fly anymore?" he inquired as he studied the dragon's leathery wings. A drab green in color, they were held close to its back by the chain harness.

I do not know, came the reply. *No one has ever offered to free me. Therefore, I have not given it much thought.*

Knowing he was walking on thin ice, the cabinetmaker said, "Think about it." He patted the dragon's side once more before turning and hurrying back to the smithy's workshop.

After purchasing the hinges, locks, handles, screws, and other metal items he needed to complete all the ordered pieces of cabinetry, Luca walked back to Rannell's Cabinet and Casket Makers.

While finishing the ordered chests and cabinets, he thought about the smithy's dragon. As surely as if they'd forged the restraining chains, the Rannell family had contributed to the animal's plight. He suspected much of the town knew about Skarsgard's treatment of the hearth dragon but chose not to speak up. Therefore, all of Comas bore responsibility for the abuse of the animal.

Haunted by the look in the dragon's eye, Luca couldn't sleep that night. *Dragons belong to the skies, seas, and forests,* he thought in the stillness of night. *But I cannot free the beast and keep my customers.*

Come dawn, Luca decided to hike to town, purchase a few more pieces of hardware he needed for woodworking projects, and again visit the dragon.

When he strolled into the smithy, Luca heard laughing and shouting below the shop area. *The dragon,* he thought. Following the laughter, he hurried to the animal's prison.

Once in the dragon's room, he saw Skarsgard and two of his friends holding wilted cabbages just out of the creature's reach. Luca spotted tears in the animal's eyes as he strained against his collar in a vain attempt to secure a mouthful of food.

"Stop!" he shouted.

The three men turned and look at him.

"Don't tease the dragon. He's starving. Please, give him the cabbages."

Dolph narrowed his eyes.

For a second, Luca feared the metal-worker would confront him, or worse.

"Pity the poor dragon, boy?" asked Skarsgard. "Then, you can feed it." The metal smith dropped the cabbage he held.

His friends followed suit. The three exited the room and strolled up the passageway.

Luca heard them laughing and joking about the dragon as he gathered the cabbages from where they had fallen. He did his best to clean away dirt and excrement before holding the wilted vegetables close to the beast's mouth.

Thank you, thought the hearth dragon. *I'm not sure they intended to actually give me the cabbages.*

"I cannot allow your situation to continue," said Luca as he fed a second head of cabbage to the animal.

I am not sure you have a choice, responded the creature as he ate the last cabbage.

"We always have a choice." Luca gently rubbed the dragon's neck. "Do not despair. I will return."

After walking up to the hearth area of the smithy, Luca selected several pieces of hardware, and paid Dolph.

"Thanks, dragon-lover," sneered the metal smith. "Did you feed the stinker for me?"

Luca nodded, turned, and left the building as the men laughed.

As he walked homeward, he began to formulate an escape plan for the dragon. Though he should have time to depart Comas before the people of the town realized he was the culprit who had released the beast, Luca decided not to take a chance that he would have to face an angry Dolph Skarsgard and his friends. He'd leave Comas with the dragon. But he knew he needed an ally for all to go well.

Since most of his grandfather's friends had predeceased Poppi, and Luca's parents had died when he was a toddler, the pool of trustworthy friends was small. He remembered Poppi had always told him, "If ever you need help in an emergency, go to Vida Zsigmond—but do not linger. Though he is a valuable customer and longtime friend, I do not agree with his lifestyle."

Luca had never given much thought to Vida Zsigmond's way of life, or anyone else's for that matter. Poppi and he had all they needed: food, home, work, and each other.

Now he *did* care about someone's lifestyle—the dragon's—and Luca was determined to change things for the better for the long-suffering animal.

With the dragon's well-being, not his own, in mind, Luca passed Rannell's Cabinet and Casket Makers and hiked the lonely road to Vida Zsigmond's stone home. Perched at the pinnacle of a steep incline, the rock structure jutted out from the hillside over the river below like the prow of a great ship.

The design of Vida's house lent itself to defense. In order to reach the front door, a person had to cross a narrow stone bridge over a frightfully deep ravine. Next, they walked between two towers. Once before the door, a visitor quickly realized the slats on the tower walls on either side of them were for shooting arrows at an enemy. And if one looked up, they'd spot a hole in the ledge above for dumping boiling water, hot oil, rocks, or some other defensive item down on anyone standing before the door.

The first time Luca could remember visiting Vida, Poppi had pointed out the defensive nature of Zsigmond House to him.

"Vida values his privacy," his grandfather had said. "It is always best to honor such a request from someone who works so hard to keep others away."

Luca had nodded, but wondered why Vida chose such a lonely existence. It mattered little now—for the time for wondering was past when Vida Zsigmond opened the stout oak and metal door to his abode.

The tall man who stood in the doorway looked exactly as Luca remembered. Vida Zsigmond was dressed in a black waistcoat, dark green trousers, brown leather boots, and a white shirt and cravat. Ebony hair swept off his forehead, exposed exceptionally pale skin. He wore a large ring with a blood-red stone on the ring finger of his right hand. When Luca glanced at Vida's hands, he noticed the man's fingernails were neatly cut and clean. Vida appeared every bit the wealthy gentleman.

"Welcome, Luca Rannell," said the dark-eyed owner of Zsigmond House. "I see, like your grandfather, you still have not purchased your own horse."

"No." Luca laughed. "Poppi always said horses were too much trouble to care for. He swore it was easier to rent a horse and cart if necessary. Since most of our customers have their own wagons and draft animals, the need for our own horse and cart is small."

"I know," responded Vida. "I tried for years to convince him that even a pair of oxen and small wagon for hauling cabinets and coffins was worth the investment. He never listened." The man smiled, motioning for Luca to step inside. "Come in and tell me what brings you to my doorstep."

~

Doing his best to accurately describe the terrible conditions Skarsgard's dragon existed in, Luca finished his narrative with, "The dragon has lived like this for thirty-two years and it is wrong. I intend to free him, but I need your help."

Vida pressed his fingertips together, leaned back in his leather chair, asked, "Luca, did your Poppi ever tell you about me?"

"Not really. He just said you were a good customer and friend."

The man leaned forward. "The reason I live alone and guard my privacy is that I am a creature of darkness. I never leave Zsigmond House during the day—to do so would be the death of me."

Luca frowned. He had never seen Vida during the day. Usually, when Poppi finished something for him, Vida drove to Rannell's Cabinet and Casket Makers in his carriage drawn by fine black horses and picked up the item himself. It suddenly became clear to Luca the item was always a casket and Vida always came at night.

"Vampire!" he exclaimed. "You are a vampire." For a moment Luca was afraid, but he recalled Poppi's assurance that Vida would help him if he was in trouble. He knew his grandfather would never have sent him to Zsigmond House if it would put Luca in danger.

"Yes," Vida nodded his head, "but you have nothing to fear. I have lived as an undead for many centuries and can easily control my blood lust."

Involuntarily, Luca shivered. Even hearing the words *blood lust* frightened him.

"Your great-great-grandfather knew my secret and provided me with many coffins. Zsigmond House has a casket in almost every room disguised as a cupboard, wardrobe, cedar chest, the base of a dining table or bed support—and the list goes on."

Vida gestured toward the wall of bookshelves to his left, "Even a part of that bookshelf is a door to a small chamber where one of my coffins is hidden. For I need to sleep in a casket each day. I move room to room in case an enemy should try to break in and destroy my resting place. They'd never be able to demolish them all in one night and leave me without a coffin come daybreak."

In an attempt to moisten his dry mouth and throat, Luca swallowed several times. "How is it you are up now?"

"Even asleep, I can hear someone approaching. And certainly, a person beating on the front door would wake me." Vida Zsigmond smiled.

Luca stared for a second at the vampire's canine teeth. They were definitely more prominent than the cuspids of everyone else he knew—except for the village dogs. *Maybe asking for help from Vida is a bad idea,* he thought.

"Sorry I disturbed you," began Luca, "I am sure you have other things to worry about. I will figure out a way to free the dragon on my own." He stood up.

"Sit," ordered the master of Zsigmond House.

Luca obeyed.

"You came to me because you need my assistance. As thanks for the generations of service and silence on the part of the Rannell family of Rannell's Cabinet and Casket Makers, I will not only help you formulate a scheme for freeing the dragon, but I will participate in the gambit. In the meantime, Luca, you need to trust me. I will require one last casket. You'll need to construct it immediately if it is to be complete for the Midsummer's Eve celebrations. For we will need to use the drunken tomfoolery of the people of Comas to our advantage if we are to free the dragon."

A fternoon light streamed through the western windows as Luca awaited the arrival of the town of Comas's most prominent weaver. He looked around the shop. To an untrained eye, it appeared no different than it had for decades, but he knew it was an illusion. Most of Luca's carpentry tools were already packed and ready for transport to a new town. Once the weaver paid for and picked up his storage chests, all of Luca's work was complete, except for the last casket. For that he needed a final set of metal hinges, a latch, a set of handles, and screws.

"Luca," called the weaver as he pulled his ox-drawn wagon in front of Rannell's Cabinet and Casket Makers.

"Pista Kornel," replied Luca as he waved the man inside the woodworking shop. "I have your three chests ready. The moths will have a tough time finding their way into these." He slapped his palm against the polished wooden lid of one of the chests.

"Did you line them with cedar as I asked?" the weaver inquired.

"Yes," answered Luca. He lifted the lid of the nearest chest. "You can smell the cedar wood."

Pista Kornel leaned over the open chest, took a deep breath, and sighed. "The moths will stay away from any cloth stored in these."

He withdrew a sack of coins from his jacket pocket and handed it to Luca. "Your grandfather would be proud of how you've upheld his business commitments. I will not only give you business in the future, but I'll send others your way."

"Thank you. I'm glad you're satisfied with my work." Luca went to the door and propped it open with a block of wood. "Now let's get these chests loaded onto your wagon. You will be home filling them with cloth in no time."

"You're not going to count the money, first?" Pista Kornel scratched his cheek.

"No, sir. I trust you," said the carpenter. He noticed the wide smile on the weaver's face. Should things go wrong when he freed the dragon, he thought Pista would help protect him from Skarsgard's wrath.

After the chests were loaded, Luca asked the weaver for a ride to the metal worker's shop. "I need some hinges and such for a piece I'm working on," he explained, "and the journey would take me less time if I could sit on your wagon as you drive to town."

"Climb up here, lad," said Pista as he pounded the wooden driver's seat. "I would be happy to drive you into Comas. We can chat on the way."

~

When the weaver's ox-drawn wagon reached Skarsgard's metal shop, Pista Kornel pulled the oxen to a stop and dropped Luca off.

"Thank you for the lift, Pista," said the carpenter.

"You are welcome. Have a good day." The weaver tipped his head, smiled, snapped the reins, and the wagon rattled down the road.

Stick to the plan, Luca reminded himself as he strolled into Dolph Skarsgard's metalwork shop. He glanced at the forge and studied the hearth. Why had he never noticed the structure before? It didn't have the classic firepot. He should have realized years ago something was amiss. Before he could study the hearth's design more fully, the smithy walked in carrying several metal rods.

"Luca," said Skarsgard, "what brings you here?"

"I have need of a set of hardware for a large chest and a handful of screws." Luca had no intention of telling the smithy the metal pieces were for a casket. Later, after the dragon was gone, Skarsgard might remember today's purchases and go searching for who might have aided in the dragon's release.

"Find what you need in the bins in the back of the shop. Once you have what you're looking for, bring them here for me to price," said the smithy as he leaned the rods against the brick hearth's chimney.

Luca stood still.

"What is it, boy?" asked Skarsgard as he wiped his brow with his sleeve.

"May I go look at the dragon again?"

The metal smith snickered. "If you want to gape at that miserable excuse for a dragon again, be my guest. Just don't linger or you're sure to stink as bad as the beast."

"Thank you," said Luca. He gave the smithy a nod before hurrying to the hallway that led down to the dragon's holding room.

Determined not to choke at the stench of dragon waste, Luca covered his nose with his arm until the last second. Once in the room with the dragon, in order to avoid coughing, Luca breathed through his mouth. Though he knew the beast must be aware of its filthy appearance and gag-inducing smell, Luca did not want to embarrass the creature further by holding his nose.

"I'm back," said the carpenter as he gently rubbed the dragon's side.

I was not certain you would return, thought the dragon.

"I gave you my word," said Luca, "and now, I have a plan."

Just in case you were telling the truth, I have been lifting my wings as far as possible every few hours. Now, not only can I lift them hundreds of times about a foot high before tiring, but I can hold them away from my body for thirty minutes. Likewise, I have been moving my legs as much as possible. Though that is not far at all.

"Good work. But I must tell you our plan before Skarsgard wonders what I am doing down here."

"Our" plan?

"Yes, I have enlisted the help of Vida Zsigmond, a family friend, to help with your escape and my departure from Comas."

Your departure?

"Skarsgard will soon figure out it was me who freed you. After he's discovered my involvement, I won't be able to stay in Comas any longer."

Why are you risking your life and livelihood for me?

"I'm not sure," responded the carpenter as he gazed into the dragon's eye. "Maybe it's because I can hear the despair in your mind. Or maybe it is because my grandfather and father knew of your situation but did nothing, and I want to prove to you that not all humans are cruel."

Or maybe, mused the dragon, *you were born to free me and together we were meant to find a life somewhere else.*

Luca grinned. "If you are talking about adventure, I think I'm too ordinary for that."

I do not think you are ordinary at all, thought the dragon before Luca told him about the plot to gain him his freedom.

"I will see you tomorrow," said the carpenter as he patted the dragon one last time.

Luca ran up the hallway, riffled through the metal smith's hinges, latches, and whatnot bin, selected a set of hardware for a casket, grabbed several dozen screws, and paid Skarsgard the price he asked for the metal goods. After pocketing the payment, the smithy turned his attention to an elaborate, decorative gate he was working on. Concentrating on the creation of the gate with fire from the enslaved dragon, Skarsgard didn't even respond when Luca said goodbye.

To ease the building excitement as he thought about the scheme, Luca whistled all the way home.

$\sim$

A fter screwing all the metal pieces onto the casket, Luca placed the last of his tools, clothing, and other belongings into two practical, sturdy chests. There was no cedar lining or decorative carving on them, for he wanted the chests to be nondescript and easily forgotten—just like himself.

Once the dragon was discovered to be missing and the smithy pointed a finger at the carpenter's grandson as the thief, Luca wanted his forgettable nature to be part of the story. When the authorities started searching for Luca Rannell, the vaguer the description, the better.

He looked around the home he had shared with his parents and grandfather. Emptied of the personal items he valued, including the five books they owned, and the practical things he would need, the cottage felt like an empty cup waiting for someone to refill it. After last night's transaction, it was now owned by Vida Zsigmond. Luca expected a new family would either rent or purchase it shortly.

His musings were interrupted by the sound of Vida's carriage pulling up in front of Rannell's Cabinet and Casket Makers. He extinguished several candles in the cottage and walked into the woodworking shop. Vida stood there with a kindly expression on his face.

"Luca, I have already loaded your two chests and the new casket into the carriage," said the vampire. "Are you ready to head for Zsigmond House?"

"You should have waited. I could have helped you carry them," said the cabinetmaker before he remembered a vampire's unnatural strength would have made moving the chests a one-man job. *Man,* mused the carpenter, *I guess he is a man in appearance, though he is undead in reality.*

"No need," said Vida. "Though it is nice of you to offer." The vampire studied him, asked, "Would you like me to take down your family's sign? I can put it in a safe place in my home should you ever want it again."

"Yes," Luca managed to choke out. Losing Poppi, then his home, in so short a period of time felt like his world was collapsing—and in some ways, it was.

But I cannot save the dragon if I stay in Comas, he reminded himself. He brushed away tears with his fingertips as his grandfather's friend placed the Rannell's Cabinet and Casket Makers sign and its hanging brackets into the carriage. Lastly, Luca snuffed out the lone lit candle in the Rannell family's former workshop.

"Climb up here," urged Vida, "and let's set our plan into action."

~

When Vida and he arrived at Zsigmond House, they unhitched the horses and put them in their stalls with plenty of hay and water. Next, they unloaded the chests and casket and carried them through the house to a heavy door located in one of the dining room walls. The vampire used a large brass key to unlock the door before swinging it inward. A pushcart waited behind the door at the top of a downward-sloping stone passageway.

As cool air whooshed by him, Luca asked, "Where does this go?" Though he did not want to doubt his grandfather's friend, walking down into a dark cellar at night with a vampire gave him goosebumps.

Vida set ablaze a torch and used it to light several other torches attached with iron brackets to the walls of the passageway before turning to Luca. He explained, "This ramp winds down into the bowels of the earth. Below us there are several levels of comfortable living space," he paused, grinned, then continued, "comfortable living space for a creature of the dark. There are also dozens of storage rooms, a wine cellar, an open area with dry-docked boats of various sizes, and finally, a stone dock I use to launch my boats. And that, Luca, is how we will get you and the dragon quickly away from Comas."

It made sense to Luca. Less uneasy, he held onto one side of the pushcart's handle while Vida grasped the other as they descended into the hill. As they walked, the vampire lit torches. Luca soon lost count of the number of torches lining the passage's walls.

Vida talked the whole time they were descending, describing one level of his underground lair after another. Occasionally, the vampire would pause, open a door, hold his torch high, and illuminate a fabulous collection of treasure. It became evident long before they reached the boats that Vida Zsigmond was a hundred times wealthier than all the other people of Comas combined.

When they at long last arrived at the boats, Luca spied a flat barge and two boats dry-docked inside the hill large enough to accommodate the dragon.

"The barge offers little protection against the elements or from the prying eyes of people we pass," said the vampire. "I think one of the boats will be a better choice."

"I agree," responded the cabinetmaker.

"We need to get the boat out of storage, into the water, place my casket, your chests, and food and water for you and the dragon aboard. But you need to sleep. If you will guide me while I move the boat to the launch ramp, I can do the rest while you nap."

"I don't need to sleep. I can help you with..." began Luca.

The vampire placed a hand on his shoulder. "Do not fear. I control my hunger, not the other way around. I won't harm you. Soon, I shall have my fill. Grandson of my friend, return to the upper rooms, find a comfortable spot, cover yourself with a blanket, and sleep. Tomorrow will be a long day."

Though heavy curtains and stained glass blocked most of the daylight, when he finally awoke, Luca knew morning was nearly over. Yesterday had taken more out of him physically and emotionally than he had been willing to admit. Today would be harder yet.

"Good morning," said Vida. He yawned, pointed to a low table nearby. "Bread, cheese, and cider for your breakfast, plus a sack of food for today's lunch. Eat. You must be going. I would take you to Comas for the Midsummer's Eve Fair, but it is unwise for us to be seen together."

Between mouthfuls, Luca thanked the vampire for his help and the meals. After swallowing the last gulp of cider, he said, "I'll sneak into the dragon's room as soon as I can. There are nuts to be unscrewed from many bolts in order for me to remove the leg irons and other restraints which have been placed on him. The trick is for me to remain hidden and as quiet as possible. I don't want Skarsgard to suspect anything is awry if he is near his forge."

"Should you be caught..."

"I won't." Luca assured him.

"Yes. Well, should you be caught, you must find a way to

delay any punishment that Skarsgard or anyone else wants to inflict. As soon as it is dusk, I will depart Zsigmond House by horseback and travel to the smithy's shop. That is where I shall meet you and we can lead the dragon to the river from there."

"We will be waiting," said Luca as he strode to the front door and opened it, just enough to slip through, but not so much as to allow the late morning light to stream in. "Thank you again," he called before closing the door.

"You are welcome," replied Vida in a sleepy voice.

The Midsummer Eve's Fair was a wonder to behold. All of the town's craftspeople had assembled tables and booths to hawk their wares. Local eateries and taverns had constructed food and drink booths as well. Many of the local farmers had stalls filled with fresh produce. The brewers had kegs of mead, ale, and hard and sweet cider for the thirsty. The vineyards had wine and grapes for sale. Not to be outdone, the bakeries not only had stacks of bread, but sweet rolls and cakes available for purchase at their booths.

Traveling musicians, jugglers, dancers, acrobats, contortionists, and other entertainers had arrived in town the day before. A family of puppeteers had built a mini stage. The structure enclosed the puppeteers, while allowing the audience to view the performance of the hand puppets and marionettes. A play about a lazy husband and his angry wife was underway when Luca arrived.

In addition, various games of chance and skill had been set up by local organizations, like the Fisherman's Guild and the Loyal Order of Civilians for the Defense of Comas. Luca saw many of the town's boys and men trying their luck at the games. Later in the day, there would be strength competitions for anyone willing to toss a heavy stone or lift a pig, horse races, oxen pulls, and team tugs-of-war.

Luca casually wandered among the throng of fair-goers as he tried to locate Dolph Skarsgard. Finally, he spotted the smithy, mug of ale in his hand, bragging about how he was destined to win all of the strength competitions that day. Glancing at the blacksmith's size and muscular build, Luca thought he might be correct.

Since his bragging and muscle display had attracted not only his comrades, but nine or ten young women, Luca was fairly certain Skarsgard would be spending his day at the fair. With the smithy away from his hearth, Luca hurried as fast as he could move, without attracting attention, to the metal smith shop. He went around to the back and slipped in through a window he had unlocked the day before.

He'd barely set foot in the hallway, when the dragon mind-spoke to him.

You have kept your word again. Even if this escape fails, know I will always be grateful for your efforts.

"Grateful enough not to roast or eat me?" asked Luca as he entered the dragon's room.

Humans are not my food of preference, thought the dragon. *Even if they were, let me assure you—you will always be safe with me.*

"Nice to know." Luca patted the dragon's left thigh. "Let's begin with the leg irons," he said as he knelt in dragon waste and began to work on the bolt threaded through the metal strap that encircled the beast's foot and the nut that held it in place. Immediately, he discovered the years of waste had corroded the nut.

"I'll be right back," he told the dragon. "I need to get a pair of pliers and several rags to help me get a purchase on the nut and to hold the bolt in place."

The animal did not reply.

A few minutes later, Luca returned with two pairs of pliers from Skarsgard's metal-shaping tool rack, a stack of rags to wipe the excrement from the nuts and bolts, and a can of lard. After working on the left leg iron for fifteen or twenty minutes, he felt the nut give and turn.

"Yes!" he exclaimed as he managed to free one of the dragon's legs.

The beast groaned.

"Did I hurt you?"

No. It is the first time in decades I can stretch my leg and I am enjoying the mobility.

"Let's see if I can free even more of you." With that, Luca moved to the right rear leg iron.

How many hours had slipped by since he began his dragon release efforts, Luca didn't know. He had taken a short break to get a drink of water and to eat the bread and cheese Vida had wrapped in cloth and placed on the table this morning —though in truth, he ate little of the vittles. Rather, he gave most of the food to the dragon. When lunch was done, he'd immediately returned to the nuts and bolts.

The vampire thought of everything. Perhaps, mused Luca, *it is because he has lived so long.*

Who has lived so long? asked the dragon.

"I didn't know you could read my thoughts!" Luca considered everything he had contemplated while in the dragon's presence.

Of course. I thought you understood when I spoke to you in mind-speak, I could also hear your mind-speak.

"Thoughts, dragon, aren't mind-speak. They are meant to be private," he said. "By the way, do you have a name? I would like to call you something other than 'dragon'?"

Bartalan, thought the dragon. *I overheard your conversations with Skarsgard, so I know your name is Luca Rannell and that you are a woodworker. But who is this long-lived friend of yours?*

"His name is Vida Zsigmond. He lives outside of Comas in a stone house on top of a steep hill above the river. He is a..."

Vampire, thought the dragon. *Only the undead live as long as dragons. I have heard of this Vida Zsigmond. Many years ago, before I was wounded and captured, the Vampire Zsigmond resided more than a week's travel from this town in a remote castle not far from the cave in which I was hatched.*

Luca did not reply. Instead, he focused his efforts on freeing Bartalan. He tried to keep his mind as empty as possible, though it was difficult not to contemplate if Vida still owned the castle the dragon spoke of, and how many more residences the vampire had abandoned over the years. It made sense. After eighty years or so, people would become suspicious if Vida not only was alive, but still looked like a man of forty.

I am sure he moves from residence to residence every seventy or eighty years, thought the dragon in response to Luca's musings. *If he has two or three homes, it would be easy to hire caretakers for watching a home while Vida was living elsewhere. When he returned after seventy years, he could tell the residents of the surrounding area he was a nephew of the original owner and had inherited the house. Who would still be alive from his earlier occupancy to question the truth of his statements?*

"This mind-speak thing is going to take some getting used to," said Luca as he stood beside Bartalan, greasing the threads of one of the harness bolts.

Just remember, when we are near one another, I can hear everything you think, and you can hear everything I think. The dragon swung his tail back and forth several times for emphasis.

"I bet it feels good to be able to move a bit."

It feels better than you can imagine, responded Bartalan. *How many more bolts do you have to go before you can begin working on my collar?*

"One more after this one," answered the cabinetmaker. "There! This nut is finally able to be unscrewed."

Luca left the metal harness spread across the dragon's back as he went to work on the final bolt securing the enormous restraining device in place. Should the smithy show up, everything must appear as usual to prevent him from becoming suspicious. Likewise, to fool Skarsgard should he appear, Luca had left the unlocked cuffs encircling Bartalan's legs.

Perhaps because it had not been soaking in dragon waste, the final harness bolt was easy to remove. A few minutes later Luca began work on the dragon's collar.

Eight chains attached to the forge were also linked to the collar. As best as Luca could tell, Skarsgard released additional links to lengthen each of the chains when he allowed the dragon to lower his head and eat or drink. It appeared the smithy retracted the linkage and locked Bartalan's fiery mouth at the base of his forge every morning. Uncomfortable didn't begin to describe how the dragon must feel with his neck stretched spitting fire and heating metal day after day.

"Why didn't he leave your head free today, since he is not working the forge?" asked Luca as he tried to loosen the nut. It was screwed tightly onto one of the collar's bolts.

I think he enjoys tormenting me. There was no reason to chain me to the forge today. I could have drunk my fill of water even if there was nothing to eat.

"I am sorry I couldn't give you a drink when I arrived," said Luca as he grabbed the iron nut with one of the pliers and held the bolt's head with the other. "But until I can free your head, it is impossible for you to reach the water trough."

Do not worry. I have gone for days without food or water. It is nothing to be thirsty for a few more hours.

"That doesn't make me feel better, Bartalan. I could kill the smithy for how he has treated you," said Luca as he felt the nut he was working on turn slightly.

You must not kill him. You will already have a price on your head after we depart Comas. If there is a murder, the reward will be increased, and more people will be interested in finding you.

The cabinetmaker patted the dragon's neck. "I am not the killing kind. Dolph Skarsgard will meet his end at the hands of someone other than me."

Me?

"No, Bartalan. Then, the price on *your* head will be too high for fortune-seekers to resist. Escape, not revenge, must be our priority," said Luca as he pulled the bolt from one side of the collar. "Now, stay still and let's see if I can slip this off your head without having to free another bolt."

As luck would have it, Skarsgard walked into the metal work shop above them at that moment. And he was not alone. A chorus of voices indicated several of his friends had accompanied the metal smith.

"I left the dragon latched in place, just in case I needed to repair one of the items I have for sale at the Fair," said the smithy. "I need to loosen the chains, let him have a drink."

"You going to feed the stinking animal, too?" asked one of the men.

"Maybe later," replied Skarsgard. "I am hoping to collect some scraps from tonight's celebrating. It would save me some money that way."

Laughter ensued.

"You are one mean son of a..."

Whatever the smithy's friend meant to say next was lost as another friend burst in. "They are lighting the bonfires and preparing to announce the winners of today's contests. Come on!"

"You all go ahead. I'll be there in a few minutes," said

Skarsgard as he began to release the extra linkage, chain by chain, to the dragon's collar.

As the last chain was lengthened, Luca struggled to extricate Bartalan's head from the collar and tangle of chains. Even though he had worked with his hands all his life, he honestly did not know if his wrists had the strength remaining to undo another bolt.

"Hello, Dolph Skarsgard," said a deep voice.

"Vida!" whispered Luca.

"What can I do for you, Zsigmond?" asked the smithy. "The shop is closed, but for the right price, I can do a little metal-shaping."

"I'm not here for metal," said the vampire. "I'm here for a meal."

"There is plenty of food at the fairgrounds. We can go together," responded Skarsgard.

"You miss my meaning," said Vida. "What I eat is not offered at the Midsummer's Eve Fair, it is in front of me."

Briefly, sounds of a struggle came from above Luca and the dragon. Next, they heard the sound of a body falling to the floor and the thuds of feet kicking. The thuds slowed, then stopped.

Luca could only imagine what was taking place in the smithy's shop.

Do not think about it, urged Bartalan. *He was a cruel man who has met the end Fate decreed for him. Now, you need to pull the harness off my back, move the leg irons away, and get in the hall. I believe I can get out of the collar myself.*

Luca did as the dragon asked. Within minutes, Bartalan squeezed out of the entrance to the room where he had spent more than thirty-two years and into the hallway. Without being told to move, Luca ran up the hall and into the metal smith's work area as the dragon followed.

Vida Zsigmond, who was standing by Skarsgard's body,

looked at them when they entered the work area. "He was a big man, so I am now well-fed."

The vampire paused. His eyes scanned the condition of the animal in front of him. "But I cannot say that is true of you, dragon. Luckily, I've brought food for you both to eat before you head for the river."

Bartalan bowed his head before grabbing a mouthful of the half dozen sheep carcasses heaped on the floor.

Between bites of a roasted turkey leg, Luca said, "You got here in the nick of time. I think Skarsgard meant to come down to the cellar to give the dragon water."

"I've been here for over an hour," the vampire replied. "Had he not shown up, I was going to have to locate the smithy at the fair and ask him to come to his shop. You see, after hearing of his enslavement of the dragon, I decided Skarsgard would be my next meal."

No need to share details, mused the dragon.

I can't say that to Vida. He is our ally. And just like you and your heap of mutton, he has to eat.

You have a point. Bartalan lifted his bloody muzzle and winked at Luca.

Luca became aware of the vampire watching them.

"It appears you and the dragon were meant to find each other," observed Vida. "Though I personally have never interacted with dragons, I'd say your future with this one will be most interesting. But before we can mull over coming days, we need to get you both into the river and swimming upstream to the boat docked beneath Zsigmond House. Do you think you can find it, Luca?"

"Yes." Luca turned to the dragon. He watched him lick up the last entrails from the sheep before asking, "Can you swim against the current for twenty minutes or more?"

The scaly beast nodded his head.

"I will light the metal work shop on fire, starting with the smithy," said Vida. "You two exit the back door. Stay to the shadows and make your way to the river. There should be few if any dockworkers about. Anyone you see has already had their fill of ale and hard cider. If they spot you, they'll blame the sighting of a dragon on their drinks. Once the fire is noticed, no one will be paying attention to the river—thus, giving you the opportunity to slip into the water. Just remember to stay near the shore as you make your way to my home."

"What about you?" asked Luca.

"I will also leave from the rear of the building and join the festivities at the Midsummer's Eve Fair. A dance or two with a town beauty is a pleasant enough diversion. All will remember me being with everyone else at the bonfire. I won't be suspected of having anything to do with the unfortunate fire that killed poor Dolph Skarsgard and burned his smithy to the ground."

Trying to think of Dolph's death as a necessary act, Luca pushed open the blacksmith shop's door. He looked back at Vida before exiting. "See you in a few hours."

The vampire raised a hand in farewell.

Turning his attention to his and Bartalan's escape, Luca scanned the area behind the smithy. *No one is near. We can make it to the back of the mill.*

I am behind you, but remember, I need much more cover than you.

Luca nodded

Without incident, they crept from one shadowy place to another. Once, a dog spotted them. The hair running down the canine's spine spiked and it barked ferociously.

A man's voice from inside the nearest house shouted, "Enough, Wolf. I've already got a headache from too much mead."

The admonishment didn't work. Wolf added snarling and howling to his barking.

Should I eat it? offered the dragon.

No. The thought of even a noisy dog becoming a dragon's meal upset Luca. *Let's just stay as far away from that house as possible.*

Six houses later, a woman saw them. She was carrying a pail of water to her goats. She screamed—a short, high-pitched scream. Then, her eyes locked on Bartalan and she froze. Her goats silently huddled together behind the woman.

Bartalan loped toward them.

What are you doing? We need to get to the river without being seen.

We have already been seen. The dragon stopped about two meters from the petrified woman and her goats. He snarled, then lowered his head to within a hand's width of her face. She gasped, then fainted. Several of the goats fainted as well.

Grinning, Bartalan trotted back to Luca. *If she remembers anything when she awakens, such a close encounter with a dragon who did not eat her or her goats will make her story unbelievable.*

Luca shook his head. *I hope you're right.*

They traveled without further sightings to the docks and slipped behind a building used for cleaning fish. Inside, were two men.

I know these men.

Luca heard the hate in Bartalan's mind.

They are friends of Dolph Skarsgard. They kicked me and kept food from me. The dragon narrowed his eyes. *I do not forgive these men.*

Remember, escape is our priority. Luca put his hand on Bartalan. He felt him quivering. *Soon we will have our chance to slip into the river.*

The dragon looked down at him. *I must do this,* he thought.

Before Luca could argue, Bartalan barged into the building. In two snaps of the dragon's jaws, the men were dead. As Luca watched, Bartalan carried the limp bodies to the river and tossed them into the water. Carried by the current, they floated downstream.

If they are found, the men will have been nibbled on by fish, crabs, and other water creatures. So you need not worry.

Luca couldn't imagine the pent-up rage of decades of mistreatment. He supposed the dragon was allowed a bit of revenge. But enough was enough. *No more killing tonight. You will need the remainder of your strength for swimming upstream.*

Agreed, responded the dragon as they plunged into the dark water.

Luca and Bartalan sat on the stone dock at the foot of the hill. Far above their heads on a rocky pinnacle perched Zsigmond House. The boat they would soon board bobbed in the water in front of them.

It is good to be clean. The dragon curved his neck around so he could look directly into Luca's eyes. *After a couple of days of enough food and rest, I will be able to fly, even with you on my back.*

"On your back! I am not sure I want to soar in the clouds."

I rarely fly as high as the clouds, replied Bartalan. *Though the vampire has offered to transport us a day's sailing distance down the river, it will not be far enough. We must travel much farther to avoid capture. There is a mountain range ten days flight from here. It would be a perfect location for us. There are towns where you can ply your trade. Wild goats and deer for me to eat.*

"I will need to carry my tools and other belongings with me. I don't think you'll be able to carry so much weight," said Luca as he scratched the dragon behind an ear.

Perhaps the vampire can create a sack for me to carry your things in, suggested the dragon.

"Like saddlebags," said the woodworker thoughtfully. "I do have two trunks of things. It would be easy to split the weight evenly." Luca gazed into the dragon's golden eyes. "But can you carry so much weight?"

I believe so, though it might take eleven or twelve days to make the journey.

"It sounds like a plan."

"What sounds like a plan?" asked a deep voice behind them.

"Vida! It took you much longer than I thought it would to get here," said Luca. He hoped his concern for the vampire's safety wasn't evident in his voice.

"I've decided to move back to a former home. I had to make provisions for a caretaker for Zsigmond House and deliver my horses to their new owner. Therefore, freed of my life here, I will be sailing you two down the river for five days. At that time, if you choose to, you may reside with me at Castle Domokos until the dragon is healthier or be on your way."

Let us sail with this vampire for five days before we decide to live with him, suggested the dragon.

You are right, thought Luca. *Though it would have been impossible for you to have escaped Comas without his help.*

That is where you are mistaken, responded Bartalan. *You would have found another way. It is you, Luca, who felt my pain and heard my voice. It is you who is my savior.*

Savior! I think not, though I now believe as you do, we were meant to find each other and travel to a new life together. Luca patted the dragon's neck.

Vida Zsigmond cleared his throat. "If you two are finished chatting, I suggest we board the boat and get moving. While it is still dark, I need to teach Luca how to guide the boat down the river since he will be the captain during the daylight hours."

"I have never steered a boat," said the cabinetmaker as they climbed onto the deck of the sailing vessel.

"True," answered the vampire, "but until today, you had

never rescued a dragon. I suspect you are capable of far more than you realize, Luca Rannell."

"I guess you're right." He glanced once more at Zsigmond House high above them. Though he wouldn't be able to see much because of the darkness, he knew after a few minutes of sailing, they would pass Rannell's Cabinet and Casket Makers and other outlying homes and businesses. Next, he should be able to spot the bonfires of Comas's Midsummer's Eve Fair and maybe even the embers of Dolph Skarsgard's smithy. After that, everything he spied would be new. He took several deep breaths in an attempt to calm himself.

Do not worry, Luca, he heard in his mind as Bartalan nuzzled him, *I am here with you.*

DRAGONFLIES

While hiking, Allen and Ori spotted a body. They stopped dead in their tracks and stared.

The body appeared to be that of a woman. She was lying on her stomach, half-buried in debris, beside a small pond. The partially exposed cadaver was fifty or sixty feet from the trail.

"You seeing this?" asked Ori. He took off his baseball cap and swatted it against his thigh again and again.

"Easy." Allen reached out, rested his hand on his best friend's shoulder. "Settle down. We can't be sure *what* we're seeing from this distance."

"You're right. There's no way to tell what happened to her from here," agreed Ori as he squinted his eyes. "We need to get closer."

"That's quite a jump from ready to run to ready to investigate." Allen rubbed the back of his neck.

"I wasn't ready to run." Skittish at first, Ori was always eager to dive into an adventure, solve a mystery, or check out a

haunted house once he'd regained his composure. As long as
Allen led the way. Ori rolled his eyes while shaking his head and
pressing his lips together in a frown.

"Maybe not, but I don't think investigating is a good idea,"
said Allen as he surveyed the lonely stretch of woodlands on
either side of the trail. "This is likely a crime scene." He pulled
out his cell phone to call emergency services. "Of course! There's
no reception here. Let's retrace our steps, then call the police
when we're closer to a cell tower."

"I suppose you're right, but..." Ori grinned, then stepped off
the footpath. "I dare you to get closer." Ori grabbed Allen's arm
and tugged him off the trail as well.

"Are we still in the sixth grade?" Allen shook his head.
"There's no way I'm going..."

"Did you hear that? She moaned."

"I think it was just the wind."

"No," argued Ori in a voice soft as a snake hissing. "I'm not
kidding. I know what I heard, and it wasn't the wind."

"Okay, but just a quick look to make sure she's beyond help."
As it he said the words *beyond help*, Allen felt his stomach lurch.
"After that, we hike out of here."

Ori nodded his head in agreement, then followed Allen until
they were about six feet from the woman's body.

"She looks young, maybe a teenager? Why do you think all
those dragonflies are circling over her?" Ori sounded less brave
than he had a minute ago.

"I'm not sure. Maybe the salt on her skin is attracting them,"
replied Allen. He glanced at his friend who had a look of horror
on his face. "From sweating, not bleeding," he added as he
studied the drift of insects whirring above the young woman and
climbing through her hair.

Allen felt his throat tighten. Though the dragonflies'

translucent wings shimmered like they were encrusted with jewels as they wandered around the woman's brown locks, they reminded him of a flock of vultures looking for meat. Silently, he hoped the dragonflies were in fact searching for midges and flies, and not actually consuming the teenager's scalp. Or worse, looking to enter her skull through her ears, eye sockets, nose, or mouth. An image of squirming maggots popped into his mind's eye.

Jeez, tone down the imagination, he warned himself.

Ori tugged on his sleeve, and they both knelt to get a better look at the partially leaf-covered body without disturbing things too much. Allen still believed this was a crime scene.

"Her skin looks weird. Do you think she's wearing body make up?" asked Ori. "Or maybe a costume sewn from sheer fabric?"

"I don't know." Allen frowned. He noticed the parts of the young woman not covered with fallen leaves appeared to be unclothed. "She's naked and dumped in the woods. She *could* have been murdered. And you're right, something is definitely wrong with her, because her flesh is tinged yellowish green."

"Do you think she's rotting?" asked Ori. "On account of the green skin and all."

"Greening of the epidermis might be an early sign of decomposition." Allen rubbed his nose. "But there doesn't seem to be a dead thing stench. Maybe the greenness is bruising."

"So you don't think she's dead?"

"I didn't say that, but I imagine we'd smell her if she'd been dead for very long."

Abruptly, the cluster of dragonflies lifted and zipped around the teen's head like a glimmering halo. Then, without warning or apparent cause, the body stirred.

"What the..." Ori gasped before he fell backwards and put a hand to his mouth to smother a scream.

"Get further away!" urged Allen as he helped his friend scramble back a few feet. He hated to imagine what hungry animal caused the woman's corpse to shift position.

Before Ori or he could stand, much less run, the reclining teenager pushed herself to a sitting position, turned to face them, and tilted her head.

Allen felt his heart beating against his rib cage like the wings of a trapped bird. Beside him, he heard Ori praying.

As the young woman sat up and the leaves tumbled from her body, Allen couldn't tear his eyes away from a large set of wings attached to her back.

She's not human, he surmised. *Probably a fairy of one sort or another.* Though not an expert on fairies, Allen did know most of them were capricious at best and brutal at worst. *I hope we get out of this predicament in one piece,* he thought.

"Look at her eyes," whispered Ori. His friend had stopped praying, but still had his hands clasped together.

Helpless to do otherwise, Allen's gaze shifted to the creature's eyes. He felt his pulse pounding in his ears when he saw they were completely black with a supernatural glint. He suspected this was *not* a benevolent fairy.

Ori stuttered, "We thought y-y-you were h-hurt."

Allen nodded in agreement. Perhaps telling the creature that their intent was kind and caring would de-escalate the situation, because things certainly felt tense.

The creature didn't answer. Instead, she held out her olive hand. It was instantly covered with dragonflies. *Her minions,* thought Allen. For that was what he now believed the throng of winged pond insects to be. He guessed the dragonflies were there to groom and protect the young woman, not harm her.

"All the dragonflies are staring at us," Ori said in a quavering voice. "I think they're deciding whether to swarm us or let us leave."

"It's unlikely dragonflies would attack," Allen assured his friend in the calmest voice he could muster. He bowed his head slightly in the direction of the dragonfly creature. "Miss, we didn't mean to intrude. We were worried about you."

Again, the green-skinned young woman didn't answer. Instead, she continued to observe them.

Allen tried to get to his feet, but found he was unable to stand. Ori must have discovered the same thing because he began praying again.

Figuring fairy-kind liked their privacy, Allen said, "Please, let us go, Miss. We won't tell anyone about you, and we won't come back."

The dragonfly woman smiled a crooked smile, parted her lips, then murmured in a voice smooth as still water, "It isn't often I get visitors. You must stay a spell."

Spell! Allen surmised that was just what rooted them in place.

The eerily-beautiful woman continued to study him. She narrowed her eyes slightly as if she read his thoughts.

"We'd love to, but we're expected..." began Allen.

"Nowhere."

The woman ran her fingers through her curly hair, sending so many dragonflies zipping into the air that, for a second, Allen feared the insects might actually descend upon them.

"You're expected nowhere, and since I haven't had guests in decades." The green-skinned teenager frowned, then continued. "Maybe it's been centuries. Even millennia. I demand that you stay."

"Demand?" Allen tried unsuccessfully to stand as he spoke.

The dragonfly woman laughed. "Perhaps the term is too harsh." She lowered her head, peered from beneath impossibly long lashes, and breathed out the word, "Request."

We're in deep trouble, thought Allen as the creature moved a few inches closer.

Finally having found his tongue and apparently oblivious to the gradual approach of the dragonfly fairy, Ori asked, "Do you live here?"

The creature nodded. Allen spotted not antenna sprouting from her scalp, but a strange ridge of flesh.

"My lair is not far." Moving her hand in a graceful arc, she pointed at the woods beyond the pond. "If you'd like to see it."

"Yes." Ori's head started bouncing up and down like a bobble-head doll.

Allen punched him in the upper arm, but when his friend turned to look at him, he saw Ori's eyes were glazed. *He's ensorcelled or at least spell-struck,* thought Allen.

"That's a very gracious offer," said Allen, "but we can't accept." Fighting the waves of magic that emanated from the creature, he stared into her dark-as-eternity eyes once more and begged, "Let us go."

The dazzle of dragonflies zipped from the creature to Allen, surrounding him in a cloud of buzzing iridescence. Each of the insects studied him as if evaluating his worthiness. Though intimidated, he didn't flinch when they landed on his hair, face, neck, lower arms, and hands. Even when he felt thousands of teeny claws grasping his skin, Allen remained motionless.

"Interesting," said the dragonfly woman as she stood. "Lucky for you two, today, I feel generous. So hurry home, but stay away from my pond and this part of the woods unless you want to become my forever guests."

She flicked two fingers, and Allen felt the weight, which had held him in a kneeling position, lift.

"Yes, ma'am," he replied as he helped Ori to his feet.

Before Ori fully regained his senses, the dragonfly creature began to sway like a cobra following a flute. Without warning, the young woman's body transformed, slowly at first, with just a blurring of features. Then, with a rapidness that stole Allen's breath, olive skin roughened into green scales and the strangely beautiful woman's face and neck elongated. Next, her black-as-death eyes enlarged and moved to either side of a newly sprouted wide-nostriled snout. Then, quick as a mamba's strike, her delicate hands grew claws where fingernails used to be, and her demure mouth widened and filled with pointed teeth.

"Time for you to leave," hissed the she-dragon as she towered above them, "unless you want to be lunch."

Now able to move and needing no further encouragement, Ori and he raced back to the path and jogged all the way home with a drift of dragonflies accompanying them. The she-dragon's laughter continued to fill Allen's ears until he stepped from the woods into his yard. As for the dragonflies, though diminished in number, a few of them still buzzed about Ori and him as they sat on the porch steps.

"Do you think that dragonfly woman will leave us alone?" asked Ori. "Or will she come looking for us?"

Allen heard the fear in Ori's voice and saw his friend's hands shaking.

"Naw, not if we keep quiet about *her*," answered Allen. He frowned as he spied an especially large dragonfly perched on the side of his father's house. The insect stared back in a most sentient manner.

"But I think we'll be watched for the rest of our lives." Allen pointed at the dragonfly attached to the house.

Yes, you will, hissed a dragonish voice in the back of his mind. One glance at Ori told him his friend had heard the warning, too.

"Let's go inside and get something to eat," suggested Allen.

Ori and he stood. His friend had already walked through the door when an uncanny feeling washed over Allen like a sudden cloudburst. He looked back at the woods adjacent to his yard.

Beneath the cedars he spotted the she-dragon, a flutter of dragonflies drifting around her like dandelion seeds caught in the wind. In a blink, the dragon vanished. But not before he heard her whisper, *See you again soon, Allen.*

MOTHERHOOD

As she curled around the magical stone, Python saw her arrow-riddled body decomposing beneath the harsh light of the sun. The dragon pulled her lips back and hissed. Such an end seemed a poor reward for her years of service guarding the sacred oracle of Delphi. But she knew the seeing-stone never lied.

"Mother," Python announced to the darkness beneath Mount Parnassus. "I have seen my decaying corpse."

Like the whisper of a thousand swallows' wings, Gaia's words rushed through her daughter's cave: "I cannot change the future. Is there something else you would ask of me?"

Python scratched her chin with one claw and thought for a moment. "I have always wondered, with no father, how was I created?"

Gaia's laughter encircled her daughter like an airy hug. "The Deluge left behind marshes filled with slime and stagnant water. Deucalion and Pyrrha, saved because of their piety, were told by Deucalion's father, Prometheus, to toss stones into the muck. Where these rocks fell, a man or woman sprang up. And so, the earth was repopulated. After Deucalion and Pyrrha finished, there remained unused mud. I wanted a beautiful daughter to guard the Delphi Stone, so I formed you."

"Humans call me a monster and run in fear," said Python. "I am *not* beautiful."

"In the eyes of a mother, every child is beautiful."

Python smiled. "I want to be a mother, too. To gaze upon my beautiful children before my death. Does a swampy place with the fertile mud of The Deluge still remain?"

In the quiet that followed, Python prayed that a bit of the creation muck still existed and that her mother knew its whereabouts. As she awaited an answer, she listened to the water dripping from the stalactites above and the scuttling of rats farther back in her chamber. Finally, her mother spoke.

"There is a swampy spot at the foot of the mountain where some ooze from The Deluge remains untainted."

The she-dragon felt Gaia's warm hand on her chest. Though she wanted to shout, "Show me! Show me!" Python patiently waited for Mother to finish speaking.

"I had thought to use the muck myself one day, but dearest, instead I will lead you to the hidden bog where you may create your children. Before we depart, you need to decide if you want them to look like you."

"Yes!" Python had always felt alone and singular. Having others who looked like her would be a blessing. "But I want them to be able to fly, too."

"I see. Then, I believe we should take some bat fur with us," replied Mother.

Python whistled for some of her cavern mates to come to her, and gentle as a springtime breeze she plucked a handful of bat hair from their tiny bodies.

～

I t was dusk when Gaia and Python reached the marsh where the fertile muck gurgled beneath the overhang of a huge boulder. The timing should be perfect, since Python suspected creation magic was best done by moonlight.

With Mother's help, Python was able to shape dozens of tiny dragons from the mud. In the center of each, she placed one of her scales and a few bat hairs. Pulling the scales from her legs hurt, but pain was a small price to pay for children.

"The stars are dimming," warned Gaia. "The children already formed will have to be enough. All that is left is for you to breathe upon your offspring to give them life."

Heart beating faster than raindrops in a thunderstorm, Python did as her mother told her.

Perhaps on Mount Olympus or beneath the Mediterranean the audacity of the she-dragon and the earth spirit angered a god, but no one intervened. Thus, with Gaia's aid, Python gave birth to dragonkind.

"Now, love them and teach them what they will need to do to survive," said Grandmother Gaia as she slipped away.

"Thank you," said the mother dragon. Then, with a toothy smile, she herded her brood up to her cave beneath the Temple of Delphi.

"M ama, Mama," called Python's sons and daughters day and night. But after centuries of being alone, the sounds of her children were sweeter to her then the songs of the woodlands.

Motherhood agrees with me, she thought as she watched her children play in the sea near the rocky shoreline. All her daughters and sons were capable of catching enough fish to survive on their own, yet she hoped they would remain with her. *Life is perfect*, thought Python just before she saw her mother walking toward her.

"Daughter, the time has come to do a favor for me in return for using The Deluge mud," said Gaia. "By order of Hera, you must pursue Leto. She has been banished to earth and cannot be allowed to rest." Then, almost as an afterthought, Gaia added, "Show her no pity. Hera has sworn revenge on anyone who helps the goddess of dark nights."

"How can this be right?"

"It is not for us to judge," replied Python's mother as she walked away with downcast eyes.

Once their grandmother was no longer in sight, Python called her children to her. She called them not by voice but using the mind-speak that is one of the special abilities of dragonkind. When she was surrounded by her sons and daughters, Python spoke aloud, "Children, the time has come for you to find your own places in this world."

The young dragons protested but their mother quickly silenced them with a roar.

"This is not my choice, but a task has been assigned to me which will take months to complete." She looked at each of their beautiful, reptilian faces before continuing. "I fear for your safety if you remain below Mount Parnassus. You must leave—not just this island, but all of Greece. Fly far from here. Even across great distances, I can hear your mind-speak, and you will be able to talk to each other."

Her children gazed lovingly at her. *I must remember this moment*, thought Python.

"Though I know not the future—" She paused as she recalled the long-ago image revealed by the Delphi Stone. "If it is within my power to do so, I will see you again."

Perhaps, the dragonets had been ready to leave her for

months. Perhaps, some of her offspring had even longed since not long after birth to be released into the sea and sky to find their futures. Whatever their reasons for a speedy departure, it took only a few minutes for her daughters and sons to launch themselves into the air. Most sailed west, some soared north, a few flew east—but none went south.

With a sense of doom weighing down every footfall, Python searched for and found Leto. As ordered by her mother and Hera, she pursued the goddess from field to forest to rocky outcrop. Though she could have caught the pregnant daughter of Coeus and Phoebe or made her run even faster, Python chose not to do so. She felt empathy for the mother-to-be. Yet, a task had been assigned to her and she could not stop the chase.

Finally, pursued and pursuer came to Ortygia. Python pretended to sleep so Leto could birth her daughter in peace. Eyes pressed closed, Python heard the new mother whisper, "Artemis," as she held the child up to the full moon. But with morning, the task of chasing Leto had to be resumed lest Python anger Hera.

Mother and daughter ran before Python until they came to the sea. At last, a god was willing to face Hera's ire. Poseidon sent a dolphin to transport the exhausted Leto to Delos, holding her daughter.

Python followed, though she was careful not to let Leto or Artemis know of her presence. Nine days of labor later, a twin was born between an olive tree and a date palm on the heights of Mount Cynthos whom Leto called Apollo. The boy was as brilliant as the sun, and Python remembered her seeing-stone vision. It had been this boy, not the sun who shone brightly on her rotting body.

With the birth of Leto's second child, Python was freed from the task assigned to her by Hera. Even though killing the newborn might change her future, Python chose to return to Mount Parnassus with no blood on her claws or conscience.

Once home, she reached out to her children, now scattered like wind-borne seeds across the earth. They all had found the places where they belonged, the places where she hoped they would thrive—some in pairs and some alone.

Python curled around the Delphi Stone and waited for Apollo. She knew not the exact day or time he would arrive with a quiver full of arrows sharp enough to piece dragon scales. She was not certain how long the battle would rage, though she knew she would lose the fight. What she did know, with a certainty more solid than the rock walls of her cavern, was that her daughters and sons were far away, safe from vengeful Olympian gods.

Future storytellers might embellish the truth, change the facts, forget the details of her life, but Python cared not. For no matter what the poets said, she knew she was a good mother.

BALANCING THE SCALES

W ith a morning breeze stirring the curtains, Lizzie
sat in the main room of the house she and Ty
Harper shared, listening to the Good Will
Redemption Holiness Church's bell ring twenty-two times.

"Ty," she whispered as she set aside the paring knife with
which she was chopping vegetables for tonight's dinner.

Although it might be a coincidence that Ty was twenty-two,
she knew with every tick of the mantel clock that her husband
was dead. In her heart, she believed it was only a matter of time
before the men brought his body home.

Maybe I'm wrong, she told herself as she reached for his
family's Bible to look for a comforting verse to read while she
waited. As she opened the well-worn Holy Book, a note fell out.

She unfolded the paper and began to read:

Dear Lizzie,

*If you're reading this, then I'm dead. I put this letter in the front page
of my Bible on the Twenty-fifth of October, knowing you'd pick up the
Good Book for comfort—not the new Sunday School Bible, but the old one*

with some of its pages taped into place. Now, I hate to add to your suffering, but no matter how they tell you I died—I was murdered.

Stop shaking your head, Lizzie. It's true.

You'll find a journal with entries starting this morning beneath the mattress on my side of the bed. I don't know how many entries I'll be able to make before he kills me. I'm hoping hundreds—but I think it will only be a few.

Lizzie, just let my family take the lead. Do what my people have done for generations when family passes. For sure, don't let on you know the truth about me being murdered. The murderer or murderers (he might have had help) will kill you, too. I don't want that. I want you to live a long life.

After mourning a reasonable time, you need to find somebody else. Someone to watch over you like I did. You can go back to the coast if you want. Just move on. It won't bother me. I want you safe and happy.

Forever yours,

Ty

Tears wetting her cheeks, Lizzie slid Ty's note into her pocket, then went to their bed. Slipping her hand between the mattress and box spring, she felt a thin book. After glancing over her shoulder to make sure no one else was there, she pulled out Ty's journal. Sitting on their bed with the sunlight streaming through the window like a slice of angel-shine, she opened it up. On the first page, Ty had scrawled, *"For Lizzie."* She sighed and began reading:

2 *5 October—*
While working at the sawmill today, I saw Alvin Cubbins hit his wife, Letrice. It wasn't like it was the first time he'd done it. I'd seen him hit her before. But this time, he knocked her out. She just crumpled like a dress falling off the clothesline.

After Alvin went back inside the mill, I went over to Letrice and splashed some water on her face. Her cheek was red. Her face was already swelling up. The poor girl's eyes were rolled back in her head and it took a couple of minutes before they went back to normal. When she finally started to come to, I told her to go tell the sheriff about it.

Letrice said, "You're so sweet to worry about me, Tyrone. Why, I wish I'd married you instead of Alvin."

I never had a crush on her when we were young, so it was quite a surprise when she said that. I'd always had my eye on Lizzie Womack. Never paid much mind to anyone else.

But Alvin heard it. I guess he'd come back down to check on his wife. And that's when Letrice reached up, grabbed me around my neck, and kissed me hard on the lips.

I stood up, stared after her as she ran away laughing, then turned around to face Alvin.

"You, too?" he said. "You after my wife like half of the boys in this county?"

I told him I'd never cheat on my Lizzie. Told him it was all a misunderstanding. Told him Letrice just said that and kissed me to upset him.

He replied, "I'm no idiot. I know what I saw. And you're gonna pay for messing around with Letrice." Then, Alvin stalked back toward the sawmill.

I think he means to murder me. I'm keeping this journal, so people will know how it began.

❧

2 *6 October—*
Last night, I had a hard time falling asleep. I suppose I should tell Lizzie about this business with Alvin Cubbins and his wife, but I don't want to upset her. Maybe I'm worrying about nothing—chasing "what-ifs"—but I don't think so. When I walked into the mill this morning, Alvin pulled an ax from the wall, pretended to be chopping something, then pointed at me. Two of the mill workers he's friendly

with watched the whole thing. They laughed when he was swinging the ax.

Lizzie, this next bit is for you. I don't know what condition I'll be in when they bring me home. Hopefully, it won't be too gruesome. I hate to think of you having to deal with a mangled body.

Get my cousin Tate to move the recliner from in front of the funeral door. Remember last fall when you asked me about having two front doors? I explained one was for everyday and the other was for funerals. I didn't think we'd be using the second door so soon.

Back to preparations. Lizzie, the deadbolt on the funeral door might need to be greased then hammered to get it to slide open. Tate will know how to get it unstuck. He and his brother, Bo, can grab the two sawhorses from the shed, then take off our bedroom door by the hinges to make a laying out board for me. Set it up in the deathwatch room. Of course, we've always called that room our parlor—but it was put there for funerals, too.

After you cover the door with a spare sheet and lay me out, I'll need to be tied down. Tate and Bo can help you with that, too. There's twine and sisal in the shed. Nothing worse than a corpse twitching while folks are sitting up with the dead.

Your parents being in Newport News, I expect my Ma and her sister, Aunt Suellen, will be over to help you clean me up and dress me in my suit. If Alvin messed me up too bad—don't fret about my face. Just drape a scarf over it.

Honestly, Lizzie, I can't write any more today. You are the best thing that ever happened to me—Ty

∾

2 7 October—
I'm still not sleeping very well. I heard an owl hooting last night for hours. They say before you die, you can hear the owls calling your name. I just heard a bunch of who-whooing and no "Tyrone" being called —so I guess I'll make it until tomorrow.

This afternoon at the mill, I overheard Alvin telling the crew chief that some of the saw blades needed maintenance. He said he feared there was going to be an accident, and somebody was going to get killed. Maybe that's the way he's going to murder me. I hate to think of a whirling blade biting into my flesh.

Lizzie, I know you're going to be upset and probably not thinking clearly, so here's some things you need to be considering when they bring my body home:

1-Buck Littrell or one of his boys will be in to measure me for my pine box. They're good carpenters and will do a fine job. Make sure and pay them—even if they don't want to take the money. If necessary, you can slip the cash under their carpentry shop's door after I'm buried.

2-Ma will talk to the preacher about putting me in the Harper section of the graveyard up on Dove Hill behind the church.

3-The mill workers will likely want to help the men of my family dig my grave. Just don't let Alvin Cubbins help. Though I expect it'd take more guts than he has to volunteer to dig a hole for somebody he murdered.

4-They'll be bringing Great-Aunt Sookie up to do the saining. I know she's a granny witch—but she's the eldest woman in my family. She never scared you before, so don't be afraid of her now. She's got the gift—her being born with a caul—so it wouldn't surprise me if she gets to our house before my body. Trust her. She'll give you good advice.

Your parents were new to the area when you started at the middle school, so I don't believe you ever saw a saining before. Aunt Sookie will light a candle, then wave it over me three times. Next, she'll put three handfuls of salt in a bowl and place it on my chest—so make sure there's salt and a bowl out and ready for her.

I'm done writing for today. Though the mountains are golden with autumn and the last of the wildflowers are bursting open everywhere, I feel a hard chill like I've been sitting in the spring house for too long. Sorry I'll be leaving you earlier than I thought when we said our vows last March—Ty

~

2 8 October—
    This morning when I punched my time-card, I felt the hairs on the back of my neck stick up. I looked over my shoulder. With a scowl worse than our Halloween Jack-o'-lantern's, Alvin Cubbins was glaring at me. When he saw I was studying him, he drew his forefinger across his throat like a buck knife.

All day, I worked careful as I could. Still, I know there are lots of chances for something to go wrong. Perhaps, I should see if they're hiring over at the big box store. Doesn't pay as much and it's farther to drive, but it'd make it harder for Alvin to kill me.

Lizzie, I've been remembering other things you'll need to do after I'm murdered. Aunt Sookie will help—or maybe Ma or Aunt Suellen—but you need to soak a dishtowel in soda water and put it over my face until the viewing. It helps keep the skin fresh-looking. My arms need to be folded over my chest, my feet tied together at the ankles, and a handkerchief should be tied under my chin and over the top of my head to keep my mouth in place.

I know this is distressing for you to read—much less do—but it needs to be done. Then, two coins need to be placed on my eyes. Some folks say it's to pay the ferryman. They may be right. What's more important is the coins help keep the eyelids closed. Don't use pennies. Copper can cause the nearby skin to change colors. Don't use silver dollars. It's a waste of money, and someone might dig me up to get to the dollars. Any smaller denomination of silver will do. While dimes are a good size for young children, quarters are ideal for a grown man.

Now, I know you're going to want to put our wedding quilt over me—don't. Use an old quilt and keep the wedding quilt as a remembrance of our time together. Besides, after you, Ma, Aunt Suellen, Aunt Sookie, and dozens of others put flowers, herbs, and whatnot on top of the quilt, no one will recall which quilt I was buried under.

I'm thinking of the day we were married—the leaves just starting to come out. That March day was the happiest day of my life. I wish I had many more springs to spend with you—but I don't. Love you forever—Ty

⁓

2 9 October—
Today, I heard dogs howling in the woods at lunchtime. Sweets Carter said they weren't dogs—they were coyotes. I hope he's correct. Because to hear dogs howling like that can be a sign that death is near.

It seemed every childhood superstition popped into my mind this afternoon. A cat crossed my path when I got out of the truck to pump gas. My breath caught in my throat until I noticed that the cat was dark gray. When I walked into the store to pay for the fuel, I carefully avoided walking under the ladder a repairman was standing on trying to fix the neon sign on the front of the store's roof.

Sweets says I'm jittery as a pig smelling a smokehouse. He probably thinks I've got a problem with alcohol. Meanwhile, Alvin and his buddies just stare, laugh, then stare some more. I don't know how much more of this I can take.

Lizzie, you asked me this morning if anything was wrong. If I was mad at you. No, my love. How could I be angry with you? A man couldn't find a better wife than you, my dearest.

Again, I must write of the day of my death. You need to cover the mirror in the bathroom with cloth—something dark like the navy tablecloth your parents gave us last Christmas. Draw the curtains closed, too. I don't want to be tempted to use the mirror or windows as portals to come back to this world and linger with my Lizzie. Though you do need to leave one window open behind its curtains, so my spirit can sail away.

Stop the mantel clock—for time will have stopped for me. After I'm buried, you can restart it.

The women will bring food to serve at the viewing. Put it in the dining room so people can grab a bite after the viewing before they leave. They'll *also bring food for the luncheon after I'm buried. Thanking everyone in-person is enough. Don't worry about writing notes.*

Ma, Aunt Suellen, Tate, Bo, Aunt Sookie, and the rest of my people will sit up with you through the death watch night. You don't need to be awake the whole time. Let the others take a turn while you rest.

In the morning, Buck Littrell will bring over my coffin. He and the boys will load me in and drive me over to the church in the back of their pick-up. Don't drive over to the church by yourself. Ride with a family member. I've enclosed several Bible verses and hymns I'd like used for my funeral. You can give them to Ma to pass on to the preacher.

You're going to do fine, Lizzie. I know sadness will be your companion for a while, but as each new season arrives, you'll begin to move forward. Before long, you'll find joy again. Love, Ty

Lizzie unfolded four sheets of paper which Ty had placed inside his journal. On the first she read:

MATTHEW 5, verse 4: "Blessed are those who mourn, for they shall be comforted."

PSALM 23: "The Lord is my shepherd; I shall not want…"

ISAIAH 57, verse 2: "Those who walk uprightly enter into peace; they find rest as they lie in death."

She folded the sheet of paper and brushed away tears with her fingertips. The second sheet of paper was a copy of the music and lyrics for *The Old Rugged Cross*, the third a copy of *How Great Thou Art*, and the fourth a copy of *The Ash Grove*. Tissue in hand she scanned the lyrics of *Ash Grove*. Her eyes lingered on the beginning of the last stanza:

"My lips smile no more, my heart loses its lightness;
No dream of the future my spirit can cheer.
I only can brood on the past and its brightness…"

"Ty, I don't think I can do this," she said to no one. After blowing her nose, she read the final entry in the journal:

30 October—

This morning, I woke before dawn and studied your face, Lizzie. I got a terrible feeling it would be the last time I saw you on this side of the veil. I hope I'm mistaken.

I've decided to apply for a job tomorrow at the big box store. They ought to be hiring with the holidays coming soon. No more sawmill for me. I will tell you after work today about Alvin, Letrice, and the whole mess.

Lizzie closed the journal. Today was the thirtieth, so Ty wouldn't be able to finish today's entry and there would be no more entries.

"Lizzie," said a voice from the front room.

She went to the bedroom door, saw Aunt Sookie standing in the everyday entrance to the house with her arms open, and ran to her.

"It's all right, child," said the granny witch as she stroked her hair. "They'll be bringing Tyrone home soon."

"What happened?" Lizzie asked—though she wanted to say *How did Alvin Cubbins murder Ty?*

"A chain came loose on a flatbed full of timber. Some of the tree trunks rolled off. Tyrone was caught beneath them. I came quick, so I can help sew him together for you."

Lizzie gasped. She realized Aunt Sookie was studying her. "He was murdered," she managed to say before she blew her nose on a tissue.

"I know," answered the granny witch. "And I brought you something to read and something to use—if you have a mind to do so." She pulled an envelope from a crocheted bag she was carrying and handed it to Lizzie. "Sit and read it quickly before the others arrive."

Lizzie nodded, sat on the sofa, and opened the envelope. Inside were a handwritten letter, plus a small bundle of hair and a black feather tied with a white thread. She looked at the granny witch. Sookie pointed at the letter. Then, Lizzie began reading:

Dear Sookie

If you've found this note, I am worm food. Do not flinch at my blunt words—for you better than most know the ways of beginnings and endings. I've taught you most everything I know about healing, birthing, foreseeing, and even a little magic. There is one more lesson, which I hesitated to teach you—but now that I'm gone, I will share: Calling a Demon.

Calling a Demon is to be done only in the most extreme cases. For once called, a demon will not depart until it has taken its prize. I have never done this magic, although the granny witch who taught me did call a demon once to deal with an evil person of extreme cruelty. On her deathbed, she told me the creature's scaly face and the screams of its victim still haunted her.

People say they hear a panther crying out in the densest parts of the mountains. But it's not a panther—it's a demon. I cannot say nor write any demon's true name—to do so would attract it to me. But you don't need to name this creature to call it forth. For safety's sake I will call it a panther.

Here is the procedure to call a panther: First, gather a few hairs from the demon's prey. Second, pluck a feather from a living raven's breast. Third, tie the two together with a thread from a stillborn baby's grave cloth. Fourth, dip the bundle in spring-fed pond on the night of a full moon. Fifth, dry the bundle on the branch of a Judas Tree. Sixth, stand by a newly dug grave with the bundle in your left hand and say the first six words of the Lord's Prayer backwards while turning anticlockwise three times. Lastly, you must stand still as a tombstone while a panther manifests itself before you.

Hold out your left hand with the bundle balanced on your palm—much like you'd feed a horse a sugar cube. The panther will take the bundle, then go fetch its prey. You must stand by the grave and wait. When the panther returns with his prey, you must witness the victim's death. The panther will come to you again. Say, "Thank you, Righter of Wrongs." Then, the panther should vanish.

Again, I warn you not to use this magic without just cause. Even then, hesitate before proceeding, for the panther you call will watch you for the *rest of your life. It is a monster of retribution. Should you turn to dark ways, it will return and claim you, too.*

Until we meet again on the other side,

Tilly

Lizzie folded the letter, placed it back in the envelope, then held up the hair and feather bundle. "Is it ready to be used?" she asked.

Aunt Sookie nodded. "Yes. I foresaw Tyrone's death, visited the barber right after Alvin got a haircut, and prepared the bundle weeks ago. But I am too old for a trek to the graveyard in the dark. So, if you seek justice, tonight as we sit with the dead, you must say you're tired. Go to your bedroom, but instead of taking a nap, change into dark clothing, sneak to Tyrone's newly-dug grave, and follow the procedure in the letter."

Lizzie pressed her lips together. She knew Ty's murder would be ruled an accident, even with the journal. The only way to mete out justice was to call a panther.

"I will call a demon tonight," she said as the vehicle bringing Ty's mutilated body pulled up beside the front porch.

Aunt Sookie smiled, patted her hands, and said, "That's my girl," before taking over the body and funeral preparations.

The sight of Ty's smashed and lacerated body being stitched together by Aunt Sookie was still fresh in Lizzie's mind when she hiked by candlelight to the graveyard on Dove Hill behind the Good Will Redemption Holiness Church. At midnight, as October thirty-first was born, she followed the instructions for summoning a demon from the dead granny witch Tilly's letter. She'd no sooner finished her third counterclockwise turn, then a hulking black form manifested before her.

The demon's eyes glinted red—like coals after a bonfire has burned down. Its long, scaly snout sniffed the bundle she held in her left hand before it grasped it between two of its shiny claws. Lizzie thought her heart would stop beating when it smiled at her before rushing away.

All she could think about was the demon's jagged teeth glistening a yellowish white in the candlelight as the minutes seemed to move slower than a dirge. Finally, the towering creature loped up the hill dragging Alvin Cubbins. Lizzie had prepared herself for Alvin's screams. But instead, the demon squeezed Alvin's neck so tightly that the man couldn't utter more than a few gasps and gurgles.

Placing itself directly in front of Lizzie, the demon hunched over its prey and proceeded to devour Alvin. After it had finished crunching Alvin's bones and swallowing the larger parts of Ty's murderer, the creature got down on all fours and licked up the blood and body bits. The demon-dragon's tongue flicked out so rapidly and with such precision that Lizzie imagined no one would notice a thing awry when her husband's coffin was carried to the grave on Halloween afternoon.

Meal finished, the panther stood before her, leaned close, and gazed into her eyes with his burning orbs.

"Thank you, Righter of Wrongs," she managed to whisper to the dragon.

The panther rumbled a purr-like sound. Then, sniffing the palm of her hand one last time, it said, "I will remember your scent," before bounding into the woods.

A week later, while waiting for her husband's cousins, Tate and Bo, to arrive to help load her things into the pick-up truck's bed, Lizzie read the obituary section of the newspaper:

HARPER, Tyrone G.

On October 30, Tyrone "Ty" Grant Harper, (22) beloved husband of less than a year of Elizabeth Ann Harper (nee Womack); and devoted son of Darla Lynn Harper (nee Sully) and the late Grant Tatum Harper, passed away suddenly. Ty was born in...

Then, she flipped back to the front page and scanned an article about a missing person:

CUBBINS WHEREABOUTS UNKNOWN

On Saturday, October 30, local mill worker, Alvin Tunney Cubbins, age 31, was last seen about midnight leaving Rock Creek Tavern. Cubbins, reported missing by his wife, is 6 foot 2 inches tall and weighs 300 pounds...

As she folded the paper, she thought, *there is no real justice— only a balancing of the scales.*

Ty was still dead, and Lizzie didn't have any interest in pursuing another relationship. Instead, she'd accepted Aunt Sookie's invitation to move in with her.

After learning about healing, birthing, foreseeing, and a little magic—she hoped to receive messages from her husband again.

For on the night of his wake, after she'd returned from her dealings with a panther, Lizzie had uncovered the mirror above her dresser. And despite the likelihood of allowing multitudes of undead monstrosities into this world, she'd opened a portal for Ty on Halloween—the day when the veil between living and dead was at its thinnest.

RICHES

I
t began with a snake. Yukio spotted the creature watching
him from the foot of a plum tree. Then, it was gone. Before
he could wonder about the creature, he saw a lovely
woman walking beneath the plum tree with the last rays of the
sun tinting her face golden.

"What is your name?" he asked.

"Takara," she responded, in a voice more pleasant than the
sound of soft rain on a koi pond.

Yukio fell in love with the lovely Takara at that moment and
married her the next day. Two weeks later, he was still enchanted
by his bride, but Yukio longed to provide a better life for them
and to have enough money to start a family.

I'm rich in love, but poor in worldly goods, thought Yukio, for he
and Takara lived a humble existence in Kyoto in Takara's
rundown family home. As his wife told the story, the house had
first been inhabited by Takara's grandparents. All of their
children had scattered—except for Takara's parents. An only
child, when first her mother, then her father died, Takara became

the sole owner of the dilapidated abode. And that was when Yukio had met her.

"We are happy," Takara told Yukio as he dressed to go look for a well-paying job. "We have everything we need. I wish you'd forget about great riches. All the money in Kyoto won't make the stars any brighter."

"Perhaps not," he replied, "but we could be looking at those stars through a nicer window. And you, my love, could be wearing pearls and dining on sweets."

"I don't need dozens of pearls or sweets," said Takara. "*You* are all I need, husband."

Yukio smiled at his wife. "You have me," he said as he cupped her tiny, pointed chin in his hand. "But I want a better job, a better life, better everything." He released her chin and indicated the whole house with a sweep of his arm.

Takara bowed her head. "As you wish," she said.

Though it didn't stop him from leaving, Yukio noticed a tear slide down his wife's cheek.

While looking for work in the city, he met Masato, an acquaintance from his youth. As he was greeting his friend, Yukio couldn't help noticing how beautifully Masato was dressed. In truth, the servant who carried several packages for his friend was garbed in finer clothing than Yukio.

"Yukio," exclaimed Masato as he embraced him. "It's good to see you."

"I'm glad to see you, as well."

"I'm only here for another week, as I've been appointed governor of Owari Province," said Masato. "Please, join me for a meal before I depart."

Yukio nodded in agreement.

The two men chatted amicably over lunch about the journey their lives had taken to this point. Yukio said he was married. Masato said he was still looking for the right woman. They both recalled shared childhood memories.

After the meal was over, Masato spoke. "I can't help but notice you've fallen on hard times. Should you be interested, I'm prepared to offer you employment. It pays well and includes the use of a comfortable home, but you must cover both your own and your wife's travel expenses to Owari Province."

"That's very generous," replied Yukio, but even as he spoke, he knew he and Takara didn't have the funds to travel to Owari Province. Nevertheless, he said, "I'll meet you here in a week's time, and we can depart together."

"Excellent!" said Masato as he rose from his seat at their table.

Where to get the money for the journey? wondered Yukio. He needed to take advantage of this opportunity to improve his lot in life, but he knew no one would lend him enough to make the journey. Unfortunately, the modest home he shared with Takara wouldn't be sufficient collateral for the money-lenders. *If only my wife had come from a wealthier family,* he thought, *then there would be no problem borrowing...*

And that's when a plan slipped into his head.

Less than an hour later, Yukio stood before Iku, the unmarried daughter of one of the most prosperous merchants of Kyoto. A year earlier, he'd worked near Iku's home. He'd delivered numerous packages to the residence, always behaving in a respectful and polite manner. Though they'd barely spoken, he believed the merchant's daughter would remember him.

Truth be told, Iku was famous in Kyoto for having no suitors. While virtuous, she was neither clever nor attractive. Worse still, she was more than a few years older than Yukio, and unlikely able to still bear children. It was common knowledge in the city her father was anxious for her to find a husband.

"Iku, I have been offered a wonderful job in Owari Province," said Yukio. He saw Iku's father listening in the shadows behind her, and almost backed out of his plan. *Be strong,* he told himself before continuing. "I have need of a wife to travel with me and live in that distant province as my helpmate. I was wondering if you'd be..."

Before he could finish asking her to be his wife, Iku said, "Yes. I'd love to come with you to Owari Province."

"Yes, yes!" added her father as he stepped from where he'd been secreted. "I'll pay your travel expenses, give Iku a generous dowry, provide a wagon drawn by oxen for your belongings, and even give you well-behaved horses for you two to ride."

"That's most generous of you," replied Yukio with a bow. Though the expression on his face gave no indication of regret, at that moment, his heart ached for Takara. *But I'm doing what's best for both Takara and myself,* he thought, though he knew he was really doing what was best for himself. If he was truthful, he'd pushed Takara's wishes to the side.

"Knowing you are pressed for time, I'll arrange for the marriage ceremony to take place later today," said Iku's father. Then, he added, "Of course, you must stay here tonight, and every night thereafter until it is time for your departure."

"Thank you," said Yukio as he studied the woman who was old enough to be his mother, but instead would soon be his wife.

That night, when Yukio held his new bride, he struggled to suppress memories of his first wife. *Takara will be fine,* he told himself. *Should she choose to, she can quickly find another husband. If*

not, perhaps in a few years Iku will have died, and I can return to Takara a
wealthy man. Then, together, Takara and I can build a prosperous future.

Y ukio's time in Owari Province was better than he could
have dreamed. Not only was it a pleasure to work for
Masato, but his friend taught him new skills which would serve
Yukio well in the future. In two years' time, Yukio had saved a
large sum of money which, when added to Iku's dowry and the
many gifts from her father, made him a rich man.

Happy to be away from the pitying eyes of Kyoto, Iku took
good care of Yukio. But her age made her vulnerable, so when a
disease of the lungs plagued Owari Province, she sickened and
died.

Yukio, who'd never stopped thinking about Takara, began to
speculate how things would go when he returned to Kyoto. He
imagined Takara's face when he arrived at their old home clothed
in well-made garments with a wagon full of gifts for her. He was
certain their life would be filled with joy, and maybe even
children.

Therefore, when Masato's term as governor was over, Yukio
could barely contain his excitement as the friends made their
way back to Kyoto.

"Why are you so anxious to return to Kyoto?" asked Masato.

"Because my true love waits there," said Yukio. "I was
married briefly before Iku, and I hope to impress my first wife
with the wealth and knowledge I've gained these last two years."

His friend shook his head. "I hope she's forgiving," he said.
"Most women would've found another husband by now."

"Not, my Takara. I'm sure she still waits for me," replied
Yukio as he urged his horse to pick up its pace.

~

As Yukio approached the house where he and Takara had lived together, his heart pounded like the thrum of frogs in the spring. It looked little different from the day he'd left. But as he drew closer, he saw that the structure hadn't been maintained very well. Vines blocked the windows, the plum tree had been damaged by storms, and a patch of bamboo had crept to within a few feet of the house.

Undeterred, he climbed off his horse. He told the servant who drove the ox cart, over-flowing with expensive cloth, household goods, and Yukio's possessions, to tend to the animals while he went inside.

The man bowed his head, then began to do as he had been instructed.

"Takara," Yukio called. *What if she has found another?* he worried. Before he could consider her marital state further or shout her name a second time, his first wife appeared in the doorway to their bedroom

"You've come home," she whispered.

"Of course," he said. "Beloved Takara, you have been and always will be my true love."

Takara, who looked slimmer than he recalled, motioned for him to join her in their bedroom.

Without a thought about the servant outside, Yukio rushed into her arms. Serenaded by the music of leaves rustling, bees buzzing, and birds chirping, husband and wife once again made love. With his eyes closed, Yukio held his beloved against his chest. In his mind he saw the two of them welcoming children, then as parents watching their sons and daughters grow, then as a wrinkled couple holding grandchildren. It was a dream made all the more pleasant by the riches he'd earned while away.

He opened his eyes and glanced down at Takara. He gasped

when he saw that curled against his side was not a woman, but a dragon—a lovely, pointy-chinned dragon.

Before he could push the animal away, her lips parted, and the dragon that was Takara spoke, "If only you'd stayed with me —all would have been well. But the heart of an abandoned dragon grows cold."

Yukio saw her brown eyes grow dimmer. "What is happening?" he asked as he sat up and pushed the dragon away.

Takara seemed to look through him as she said, "Had you stayed a few days longer, I'd planned to tell you I was adopted, and reveal the wealth I'd hidden away years before." Then, the dragon who was his first wife gazed into his eyes and said in a voice soft as a butterfly floating to the ground, "Yukio, you betrayed me. You betrayed us."

He watched in horror as, within a minute, her scales fell away, her flesh decomposed, her bones were exposed, and her skeleton crumbled into ivory bits.

"No," Yukio screamed as he sprang from the bed, grabbed his clothes and, still wearing nothing but a look of shock, backed out of the house he and Takara had shared. He dressed quickly and, waving away his servant's questions, Yukio ran to their neighbor who was working in her garden.

"Excuse me," he said. "The woman who lived here," he pointed at Takara's house, "what became of her?"

His neighbor, who obviously didn't recognize Yukio in his expensive outfit, replied, "Takara's husband left her. She lived alone for a while but grew thinner than a river reed. Soon, no one saw her anymore. She is dead."

"Why didn't someone check on her? Help her?" asked Yukio.

The woman stood, brushed soil from her clothing, then answered, "We were afraid. That place was always strange. They say a demon, or worse, lived there years ago. With my own eyes, I've seen the shadow of a dragon upon the front door."

The neighbor stopped speaking and studied Yukio's face. "It wasn't my responsibility to take care of Takara. It was her husband's. He's to blame." She squinted before adding, "I think I know you."

"No," said Yukio. "You don't know me."

"Yes, I do." The neighbor woman stepped closer. "*You* are the husband who left her—*you* are Yukio!"

"No. I am just a distant relation who stopped in," said Yukio. "Sorry to have troubled you."

Yukio felt his former neighbor's eyes boring into his back as he hurried back to his horse, oxen, cart, and servant.

I suppose I'll find a place to stay in the city—perhaps with Masato, he mused. *We are, after all, good friends.* As he looked once more at the ramshackle building where he and Takara had shared a few magical weeks, he thought, *Although, I'm now a man rich in worldly goods, I am without Takara. I hope she believes the emptiness I feel is enough punishment.*

But he doubted a dragon would be so forgiving. He glanced back at Takara's house one last time. Then, though his servant—when questioned later—would say he saw nothing, Yukio witnessed a dragon, greener than a pine bough, emerge from the shadows. The magical creature peered at him from behind the plum tree. She stared at him with eyes red as blood, raised one razor-sharp claw, pointed it at Yukio, then drew the claw across her throat like an assassin's dagger.

Coldness creeping up his spine, Yukio watched the dragon. She lifted her pointy chin. Her red eyes returned to the umber of his first wife's eyes. The dragon, whom he knew was Takara, smiled before vanishing quicker then a stone tossed into the sea.

Sure now that the penalty for his betrayal was death, Yukio climbed onto his horse and motioned for his servant driving the ox cart to follow him.

How much time is left to me? he wondered as the clicking of the locusts in the treetops reminded him of the ticking of a clock.

In answer, a locust fell from the branch above Yukio and landed on his pants' leg. It buzzed loudly as he pulled it from his clothing. He looked at the insect's red eyes. They darkened. Then, the locust shriveled and turned to dust.

A sudden wind, laden with the scent of plum blossoms, scattered the locust's remains. A familiar voice rode the dancing air. It whispered, "Tonight, Yukio, I shall embrace you for the last time—with claws unsheathed."

WOLFBANE

O n the first day of spring, Maud heard the cries of the
creature before she spotted the featherless body
struggling to crawl from its shell.

"Poor baby," she said when she saw the tiny hatchling.

She looked around the weedy spot of ground under the
climbing rosebush at the corner of Mordiford Manor's garden
where the youngling lay but saw no fallen nest. Determined to
discover from whence the baby had come, she tilted her head
back and searched the oak branches above her. Nothing. No nest.
No frantic mother bird chirping for her nestling.

"You're an orphan, aren't you?" she asked, expecting no reply.
Then added as she scooped up the naked baby and hurried across
the lawn, "Don't worry, I will take care of you."

After wrapping the hatchling in her handkerchief, Maud
showed her mother what she had found.

Mother shook her head. "It won't live. It is too little."

"May I keep him? Try to save him?" asked Maud.

Mother sighed. As the only child of the Lord and Lady of
Mordiford, loneliness filled Maud's days. It was deemed

unseemly for her to interact with the village urchins, so she spent her free time amusing herself with books, dolls, and embroidery. And by playing in the manor's garden.

"I've been asking for a pet for months, Mother."

"You know your father is opposed to cats and dogs in the house," replied Lady Mordiford.

"He's neither cat nor dog," said Maud.

"If the bird lives," said the mistress of Mordiford Manor, gazing down at the scrawny nestling, "I suppose your father won't find it objectionable."

"Thank you, Mother!" exclaimed Maud.

"Just keep the creature in your room and don't let it bother your father."

"Don't worry. It won't cause any trouble," Maud called over her shoulder as she scampered to the kitchen to find something to feed the baby.

Cook had no use for the hatchling. "Take that pitiful beastie out of here," she said. "It's bound to get feathers in the meat pies."

"It doesn't have feathers yet," replied Maud. "I was hoping you would help me find something to feed it."

Cook rubbed her brow with the back of a flour-covered hand, then picked up some of the meat not yet placed in a crust. "Here are a few scraps of flesh from the pies. Now, off with you."

Maud took the proffered meat bits, a mug of milk, and a small wedge of cheese, and climbed the back stairs to her bedroom. With gentle hands, she unwrapped the hatchling and fed it tiny bits of meat and cheese. The creature eagerly gobbled the food. The shape of the mug didn't offer the baby a way to get a drink, so Maud took the lid off of a jar she used to store her trinkets in and turned it upside down. It was shallow enough that when she poured a spoonful of milk into it, the little creature could lower its head and lap up a drink.

Lap! The word seemed wrong for how a bird dips its beak into water for a sip.

Neither Mother nor Cook had really looked at Maud's pet. Little legs with clawed feet, two undeveloped wings, and a scaly, naked body were all they saw. But now, Maud realized the head wasn't a bird's head.

Upon closer inspection, she saw the skin wasn't rough because it lacked feathers. It was rough because it was finely scaled. The creature's oversized eyes had distinctive eye ridges above them. Its mouth wasn't a beak, but a long, narrow snout. Studying the nestling's feet, she noted they weren't bird feet, rather they had the toes of a lizard's foot.

"You're a wyvern!" exclaimed Maud. She wondered if he had fallen from a star rather than a nest. Then, as the reality of the situation set in, she whispered, "We can't let anyone else see you. Wyverns aren't welcome in Mordiford—or anywhere else in Herefordshire."

The wyvern squeaked.

With a laugh, Maud cupped the dragonet in her hand and stroked his neck with her forefinger. "What shall I name you?"

Suddenly, she thought she heard someone whisper, *Wolfbane.*

"Is that you?"

The creature gazed at her with otherworldly, yellowish-orange eyes and blinked three times.

"Wolfbane it is! I suppose that means wolves are your enemy. Well, that should make Father happy. He is always saying we must be careful, because the world is full of wolves trying to steal from us."

Later that day, and several times each day for weeks, Maud retrieved meat, cheese, and milk from the kitchen for Wolfbane. Neither Mother nor Cook checked on her new pet. Involved in their everyday activities and seeing to their many responsibilities, both women assumed the bird must have survived and now thrived under Maud's constant attention.

And Maud did pay constant attention to Wolfbane. The wyvern slept on the pillow beside her head at night and perched on her shoulder when she was in her room or in the garden far from the prying eyes of servants. In order to transport her pet from bedroom to garden, Maud carried him in a basket covered with a green scarf. Since the color of the fabric nearly matched his scales, Wolfbane was well hidden should someone stop and ask what it was she carried in her basket.

The girl and her dragon played games of catch, fetch, and hide-and-seek. Maud noticed as they engaged in various games of make-believe that Wolfbane was adept at hunting and consuming spiders, flies, crickets, and other garden pests. Soon, the wyvern graduated to catching and eating mice, moles, voles, and chipmunks. Though Maud dared not tell Cook why the pantry seemed rodent-free—it pleased her to know her pet was benefiting her parents' estate.

Weeks turned to months, and Wolfbane outgrew his basket and Maud's ability to feed him with kitchen scraps and captured rodents. After shedding a few tears because her pet could no longer stay in her bedroom, Maud located a close-by alternative: a small abandoned stable not far from the garden's edge. The forgotten building was hidden by a thicket of willow and thorns. It would be a perfect home for her wyvern.

Maud and Wolfbane walked there at dusk that evening when Mother thought them already abed. Carrying two old blankets, a bowl for water and one for food, a sack of meat scraps, a pitcher to dip water with, and a candle to light Maud's way back, they set to work making the stable comfortable.

Accessed by a sturdy door, the building had a storage loft and three stalls—each with a window. The windows had shutters and the stable had a wooden floor, so it was already a remarkably cozy abode even before Maud freshened it up. After adding the blankets and bowls, she made a mental list of other things she would bring to the stable to make it even nicer.

"You will be fine here, Wolfbane," she told her wyvern as she scratched his eye ridges and under his chin. "I have filled your bowls and you are welcome to wander the forest at night when no one can see you."

Wolfbane sighed.

"I know. I would much rather keep you in my room, but you need to hunt for bigger prey."

The wyvern blinked three times.

"Just remember—only wild animals. Stay away from father's sheep, cattle, horses, and chickens. But now, you'll be able to hunt rabbits, geese, ducks, and squirrels."

As you wish, Maud heard in her mind.

"I love you," she whispered as she gave Wolfbane a hug. Then, the girl exited the door—leaving it slightly ajar so her wyvern could easily slip in and out of the building.

And I you, came the response as she hurried back to the manor house.

In the morning, Maud ate a quick breakfast, grabbed several extra biscuits, and ran to the stable to check on Wolfbane. She burst through the door expecting to see a hungry dragon, but instead she found a slumbering wyvern with an obviously full stomach.

Wolfbane lifted his beautiful head, yawned, and smiled a toothy smile.

Rabbits are very tasty.

Maud made a face. "When one of Father's men brings in a brace of hares, we have to eat them. I don't like the taste of rabbit."

Slip the rabbit meat into your pocket and bring it to me! I will not turn down rabbit, thought Wolfbane.

"Don't worry, I will surely bring you any rabbit that lands on my plate!"

The girl and her dragon laughed.

Summer became fall, and with the chillier autumn winds, the stable didn't seem as cozy. Basket full by basket full, Maud carried several bales of straw to Wolfbane's stable. She heaped the bedding in the center stall, then covered it with the blankets. After securely latching the window shutters, she hung old animal hides she had located in a storage room in front of the windows.

They should be nailed down, suggested Wolfbane.

"You are right. I will get a few nails from one of Father's workers each day until we've got those hides secured. But," began Maud, "I can't borrow a hammer, or someone is sure to follow me to see what I am doing."

A flat rock should do.

"Brilliant idea," said Maud as she scurried out of the shed to look for a handful of nails.

Had Lord and Lady Mordiford, Cook, or anyone else been paying attention to Maud, they would have noticed her frequent absences. But no one was watching her closely. Had a servant followed young Mistress Mordiford, they would have been shocked at not only the transformation of the abandoned stable into a wonderful abode—but at discovering a fully grown wyvern residing on the property. And most certainly, had even the bravest man seen the dragon resting his scaly head in Maud's lap while she itched behind his ears and told him stories—they would have been in awe of the fearlessness of the girl.

But the friendship of Maud and Wolfbane remained undiscovered through early winter. At Yuletide, the heavy snow clearly showed footprints leading out of the garden and into the thicket which hid the stable. A trail of footprints Thomas, the servant in charge of stoking the fireplaces throughout Mordiford Manor, decided to investigate.

Thomas's shouts brought a throng of servants and Lady Mordiford out of their warm dwelling into the wintry cold.

All gasped when they beheld the emerald-scaled dragon standing in the snow beside his stable. Several of the women screamed. The blood smeared around the dragon's mouth deemed him guilty of slaughtering several of Lord Mordiford's prize sheep—sheep that had gone missing only the day before.

"Sir Garston. Call Sir Garston," cried the crowd. "He is a swordsman."

"Get Lord Mordiford and our dinner guest," ordered Lady Mordiford. "Tell them a wyvern has been killing our livestock and living in the old stable." Almost as an afterthought, she added, "And bring me a warmer wrap. I am quite cold."

By the time Lord Mordiford and Sir Garston raced through the kitchen door, across the garden, and to wood's edge where the crowd stood gawking at the dragon, Maud had run to Wolfbane. She leaned against his chest with her left hand resting on his scales.

"He is friendly. He never kills any of Father's animals—only wild creatures. Please, don't hurt him," begged Maud.

"The blood on his muzzle proves his guilt," said Lord Mordiford. "Move away, and let Garston put an end to the star-beast."

"Father, no! He is my pet. I raised him from the day he hatched. Mother said I could keep him last spring and..."

"Silence!" shouted her father.

Lord Mordiford glared at his wife. "Did you know it was a wyvern? A spawn of another world?"

"Heavens, no," replied Lady Mordiford. "Had I known, I would have drowned the creature myself."

"Mother, please."

Distracted by Maud's pleading and the crowd of people, Wolfbane didn't notice Sir Garston circling the stable. The creature was taken by surprise when the warrior rushed at him from behind and thrust a sword between his ribs.

As he roared in pain, Maud dropped to her knees and covered her ears with her hands. Rather than attack Garston or the crowd —the dragon wrapped his wing protectively around Maud and collapsed.

Still determined to end Wolfbane's life, Garston shoved his sword's blade deeper into the dragon. Then, certain he had mortally wounded the beast, he withdrew the dripping weapon from the wyvern's side.

"No," sobbed Maud as Wolfbane groaned. She cradled his greener-than-ivy head in her lap.

The wyvern gazed at the girl with his lovely yellow-orange eyes as she caressed his cheek.

I would never eat your father's animals, thought the dragon. *The blood on my mouth is from a wolf I caught stealing Lord Mordiford's sheep. I saved the wolf's body to show you. It is in the stable.*

"I am sorry they hurt you," said Maud as the winged dragon closed his eyes.

Do not blame yourself. You saved me, gave me love. I am grateful to have known you, dear Maud, came the reply.

The servants, Lord and Lady Mordiford, and even the usually swaggering Sir Garston stood silent as the dragon seemingly exhaled for the last time and Maud cried as if her heart was torn in two.

Eventually, the girl placed the wyvern's scaly head upon the snowy ground, stood, and pointed an accusing finger at her father. "You have killed not only my friend, but the guard beast that was protecting your sheep. Look inside the stable. There lies the wolf who savaged your herd—killed by my beloved Wolfbane."

Sir Garston checked the stable. "She speaks the truth," he said gruffly. "It appears the wyvern was guarding your animals."

"I have done nothing wrong," said Lord Mordiford with a wave of his hand. "By law, the wyvern had to be killed and its hide hung on the side of a barn as a warning to all such beasts to stay away."

Maud said nothing as her father ordered the wyvern to be skinned and its hide to be nailed to the side of the barn closest to the public road.

"As for its head," said Lord Mordiford as he turned to return to the dining hall for dessert, "it will be mounted and displayed in my library as a sign of the power of the Mordiford family."

"A power that will end with me," said Maud.

Her father stopped, then whirled around to face his only child.

"I will mourn all of my days the loss of Wolfbane, my one true friend. I will take no husband. I will bear no children. Upon your death, I will give away your wealth."

"Perhaps we will have another child," replied Lord Mordiford in a voice filled with loathing.

Maud gasped. She knew without question she had never been wanted or loved by Father.

"Dear, let us not be hasty in condemning..." began Mother.

Father shrugged Mother's hand from his arm. "She is your daughter. Deal with her." Then, without another glance at his daughter, Lord Mordiford strode into the manor house.

When the guards went to retrieve the dragon's body—it was gone. It appeared that while everyone's attention was focused on

Lord Mordiford, Wolfbane had vanished. No beheading had been accomplished. No wyvern-skinning had occurred. And no one dare speak of the missing dragon.

~

The following month was not kind to Lord Mordiford. He fell from his horse while hunting winter boar and was gored. After a week of suffering, he succumbed to his wounds. Lady Mordiford sickened from the pox in early spring and was dead and buried before the first blooms of May.

As for Maud, once she became Lady Maud, she divided the Mordiford lands, animals, and possessions up between the servants. For herself, she kept the garden and land surrounding the stable. After selling the manor house, Maud built a small cottage beside the stable where she had spent countless happy hours with Wolfbane.

The servants kept an eye on their former mistress. They observed that each day, Maud gathered a bouquet of greens and flowers which she laid upon the spot where the wyvern had last been seen. And every day, she sat on the ground and cried for the star-beast.

~

Autumn came and went, but the servants saw no lessening of Maud's terrible sadness.

One snowy evening, nearly a year after the dragon's disappearance, the former servants observed no smoke coming from Lady Maud's chimney. Fearing the worst, Cook, a retired groom, and several farmhands knocked upon the cottage's door. When no answer came, they opened it and entered Maud's cottage.

By lantern-light, Cook and the others saw large, wet footprints on the cottage's wooden floor which led to the open back door.

"Oh, no," Cook screamed. "The beast must have survived. The dragon has healed, returned for revenge, and taken Lady Maud!"

"Wait," said the old groom as he pointed at a small clearing behind the cottage. There beneath the starless, winter sky Maud climbed astride Wolfbane. "She goes with him freely."

Mouths gaping, the servants stood in the doorway and witnessed the dragon lift into the air with several strokes of his green wings. They tilted back their heads and gazed up at the fearsome wyvern soaring above the trees. Eyes wide with wonder, they saw Maud, bundled in warm clothes, riding on Wolfbane's back.

Before they could call out to their former mistress to return, the star-beast roared, and the pair vanished in a swirl of snow.

KINDNESS

Though he seemed destined to be poor from birth to death, Makoto worked hard, honored the gods, and took care of his crippled mother. It was a lonely life for a young man, but he tried to make the best of things and was known in his village, despite his poor circumstances, for being helpful and pleasant.

Determined to find a way to improve both his and his mother's lives, Makoto regularly visited the temples of Kannon, goddess of mercy, and prayed to her for a miracle. But no miracle happened.

One autumn morning, while walking through southern Yamashina to yet another one of Kannon's temples, Makoto met a man coming in the opposite direction carrying a pole with a small snake tied to it. To no avail, the reptile squirmed and flopped about in an attempt to free itself.

After exchanging greetings, Makoto asked, "Why are you carrying a snake?"

The man, who'd said his name was Kenji, explained, "I need the oil from this snake to work into ox horns which I carve and shape into wands." Kenji moved the pole back and forth causing the snake to writhe all the more. "Monks use the wands in various sacred rites. I hate to kill it, but a man's got to earn a living."

Makoto looked at the snake and would have sworn the creature stared back at him with an intelligence akin to that of a human. "Is there no other oil you can use?"

The wand maker shrugged his shoulders and tilted his head. "Yes, but I spotted the snake curled by a pond just up the road— so why not grab a source of free oil?"

"So, there are other oils that would work as well?"

Kenji nodded.

"Then, let me buy this snake," offered Makoto. "It's so young, I hate to see it killed."

"How much will you pay?" asked the wand maker.

"I have no money, but I'll trade my coat for the snake." Makoto removed his coat. He hoped warm weather lingered long enough for him to earn the money to purchase another one.

Kenji laughed. "I can sell this coat for more than the cost of oil, so I'll make a profit on the deal." He laughed again. "Here's your snake."

"Thank you," answered Makoto as he knelt, untied the string which bound the snake to the pole, and carefully held the serpent with his right hand. As he studied its face, he saw the creature had ruffled flesh above its eyes, a few whisker-like feelers near its rather elongated face, and a mouth which seemed more fitting for a lizard then a serpent. The pattern on the snake's back was just as strange—an intricate weave of diamonds, hexagons, ovals, and stripes in shades of peacock, indigo, and forest green.

With Kenji gone, Makoto spoke to the serpent, "Little one, let's find that pond and put you back where you belong."

The creature blinked its orange eyes.

After hiking for no more than five minutes, Makoto spotted a large pond. The reeds and other water plants along the pond's edge grew nearly to the road upon which he stood.

"Here we go." He bent down and released the snake which slithered quickly into the still, emerald water.

Without another thought about the beautiful serpent, Makoto resumed his journey to Kannon's temple. As the road wound around the pond for some distance, he'd not yet passed the end of the water when he saw a young girl, beautifully dressed, coming towards him. He frowned. The woods were a dangerous place for a child to be alone.

Before he could voice his concerns to the girl, she said, "I'm here to thank you."

"I don't know what you're referring to. I've never seen..."

"But you have seen me before, Makoto. Just a few minutes ago, you released me back into my parents' pond."

He was speechless. Like all of the children of his village, Makoto had heard tales of shape-changers. Some were evil, some tricksters, and a few were kind.

"Come," said the girl holding her hand out to him. "My parents want to meet you."

Makoto's heart raced, but fearing he'd offend the snake-girl if he declined her offer, he took her hand. "Do your parents live around here?" he asked, afraid of the answer.

"Of course," the child responded. "In the depths of the pond."

Feeling weak-in-the-knees, he whispered, "I cannot swim."

"There's no need. Close your eyes, and I'll take you to them."

Makoto had barely lowered his eyelids when he felt himself slicing through water.

Before he could open his mouth to cry out, the girl said, "Open your eyes."

When he did so, Makoto found himself standing inside a courtyard. Rather than dirt or pebbles, the stones beneath his feet were semi-precious gems. Before him rose a gate of wrought gold and silver. The metalwork was shaped into images of every fantastical creature he'd ever heard about from the storytellers and more. Animals and magical beings that his imagination had never before conjured were woven into the gate before him.

The girl pushed open the gate and grabbed his hand again. She led Makoto to a central pavilion built of jade from the purest white to a green so dark, it was nearly black. There stood a man and woman with crowns upon their heads.

Makoto bowed and started to kneel.

"Do not kneel, Makoto," said the man. "As the person who saved our daughter, it is we who are honored to be in your presence."

"I did nothing special," responded the coatless young man.

"That is where you are wrong," said the woman wearing the crown. "Kindness such as you showed is rare and deserves a reward."

"There is no need for reward," said Makoto. "Though, should you have an old coat or jacket about, I'd appreciate the loan of it while I continue on my way to..."

"I think we can afford a better reward," said the man in the crown.

In less time than it takes a carp to flick its tail, the man, woman, and girl transformed into dragons. The king, for that was whom Makoto knew him now to be, was the largest dragon with scales of indigo and ultramarine. The queen was covered in scales of malachite and spring green. And the girl's scales were the same beautiful colors as the small snake's scales had been. Their eyes were reddish orange, and upon their heads all three wore golden crowns.

Despite the king's early request to remain standing, Makoto fell prostrate.

"Rise," ordered the Dragon King. When Makoto had done so,

he continued, "For your kindness, we give you not only a new coat—one which will never fray, never need to be repaired, and will never allow itself to be taken from you by another—but also this rice cake."

As he spoke, two servants appeared. One helped Makoto into a perfectly-fitting coat. The other placed a thick, golden-colored rice cake in his hand.

"I don't know what to say but thank you."

The Dragon Queen reached down, tapped the rice cake with one of her needle-sharp claws. "Break off a piece and eat it."

Makoto did as she directed him to do. As he chewed, he decided this was the most delicious thing he'd ever tasted. He was about to tell the Dragon Queen so, when he noticed the place where he'd broken off a bite had repaired itself. The golden-colored rice cake was again whole.

"Never again will you be cold or hungry," promised the Dragon King.

"Or poor," added the daughter of the king and queen as she gave him a heavy sack. "Coins and gems enough to last a lifetime are within, but do not check the bag until you have left our palace."

"Speaking of which—" The king clacked his claws together. "Our daughter will now take you to the pond's edge, then return *immediately* to the palace. No resting on the bank near the road again."

The smallest dragon grinned, then faster than the twitch of a dragonfly's wing, she morphed into a young girl. As Makoto's hands now held the sack of riches and the rice cake, the Dragon Princess grasped his arm, led him to the palace's entrance, and told him to shut his eyes.

In less time than it takes a nightingale to open its beak, Makoto found himself standing on the edge of the pond with his new-found riches.

"Thank you again, Makoto," said the dragon-girl. "Go home, live a good life, and always remember to choose kindness."

"I will try," he replied as she changed into a small snake, squirmed into the pond, and vanished below the water's surface.

U pon returning to his village, Makoto built a modest home for his mother and him. He soon met, fell in love with, and married a shy, but intelligent woman, and they had five children. Countless times, he showed kindness and generosity to friends, neighbors, and even strangers. In fact, it was said by all who met him that Makoto was the kindest man in all of Japan.

As the years unwound like silk thread from the spool of their lives, Makoto and his wife, their children, grandchildren, and great-grandchildren were never hungry or cold or poor. Upon Makoto's death, the golden-colored rice cake and his favorite jacket vanished. But having been wise in his investments and passing that wisdom on to his offspring, Makoto's sack of coins and gems was never empty. And, it is said, his descendants have a bit of dragon wealth still.

BLOODGUILTLESS

I n order to dip their oars in the Nodin in a synchronized
manner, Paco, Grandfather, and Nina sang a seafarer's tune.
Using the rhythm of the song, they were able to smoothly
row to the sacred beach where they would honor Anna Tuwa, the
spirit of *this* world. Nina knew that in the Olden Times, her
People had honored the first Mother in a similar way. But things
were changing, and fewer and fewer of the kelp farmers, fisher
folk, clammers, shipwrights, and nest-gatherers of the city of
Halona acknowledged their heritage.

"There she is." Grandfather gestured toward a rock
formation.

Paco, Grandfather, and Nina guided their boat to the pebbly
shore, climbed out, and dragged the craft above the tide line.
They took a few items from their gear and stood reverently
before the sacred stone.

"Begin, child," said Grandfather in a voice as solemn as the
cry of a lone osprey.

With a nod, Nina knelt before the enormous stalagmite that
guarded the mouth of Hassun Cave. "Anna Tuwa, loving

Goddess, we thank you for protecting your children." She placed a nosegay of spring blossoms at the base of the rock formation which resembled a broad-hipped woman with her arms by her sides.

"Anna Tuwa, Mother to us all, we thank you for sharing your bounty with your children," said Nina's grandfather, Old Kuruk, as he knelt, then poured a flask of wine on the shell fragments at the foot of the tall boulder.

Nina studied the womanly-shaped rock. Perhaps it was the way the sunlight shadowed the front of the formation, but she thought she saw the Goddess bend her head slightly.

"Anna Tuwa, spirit of our world, we thank you for welcoming your children to this new home," a kneeling Paco said as he sprinkled a bag of corn kernels before the mammoth rock.

Again, Nina thought she saw the Goddess rock move.

With heads bowed, the three nest-gatherers touched the sacred stone with the prongs of their nest-gathering tools. Named for the five-toed cat, their *mosi* was the only safe way to remove the bodaway nests from the cave walls. Then, they stood, backed away from Anna Tuwa, and boarded their skiff. After wrapping their tools in sailcloth and stowing them in a compartment in the bow of the boat, they paddled toward the nest-gatherers' platform.

"Look," whispered Nina as the dorsal fin of a cave shark sliced the water's surface near the boat. She could see countless dark forms swimming around them just below the foam.

"Don't worry," said her grandfather. "They wait for the careless and the weak. We are neither."

She nodded, but continued to gaze at the sharks' sleek bodies. "I'll be glad when we reach the gatherers' platform."

Paco, who cooked for the nest-gatherers, agreed, "I can't wait to reach the platform as well. There is much work for a cook to do, but there is also much cook for a shark to eat." He patted his prominent belly and chuckled.

Nina and her grandfather laughed along with their friend.

Within minutes, Nina, Grandfather, and Paco glided into the sea-cave and docked their skiff below a suspended wooden deck. Once the vessel was secured with multiple ropes, they climbed the pinewood ladder up onto the gatherers' platform. The other four nest-gatherers on their crew were already unpacking supplies and personal gear.

"Finally here," said Chayton. "Well, Old Kuruk, did Anna Tuwa appreciate your gifts?" The crew chief's disdain for the old ways colored his words. "Did she bless your *mosi*, so you will gather more nests than the rest of us?"

Nina opened her mouth to reply, but Grandfather placed his hand on her arm, and gestured for her to remain silent.

"Chayton, you tempt the cave spirits with your words. We appease them with our humbleness. Let's hope that balances things out," said her grandfather.

"Old man, you waste your time. Storms have put us two weeks behind schedule. We need to be working, not worshiping."

Chayton turned to the rest of the gatherers. "Drag your gear up, get your *mosi* in hand, and climb. Each of us must have fifty nests in our sacks at the end of the day, no matter how late the hour we begin working. Remember, the Guild depends on us."

The other gatherers pulled their remaining gear up from the boats below, picked up their nest-bags and *mosi,* and began to climb hand-over-hand up the hevataneo vines to the wooden scaffolding above.

Nina watched them. Team Two, the first team to climb today, consisted of Tupi and his sister, Meli. Meli was the only other female nest-gatherer sent to Hassun this year. The second team to scale the vine pillar and reach the first platform was Team One: Hinto and the crew chief, Chayton.

"See you later, Paco," said Nina as she began her ascent.

Nina, Old Kuruk, and Paco were Team Three; although Paco would not begin to harvest any nests until after he had prepared, served, and cleaned up breakfast. In order to begin supper for the crew, he also had to stop harvesting early in the day. His daily quota was only twenty-five nests. And some days, it was hard for Paco to meet even that small number.

"Keep safe, little Nina," answered the cook as he began to unpack his pots and utensils.

She smiled. Even though she was seventeen and over five feet tall, Paco still saw her as the dark-eyed little girl that lived next to him in Halona. This served her well when his younger son, Wade, bothered her.

While she waited for her grandfather to reach the first platform, Nina held onto a braid of hevataneo vines and adjusted the nest-bag and *mosi* that she carried on her shoulders. She tilted her chin and studied the intricate network of walkways and hevataneo vine bridges that crisscrossed Hassun Cave.

Above her, each gatherer carried a torch in one hand as they worked. As Nina watched Teams One and Two weave their way through the main chamber, she thought of stars twinkling at mirknight.

"Wake-up, granddaughter."

Nina started at the sound of Grandfather's voice in her ear. "Sorry, I was thinking of home."

"Halona will be there when we return."

Nina nodded, then began to work her way up to a narrow passageway which would lead them into another part of the cavern. Under her feet, pine boards creaked and complained as she reached the entrance to the tunnel. The acrid stench of bodaway and bat guano that wafted out of the next chamber caused her to gasp, and then, cough. It had been the same last year and the years before. The first day in Hassun was a readjustment period. During the year in Halona, the memory of the smells, sounds, and sights of the cave faded in the minds of the gatherers.

"Listen," said Grandfather.

Nina heard the muffled sounds of the bodaway: thousands of wings flapping, thousands of small mouths tittering, thousands of toenails clicking against limestone.

"They're frightened," she whispered.

"Yes. The others have begun the harvesting."

With sinuous movements, Nina and her grandfather traversed several bridges and platforms which snaked through the chamber where the other nest-gatherers were hard at work. They reached the opposite side of the dark pit and scooted through another cramped passage. Thus, they continued through seven more wells of darkness, their twisted path lit only by the gleam of torchlight and the faint sparking of the bodaway at work on their nests.

Upon entering the ninth cavern, Grandfather spoke. "We will begin here." He lifted his torch and pointed to the uppermost walls of the chamber that bulged above the abyss.

Nina pressed her lips together. She concentrated on the hairy, rope-like hevataneo vines and pinewood trellises banded together by generations of nest-gatherers who had worked Hassun Cave since before Old Kuruk was born. This deep in the cavern, Nina paused and tapped the boards before she stepped onto the bridge in front of her. They sang the ringing sound of good wood, so Nina trusted her weight to the pine and climbed up to the highest niche of the chamber.

"Ah." Grandfather raised his torch to illumine a cluster of bodaway nests. They glowed with a milky translucence.

The bodaway were frantic. They chattered and squawked.

Usually excellent navigators, using their rapid chittering and echolocation to find their way in the dark maze of their cave, the panicking bodaway flew into Nina and Grandfather. Then, stunned by the impact with the gatherers, the reptiles fluttered in silence to the nearest vine.

Before collecting a nest, Nina looked inside each one to make sure there were no early eggs. To take an occupied nest was a sacrilege, and the spirits of the cave were sure to turn an evil eye on a gatherer who committed infanticide. Next, using her five-pronged *mosi*, she pried the pale nests from the walls and dropped them in her nest-bag.

Below her, Grandfather did the same. They were careful never to touch the bodaway nests with anything other than a *mosi* until after they had been removed from the slick limestone. To do so would be stealing from the cave spirits and from the Goddess.

"Oh, no."

"What is it, child?"

"There are two eggs in this nest." Nina pointed to the shimmering cup around which an angry bodaway hovered.

Grandfather climbed up to Nina. He looked into the nest and at several others nearby.

"Check for eggs carefully. Four other nests on this stalactite are occupied."

Nina frowned. "What is happening?"

"We have begun too late this spring. We'll be lucky to get one full harvest before we must leave Hassun." Grandfather rubbed his forehead, then continued, "We will have to return at the end of summer for a final harvest."

"We usually get three batches of nests."

"Not this year," her grandfather observed.

Nina and Grandfather worked for four more hours. Grandfather kept count of the nests they placed in their nest-bags.

"The work is harder, because we must avoid the occupied nests, but there are still plenty of empties to make our quota and beyond," he said as they ate their lunch of dried seaweed, fruit, and nuts.

"But we don't eat any nests, so it's easier for us to make quota."

"Do you really like them raw?"

Nina wrinkled her nose. "No." She thought about how gummy and tasteless the nests were when she ate them raw. "They remind me of chewy jellyfish."

Grandfather laughed. "Chayton and the others believe it gives them the strength of the bodaway."

"They're just too lazy to carry food and water when they climb."

"True, but I would keep that to myself. We'd all like a peaceful evening tonight."

"Look," whispered Nina as she pointed to a spot on the cavern's wall where she had removed a nest before lunch.

A bodaway was rebuilding her nest. They sat watching the industrious reptile. She withdrew a strand of saliva from a pale pink gland under her tongue with her claws and pressed it onto the limestone. After uttering a series of clicks, she exhaled a burst of flame that dried the glutinous string. The bodaway repeated the process again and again. By the time Nina and her grandfather finished their lunch, the little fire-maker had woven a thin webbing shaped like a small soup bowl. The skeleton of a nest glistened in the feeble light of her fiery breath.

"It is like a miracle."

"No," said Grandfather. "It *is* a miracle."

Nina and her grandfather continued to fill their nest-bags for several more hours. In the torchlight, she noticed Grandfather's forehead glinting. His wrinkles became deeper, more pronounced as the day wore on.

"I think we should finish our water and head back to the gatherers' platform," she said.

"Yes," he answered. "I need to rest for just a moment, then we can start back."

Grandfather and Nina sat on a pinewood and vine bridge hundreds, perhaps thousands, of feet above the cave bottom. They were careful not to sit on a knot of hevataneo vines, for small cave sprites were said to inhabit the knots. Small cave sprites, whom she'd been told, could trip a nest-gatherer as she scampered down a ladder and send her plummeting to her death. Before she could conjure up more images of the cave sprites' faces flashing by as she fell into the deep pit of Anna Tuwa's belly, her grandfather stood.

"Lead the way," he said, and slipped his bag of nests back onto his shoulder.

She nodded but noticed before she turned to head back to the gatherers' platform that her grandfather's legs quivered, ever so slightly. This would be the last year Grandfather gathered the nests.

Like skilled rope-walkers, Nina and Grandfather traveled the underworld chambers on a serpentine trail of pinewood and hevataneo, always careful to grasp four or five of the vines. "Never trust your weight to just one vine" was the favorite saying of the nest-gatherers. And Grandfather made Nina recite that rule every day during nest-gathering season three times before they climbed up to the first platform.

Almost an hour later, they emerged from the labyrinth of deep caverns. Below them, Nina saw the bright torches of the gatherers' platform. They washed the sweat and filth of the day from their bodies at the cleaning station, and then, stepped onto the main section of the wooden deck.

Paco ladled a thick fish stew into two wooden bowls. "You are the last in tonight," he said as he handed them their dinner.

"There were eggs in many of the nests, so it took a little longer to make quota," replied Grandfather before bowing his head.

Nina bowed her head, too, and thanked the Goddess for her protection and generosity. Then, she lifted her chin and told the cook, "We saw a bodaway rebuilding her nest."

"You are a lucky girl. Not everyone gets to see such a thing."

"And they had better rebuild them fast, because we'll be harvesting again soon," mumbled Chayton, his mouth full of fish.

Her grandfather shook his head. "I don't think that will happen this year. More nests will fill with eggs each day that we are here. The harvest will be smaller."

"I am Chief Harvester, and *I* say we will do two spring harvests before we let the bodaway raise their young. We've got to think of what is best for the nest-gatherers and their position in the Guild," replied Chayton.

Nina saw the challenge in his eyes. *He knows this is Grandfather's last year as a gatherer*, she thought.

"And it is the last year anyone is gonna waste drink on a boulder." Chayton lifted his mug, filled with honey wine, as if toasting Grandfather's retirement.

"Agreed, agreed," cheered Tupi and Hinto. Meli, as usual, remained silent.

"Hush," warned Paco. The cook lifted his hands to the cave ceiling. "The cave spirits and ghosts of the nest-gatherers of old will hear."

Everyone grew quiet. Even Chayton glanced at the human-shaped shadows cast by the stalactites, stalagmites, and columns.

"Tell us a tale, Old Kuruk, while we prepare tomorrow's torches," urged Paco. "It will chase away this feeling of ill-luck."

"You have all heard them before."

"Tell them again," said Meli.

Nina's grandfather raised his eyebrows. Meli rarely spoke, and when she did, it was usually to complain or scold.

"Since you ask, child, I will tell the tale of the Great Migration."

The gatherers settled on their sleeping mats and watched the firelight dance across Old Kuruk's face as he retold their history.

"In the Olden Times, on Terra, the First Mother, there were many tribes and many nations. As mankind mistreated the First Mother, she grew weak and tired. Too tired to take care of the millions of men and women who were her children.

"It was decided that a Great Migration would be embarked upon. All the tribes of Our People combined their languages, their power, their wealth. When the Seed Ships were cast upon the Ocean of Stars, Our People had a place on each ship. It was the time of the Long Dreaming.

"The Seed Ships sailed for almost forever in the Ocean of Stars, and Our People and all the other tribes of men slept the sleep of the dead. Finally, near the shores of forever, the Seed Ships each found their island. Our Seed Ship found Earth Settlement Five, our new mother. Known to Our People as Anna Tuwa."

Old Kuruk paused, pointed out the mouth of Hassun Cave. "The bodaway, who swoop over the ocean feasting on small fishes, were only one of the new and strange creatures that humankind discovered on ES5. But we did not come unprepared. We brought many animals with us, stored in glass bottles.

"When Our People and the rest of humankind on Seed Ship Five reached ES5, we planted the animal seeds and grew the cattle, sheep, horses, and chickens of the First Mother. But did we just bring these few practical animals?"

"No," murmured the nest-gatherers.

"No," repeated Nina's grandfather. "We brought seeds for the totem animals of Our People, too. We brought the Wolf to remind us to persevere, we brought the Squirrel to make us laugh, we brought the gentle Deer, we brought the wise Whale, the powerful Bear, and many more."

"Don't forget Turtle," said Nina.

"No, we never forget Turtle, who reminds us of creation and eternal life." Her grandfather smiled.

"And so, Our People settled with the other nations of men and women on our new home and honored our new mother, Anna Tuwa of the Thousand Islands. For Anna Tuwa has many islands no bigger than a few rocks poking their heads above the Nodin Sea, where black iguanas munch on sea plants and ocean birds stretch their white wings in the daylight. And Anna Tuwa has islands so large that they hold a land like Gad, with cities, towns, great mountains, and vast deserts. But wherever men go on Anna Tuwa, there is always the Nodin Sea—swirling with angry winds and stirred into a bubbling soup by storms. Always the sea.

"But the men and women of the fortunate city of Halona, that rests between the banks of the Donoma River and the Nodin Sea, rejoice in the ways of the waterman. We are the fishermen, the kelp farmers, the nest-gatherers, the gleaners of shellfish. We are the custodians of the rich shores of Gad."

"Tell of the nests," urged Tupi.

Nina's grandfather cupped his hands into a bowl shape. "In the Olden Time when Our People first came to Halona, to the shores of the sparkling waters of the Donoma River, to the shores of the white-capped Nodin—two brave fisherman set sail for a small island not far from the edge of Gad. They named the island Moki, for it was as beautiful as a doe. It was they who first saw the bodaway, the little fire-makers, soar in and out of the caves. It was they who gathered the first nests.

"The fishermen brought the nests back to their wives, who decided to wash away the impurities and cook the nests in the sweet water of the Donoma. The broth made by the fishwives of Halona was discovered to be a magical cure for diseases of the skin and stomach. Its healing ability was without end.

"We must protect this secret, decided the fishermen and their wives. They decided to add the nest-gatherers to the Sea Guild. Like the fisher folk, kelp farmers, shellfish harvesters, and shipwrights, they swore to preserve and pass down to the next generation the secrets of their trade. And so, the nest-gatherers of Gad began. And through the long years, the gatherers have kept the secrets of the caves, protected the flocks of bodaway, and prepared the broth.

"It is an ancient trust handed down from parents to children, from grandparents to grandchildren, from uncle to nephew. A sacred trust, which the nest-gatherers are sworn to uphold."

The seven gatherers sat motionless, gazing at the flames of the cooking fire, thinking of the traditions of their ancestors.

"No one has made even a single torch," said Paco after a few minutes of fire-gazing.

Chayton looked around the platform. "No more fireside tales. Get tomorrow's torches completed."

Without argument, the nest-gatherers broke into their teams and began to make their torches. They each pulled strips of pine bark, which had been soaking in sap, from a crock located on the back corner of the gatherers' platform. They wrapped the pliable bark tightly around their torch sticks and bound it with string. It was a tedious job, but a well-wrapped torch burned longer and more brightly.

"I gathered only twenty-five nests today," said Paco to Old Kuruk as he worked on his torch. "A late start, a flabby body, and some full nests left no time for an extra nest or two."

"We did well, though the gathering was slow because of the early eggs," her grandfather replied.

Grandfather had warned Nina not to brag to Paco or the

others, but he had told her they'd managed to collect one hundred and seventeen nests between them.

"Of course, we do not eat the nests," said Nina as she finished binding her torch.

"And why is that, granddaughter?"

She sighed. "We must save the extra nests to take home to Halona. There, we will make ointments and home remedies from our extra nests. For people come not just from Halona, but from all over Gad for Old Kuruk's ointments and remedies."

"And for Nina's," her grandfather added. "And why is that?"

"Because our ancestors were medicine men and women. Many of The People who still honor the ancient traditions know Old Kuruk and his granddaughter continue the healing ways of the ancestors."

Her grandfather nodded. "The other nest-gatherers will sell the extra nests beyond their fifty-per-day quota to the nest-dealers. It is bonus money above salary."

"We have no choice," said Paco as he sipped a mug of honey wine. "I support my wife, two sons, my mother-in-law and her sister. Most nest-gatherers support an assortment of relatives. And most of us haven't the knowledge to make our own ointments. So we must also work for the kelp farmers."

"True," said Grandfather. "But nest-gathering is a reliable source of income, and work in the rendering halls goes to Guild members first."

"I hope my sons are offered a Guild membership." Paco wrapped a blanket around his shoulders and studied the fire.

"If that is what you wish, then I hope it, too," Nina's grandfather said to his friend.

Nina unbraided her long dark hair, curled up on her sleeping mat, and pulled a light shawl over her body. She could see the reflection of Grandmother Moon on the glassy surface of the Nodin. The edge of the cave entrance overhang blocked her view of the real moon, but she was satisfied to gaze at her wavering twin.

She wondered if the night fishes thought the reflections of the stars were glowbugs. In answer to her question, she heard the splash of a fish as it leaped from the tidal wash, and then, plopped back into the water. She fell asleep listening to the deep-voiced conversation of her grandfather and Paco.

~

"Nina, Nina," called Grandfather as he tapped her shoulder. After rolling onto her back, Nina wiped the sleep out of her eyes. "Morning already? I was dreaming about the bodaway again."

"Perhaps they are your totem. Though, I have never heard of bodaway being anyone's totem before. Totems are usually the animals we brought from the First Mother."

"How will I know for sure which animal is my totem?"

He patted her hand. "You will know, granddaughter. You will know."

She smiled at her grandfather, then crept to her washbowl, dipped her hands into the chilly water, and splashed her face.

Most of her crewmates were just waking up, but not Paco. The cook had risen early and was currently stirring a kettle of hominy. The eating table was already laden with a platter of dried fruit and nuts, a large pan of cornbread, and mugs of steaming tea.

"Need help?" asked Nina after she had re-braided her hair.

"Bring the bowls over to me before the grits scorch," said Paco.

She did as she was told.

"Now, hold them steady while I dish out the hominy."

After the cook filled each bowl, Nina carried it over to the table and set it down. By the time all seven bowls were ready, most of the crew were sitting cross-legged around the low pinewood table, beginning their meal.

"An early start today. That's good," said Tupi as he stuffed a chunk of cornbread in his mouth. "More time to gather."

"Everyone make quota yesterday?"

Hinto frowned at Chayton. "Barely. Too many nests have eggs in them. There will be little profit for us at this rate."

Chayton rubbed his chin. "A dropped egg or two is not a tragedy."

"Blasphemy," hissed Meli.

Nina stared at the scowling girl. She was surprised Meli still honored the old ways.

"Do what you wish, Meli. But if you do not make quota plus bonus, I don't want to hear your whining." Meli scowled at the crew chief as he continued, "How about you, Tupi? Empty nests only?"

Tupi glanced at his sister, and then, at the crew chief. He shrugged his shoulders. "Our team works together. If Meli doesn't want to dump the eggs, I won't either."

Chayton snorted. "Suit yourselves, but I'm not paddling back to Halona for salary alone. I am going to get a fat bonus from the nest-dealers, and if that means dumping a few eggs—so be it."

"Greedy nest-gatherers chased the bodaway from Kaliska Island. Over-harvesting chased the bodaway from Moki Island. Now, we paddle by them on our way to Hassun. Even if the Goddess allows you to desecrate this cavern, the bodaway will leave. How far then will we have to paddle to find nests?" asked Nina's grandfather.

"Some of us have big families to support, but if you're afraid of ghosts and angry bodaway, you can stay with the cook today. We would not want you to fall, Old Kuruk."

Meli gasped. Nina took quick shallow breaths. Tupi made a warding sign.

"Fool," whispered Paco. "Such language wakes the spirits. They will cause an accident."

"Ha." Chayton grabbed his nest-bag and strode to the hevataneo pillar. Hinto hurried after him. The rest of the nest-gatherers watched as Team One reached the first platform and dashed across a vine bridge.

"We will honor the bodaway. There will be no eggs discarded by Team Two," said Meli. Her brother nodded in agreement.

"I hope that will be enough," sighed Grandfather.

As Nina and her grandfather climbed the pinewood and vine webbing, there was no talking or joking. Nina led them through the same maze of tunnels and bridges until they were once again in the heart of Hassun Cave. From a smallish platform, she shimmied up a hevataneo braid and tightrope-walked across a slender bridge.

"There are hundreds of nests here," she called back to her grandfather. There was no answer. "Grandfather?"

"I am here, Nina, but it takes time now for me to pull myself up to the top of a cavern room."

Though it was early in the day, she could hear the exhaustion in his voice. This wouldn't do.

"See," she pointed with her torch at a dark spot on the chamber's wall. "Just to your right is an alcove filled with nests. You gather those while I work up here."

"Seems like a wise choice," he answered. "When it is time for lunch, you can climb down and join me. There is room enough in there for us both to sit and rest."

Nina tied her torch onto the end of her *mosi*. With the extra illumination, she was able to chisel one nest after another off the face of the vertical shaft in front of her. The shaft was white with nests, and none of the nests contained eggs—though she was careful to check every one before touching it with her *mosi*. The morning slipped by quicker than a mudslide.

Although she had not counted her harvest as she dropped the nests into her bag, Nina suspected she had over fifty by the time she heard Grandfather call, "Time for lunch."

"Coming," she answered, and slid down the vines and crossed the pinewood bridge. From the tiny platform, she scurried across a short span of hevataneo, and crept into the alcove where her grandfather was working.

"Any eggs up there?"

"No," said Nina between handfuls of nuts.

"Not here, either."

"Perhaps," she ventured, "no one will find eggs in the nests today. Wouldn't that be wonderful?"

Her grandfather frowned, then said, "I am afraid for you. Chayton will not be satisfied until he has boats over-flowing with nests. And if not this season, then next, he will push the Goddess too far."

"Let's just gather our nests and let Anna Tuwa worry about Chayton."

"That is the problem. The Goddess's solutions can be larger than one foolish man."

They said nothing more until they finished their lunch. Then, Nina handed her nest-bag over to him.

"How many nests did you glean? I think I have over fifty already," she said as Grandfather counted her harvest.

"Good girl, you have gathered fifty-seven. I've been lucky, too. I collected forty-one. Another hour, then I say we head back to see Paco and help him with supper."

Nina hugged him, slipped out of the alcove, and scampered up to her previous perch. Her *mosi* seemed to truly have magical powers as it plucked nest after nest from the chamber's wall. As promised, an hour later Grandfather summoned her back to the alcove. Without counting, they both knew today's harvest would be their best in the last two seasons.

They were nearly to the entrance chamber when hundreds of bodaway came swooping into the tunnel they were trying to navigate. To avoid falling, Nina and her grandfather flattened themselves against the tunnel's floor. She couldn't stop gagging as the ammonia fumes from the guano assaulted her nose. Worse still, her torch flared, then was extinguished by the thick layer of animal feces.

"Grandfather," she cried out as her eyes teared.

"Hush, I am here," he comforted. "We need to hurry. Something is wrong with the bodaway."

"I know," she sobbed. "I can hear them."

"Their chittering can be overwhelming, but it will be okay."

"You don't understand. I can hear them," Nina repeated.

"You can hear what they are saying?"

"Yes. They are screeching: 'Murderers! Murderers!'"

Grandfather grabbed Nina's hand and led her through the tunnel. The entrance chamber spread before them. It was dimly lit by torchlight and the sunshine that streamed in through the cave's mouth. "Can you see well enough to get down to the gatherer's platform?"

"Yes," Nina answered.

"Then go as quickly as your legs will carry you."

Nina descended the web-works with such speed, that upon reaching the gatherer's platform, Paco said, "For a moment, I thought you must have wings. I've never seen anyone move through the cave like that."

"Paco," Grandfather called from the first platform. "Have any of the others returned?"

"No, you're the first. But it is still early. I haven't even prepared the evening meal."

"Did you climb today?"

"No. I started up the vines and realized I had forgotten my *mosi*. The spirits didn't want me to climb today, so I spent the hours organizing the gatherers' platform and preparing things for tomorrow's meals. It will take me a couple of days to make up for the lack of nests, but I think I can make quota by the end of our time on Hassun," said Paco. "How was your day?"

"Anna Tuwa was very generous. We can give you some nests to help make up for your bad luck."

Nina's grandfather crossed to the pinewood and rope ladder. "I need to check on the boat," he said and vanished.

Nina ran over to the ladder.

"Stay with Paco. I will be right back," her grandfather called up to her.

Nina watched him paddle towards the shell-strewn beach of the Goddess stalagmite. About ten minutes later, he paddled back.

"Pack up anything you value, Paco. We need to leave as soon as possible," he told the cook as he climbed back onto the gatherers' platform.

"What's going on?"

"Swarms of cave beetles are rushing out of Hassun. Bats are circling above the cliffs in broad daylight. There are no cave sharks to be seen, and Nina can hear the bodaway."

"We all can hear the little fire-makers."

"No, Paco, that is not what Grandfather means. I can understand what the bodaway are saying, and they're screaming, 'Murderers, murderers.'"

The color left the cook's face. "I'll pack," he said, and slid his *mosi* into his nest-bag along with the harvest from the first day.

"Did you bring your nawkaw sticks with you?" Grandfather asked Nina.

"Yes." Nina cocked her head. She wondered what he wanted with a toy.

"Give them to me, Nina, and pack our belongings."

"What are you going to do?"

"Team Two is working in The Ear today and Team One is harvesting in The Gallery. I am going to climb to The Crossway and warn them."

"*The Leaving Song!*" Nina exclaimed.

Grandfather nodded. "They should be able to hear the clacking of the nawkaw sticks echoing through the cavern. When they draw closer, they will recognize the song. I'll tell them it is time to abandon Hassun; then, hurry back to you and Paco. But you must be ready to cast-off as soon as I return."

"No," said Nina. "You're too old, too tired to make the ascent. I'll go. I am the quickest climber in the crew. You and Paco pack the nests and pots and pans. Be ready to cast-off when *I* return."

Her grandfather held her face between his hands, kissed her on both cheeks. "Brave girl." And then, he lashed the hollow wooden nawkaw sticks together and tied them to Nina's back. "Go, but do not wait too long for the others. Chant *The Leaving Song* five times. If no one answers, chant the song five more times, then hurry back."

"Fly, little Nina," said Paco. "We will be ready to paddle away from Hassun as soon as you return to the platform."

Nina scaled the hevataneo and darted across the bridges and scaffolding. She slipped through the first tunnel, and nimble as a cat, Nina hastened to The Crossway. The Crossway was a complicated crosshatching of pinewood poles and hevataneo vines that resembled a great wheel turned on its side. Vine and wooden spokes shot off of the central platform in more than twenty directions. Most of the chambers in Hassun Cave could be reached from this spot. No one knew how deep the void below The Crossway was. And Nina didn't want to know.

Nina sat cross-legged on the central platform. She untied the nawkaw sticks and holding one in each hand, began the rhythmic tapping of *The Leaving Song*. Tap-tap on the platform, clack-clack the nawkaws kissed, tap-tap on the platform, clack-clack the nawkaws kissed. Next, Nina began to chant the words to *The Leaving Song*. It was an ancient farewell song that warned of disaster and promised escape. The People believed it had been sung millennia ago on the First Mother when the Seed Ships were being filled with humankind. Some had ignored *The Leaving Song*. They'd stayed with the First Mother and held tight to her when death came.

Nina sang *The Leaving Song* for the fifth time. Paused. From down the winding tube called The Ear, she heard shouting. Nina resumed chanting, resumed the wooden rhythms of the nawkaw sticks. She had not quite finished the final chorus of *The Leaving Song* for the seventh time, when she spotted pinpricks of light deep in The Ear.

"Hurry," she called. "Old Kuruk said to abandon the cave, because..." Before Nina could finish, there was a rumbling from the heart of the cave. She grabbed onto The Crossway's framework. The quake only lasted for two or three seconds, but she heard the hevataneo groan. Nina's eyes searched the entrance-way to The Ear. Two torches held by two frightened nest-gatherers burst into The Crossway.

"Have you seen Team One?" she asked Meli, as the young woman paused beside Nina to catch her breath.

"They are in The Gallery. I'm sure they heard you, and I know they felt the quake. Come with us to the boats." Meli extended her hand to Nina.

Nina wanted to run but had promised to sing *The Leaving Song* ten times. "I'll come as soon as I finish singing."

"Then, you will wait alone," said Meli before bolting after her brother.

She cleared her mind of fear, began the clacking of the nawkaws, the chanting of the song. As she started the final singing of *The Leaving Song,* Nina saw Hinto and Chayton enter The Crossway.

"Quick," she called, and fled across the hevataneo to a pinewood walkway near the tunnel which led to the entrance chamber.

"Hinto is hurt. Wait for us in the tunnel," Chayton yelled.

Nina paused in the tunnel. Grandfather had told her to come back after all the gatherers had been warned, but crew chief Chayton had ordered her to wait. According to Guild rules, she must obey an order from Chayton. So she waited.

As the men entered the tunnel, she saw they were scratched and bloodied. Hinto's right eye appeared to be gouged out.

"What happened?"

"We took nests with eggs. And then, the bodaway attacked with claws and teeth and beating wings. We had to stab at them with our *mosi* to escape. We are cursed," moaned Hinto.

"Shut up, you worthless..." But the remainder of Chayton's words were swallowed by Anna Tuwa stirring.

This time, the quake lasted for six or seven seconds. The gatherers had thrown themselves to the tunnel floor when the tremor commenced and remained there as countless bodaway and bats winged their way out of the caverns.

As soon as the creatures had vacated the tunnel, Chayton yanked Hinto to his feet. "Come on. We've got to get out of here."

"Wait." Nina threw her arm in front of Chayton. "The bridge from the tunnel to the scaffolding is damaged."

The nest-gatherers gazed at the hevataneo vine bridge that separated them from the path to the Platform. Only one strand of vine still held true. The gap between the tunnel and the well-woven scaffolding was at least eighteen feet. Too far to leap.

"Someone must become the bridge," said Chayton. "Nina isn't strong enough, and I am Chief Gatherer."

"I'll be the bridge," said Hinto. "The bodaway have blinded me because I was blind to Anna Tuwa. I beg her forgiveness and offer my life in payment."

"The ancestors will welcome you home, Hinto," whispered Nina as she patted his back. "And your sacrifice will be acknowledged by the Goddess."

Chayton snorted. "We'll need some vines to secure your feet." He took a knife from his belt, hurried to the other end of the tunnel and ripped some hevataneo from a walkway.

Nina thought about warning Chayton he risked the ire of the cave spirits for destroying the old vine-work. That he was violating the magic of their forefathers. But she kept quiet.

Chayton returned with the now-cursed vines. Hinto got on his hands and knees and crawled out onto the weakened bridge. He lay flat. Chayton lashed Hinto's feet tightly to the hevataneo braiding about two feet from the lip of the tunnel. Hinto stretched out. A tall muscular man, he was able to grasp the vine bridge where it returned to a thick braid with his hands. But between Hinto's calves and elbows, there was only one strand of hevataneo.

"As Chief Gatherer, I'll go first." Chayton swiftly crossed the man-vine bridge.

Hinto prayed to the Goddess in a calm voice as Nina walked upon his legs, back, and arms. Never looking back, Chayton sprinted down the scaffolding to the platforms.

Nina paused, turned around, and called to Hinto, "Is there no way for you to escape, too?"

"No."

"I will remember you," she said, and flew down the scaffolding. She could still hear Hinto's prayers as she approached the first platform. Then, they stopped. Nina looked up at the tunnel entrance. The bridge was gone. She slipped down the hevataneo vine pillar and ran to the other end of the gatherers' platform.

Grandfather was kneeling by the ladder. He looked up at her. "You are late. The boats are ready to depart."

"Where is Paco?"

"A bit of the roof fell. It damaged one of the skiffs," said Grandfather as he pointed to a gaping hole in the wooden deck. "Paco was hit on the head by some smaller rocks."

She knelt by her grandfather. Below them, Tupi and Meli were in a boat loaded with gear and nest-bags. Tupi was tying the final knot in a rope that attached his boat to the one containing Paco. Strapped to a makeshift stretcher of twined pinewood poles in the second boat, Paco appeared unconscious. The second boat had sustained damage, but with only one man on his pinewood bed, it should make it back.

"We will see you at Halona," called Meli as the siblings paddled away from Hassun pulling the skiff with Paco in it.

Grandfather lifted his hand. Waved.

Nina watched Chayton pack his gear and nests into the last boat. In the dimness of the tunnel, she'd failed to notice the depth of the gashes on his back and legs, but here she could see them clearly. She couldn't imagine what he had done to provoke the bodaway into attacking with such ferocity.

"Hand down the last of your nest-bags," shouted Chayton from the boat.

"Put Nina in the boat first," said Grandfather.

Chayton frowned, then clamored up the ladder. "I'm tired of dealing with your arguments, old man. Give me the nests."

Grandfather took a step back from the crew chief. But before he could say a word, Chayton slipped the knife from his belt and slashed the old man's throat. As Nina's grandfather crumpled, Chayton snatched the nest-bags and descended to the waiting boat.

Nina screamed and tried to break her grandfather's fall. "Wait, help him."

There was no answer. Below her, she heard Chayton push off. Then, she heard the sound of his paddle dipping into the Nodin.

Nina cradled Grandfather's head in her lap. He tried to speak, but could not. He gazed into her eyes and grasped her wrist with a bloody hand. Nina leaned down. His mouth trying to form a word. Again and again it shaped the same word: *bodaway*.

"No, Grandfather. I cannot leave you."

Her grandfather could no longer hold his eyes open, still his lips said: *bodaway*.

Deep in the bowels of Hassun, near the heart of Anna Tuwa, there was another stirring. What was left of the gatherers' platform, swayed. Stalactites and ceiling debris showered down. Another section of the wooden deck broke away and fell into the sea.

Nina looked at her grandfather again. He was dead.

She stroked his sparse hair and sobbed, "Grandfather, don't go."

Nina remembered the happy times spent together harvesting nests, preparing ointments, and tending the garden. She remembered the stories told to her by her grandfather—not once, not twice, but dozens of times. And she knew what the granddaughter of Old Kuruk must do, for she knew what the granddaughter of a medicine man must do.

"Anna Tuwa," she called. "Loving Goddess, your servant sleeps the sleep of the dead. As you welcomed The People in the Olden Times, I beg you to welcome Old Kuruk at the Gates of Forever. Fold your arms around him, keep him safe from storms, and warm him in the bitterness of the star-cold night."

Nina lifted her chin, cried to Anna Tuwa, "Old Kuruk honored you and protected your bodaway. Honor Old Kuruk by punishing he who spilled his lifeblood."

Hassun Cave quaked in answer.

Nina bowed her head, leaned over, and kissed her grandfather. She touched his forehead, lips, and chest lightly with her right hand, while touching her own forehead, lips, and chest with her left hand. She keened a final lament, and then, stood.

Nina spread her arms wide and called the bodaway. She summoned them not with sound alone, she summoned them with her thoughts—for that is how she heard their voices.

"Come back. Rescue me—for I am bloodguiltless. Little servants of the Goddess, I am your sister. Come back," called Nina with her tongue, her mind, and her heart.

The cave thundered with a great flapping of wings and a wild chiming of bodaway screeches. The reptiles surrounded Nina. She felt their talons grasp her clothing, her hair, and even her flesh. Their wings moved in a blur, and Nina knew she was airborne.

Out of the Hassun Cave they glided. Nina glanced back, witnessed the collapse of Hassun Cave, and saw the cave-in send a tidal wave rushing across the Nodin Sea.

Onward they sailed.

Below her, Nina watched the tidal wave wash over the skiff with Chayton. He would pay a high price for Grandfather's murder. The sharks should find him before he reached shore.

Then, Nina spotted the two skiffs roped together. They twisted and bobbed but didn't sink when the great wave reached them. Silently, she thanked the Goddess for her mercy. Meli, Tupi, and Paco would make it home.

The bodaway turned landward.

Nina beheld Kaliska curled around Moki. First home to the bodaway. First islands they abandoned when their nests were over-harvested. Next, Nina spied the fishing boats skimming across the waters of the Nodin Sea towards the docks of Halona

—their sails shining orange in the fading sunlight. Beyond Halona, Nina saw the Donoma River curled like a golden necklace across the flatlands of Gad all the way to the Zaltanas.

It was towards those towering peaks the bodaway fluttered. As Nina and the bodaway rode the updrafts to the high meadows of the Zaltanas, she saw an azure body of water cupped in the center of the mountains.

Glimmerglass! She had thought the lake a legend like the Great Migration, like the tale of the coyote who never catches the deer, like the turtle who raised Gad up from the depths of the Nodin Sea.

Downward the bodaway spiraled. Nina's breath caught in her throat. The bodaway and their sister skimmed above the sparkling waters of Glimmerglass, hovered over the grassy shore, then circled over a forest thick with evergreens. As they approached the cliffs of one of the Zaltanas, Nina realized it was dotted with caves.

"Home," she heard thousands of bodaway whisper in their hissing voices. "Home at last."

BAYOU

There are things living in the bayou which nobody wants to know about. At least that's what Latrell's grandfather said.

Pappy had told him stories about were-gators who walked like men, snapping turtles big as tables who'd bite your leg off, and bobcats roaming the marshlands searching for a person walking alone. But Pappy's tales weren't needed to make a boy mindful when he lived beside the bayou. Mother Nature did that.

Just this afternoon, Latrell had found a copperhead curled among the sweet potato vines. Using a shovel, stick, and a great deal of care, he'd scooped up the serpent, carried it to the bayou, and tossed it into the water. It wasn't the first poisonous snake he'd discovered on the grounds of Swamp Oak Manor this summer. And it wasn't the first time he'd felt someone watching.

"Shake it off," Latrell told himself. He was allowing the superstitions of the heavily-vegetated swamp lands to spook him. Nobody spied on him but bayou critters.

"I wish you were still alive," said Latrell as he studied the moonlight reflected by the eyes of dozens of alligators floating in the brackish water on either side of Swamp Oak Manor's wooden wharf. The reptiles poked their snouts just far enough above the surface of the murky bayou to spot a careless muskrat or marsh rabbit.

"The buildings are falling into worse disrepair without your know-how," he added. The gators continued studying him with hungry intent.

Pappy had died of a heart attack on June sixth. Seven days later, when school closed for summer vacation, Latrell had moved in with Nana. With Pappy gone, Nana and Latrell did what work they could around the manor, but they didn't have the time or skills to do most of the much-needed maintenance.

Laden with the odor of decomposing plants, a slight breeze from the bayou caused Latrell's shirt to press against his chest. "Swamp Oak Manor gives me the creeps," he told his grandfather's spirit—wherever it floated. "But Nana won't leave Miss Coralee. She says she can't abandon her to Mr. Judson's cruel ways."

Latrell tossed a pebble into the center of the moon's reflection. "And I won't leave Nana to do all the cooking, cleaning, and waiting on the Beauregards by herself."

A part of him hoped Pappy would appear as a misty figure drifting above the duckweed and cypress knees to offer Latrell some sage advice. No such luck. An increase in the intensity of the bullfrogs' croaking and the cicadas' song was the only response.

Latrell sighed, turned around, and strode back to the decaying manor house. He glanced up at the once opulent three-story structure. More than a hundred-years-old, the main house and both wings were slowly crumbling away. The covered veranda where, according to Nana, dozens of guests would in the past sit, sip lemonade, and discuss the news of the day was moss-covered and in disrepair. The latticework below the veranda was broken, entwined with kudzu, and infested with vermin of all sorts. The window shutters, needed when a bad storm blew in from the swamp, were missing some slats and shutter-dogs. No longer secure, they'd be of little help if a hurricane arrived.

His musings on the shabby condition of the once-grand estate were cut short by a hair-raising wail.

Latrell's eyes searched the back of Swamp Oak Manor for the source. His gaze finally stopped on a slender figure dressed in a long gown of pale fabric staring into the bayou with arms outstretched. He whispered, "Miss Coralee, don't you go jumping."

As if she'd heard him, though he spoke no louder than a cottonmouth's hiss, Coralee Beauregard grasped the third-floor balcony's railing and looked down at Latrell.

He froze. The strangeness of the Lady of Swamp Oak Manor was not lost on him. Since moving in with Nana three weeks ago, Latrell had only seen Miss Coralee at mealtimes and tonight on her balcony calling to the swamp. And there was no doubt in his mind that was exactly what she was doing—calling to the bayou.

Miss Coralee didn't smile or wave, instead she straightened her back, spread her arms, and for a second time, wailed an inscrutable message that sounded more like a wounded animal's cry than something uttered by a human. The pain in her cry rang in his ears as Latrell hurried to the door to the east wing where he and Nana had their rooms. A split second before entering the structure, the Lady of Swamp Oak Manor wailed a third time.

Before he could say anything to Nana, she looked up from her mending and noted, "It's almost a full moon. Miss Coralee calls to the swamp sometimes on waxing moons."

"The sound makes my skin crawl."

His grandmother nodded. "Mr. Judson will make her stop. He doesn't tolerate her keening."

"Keening?" There was a familiar sound to the word, but Latrell didn't remember hearing it in conversation before.

"It's a pitiful lament," explained Nana, "for things lost or taken away. Though I don't know what Miss Coralee is mourning after."

"Probably her freedom," said Latrell as he grabbed a handful of molasses cookies from a large, covered glass jar on the sideboard.

"Could be true," agreed his grandmother as she set down her darning egg and several newly mended socks. "Mr. Judson keeps her hidden away, even from you and me. Sad life for a woman to be caged."

"You don't really mean *caged?*"

Nana smiled, though her eyes weren't happy. "I clean the private rooms. There are no iron bars or padlocks, but something keeps that woman chained to this place and Mr. Judson."

"I'd free her if I knew how," replied Latrell. "The noise she made tonight was filled with more suffering than I've ever heard in another person's voice."

"As would I," said Nana. She pushed up from her rocking chair. "I don't understand their relationship. Despite Mr. Judson's meanness, she stays. I swear, I never saw love between the two of them. Ever."

"She's so much younger than him, too," said Latrell thinking of the thin-as-starlight woman whose footfalls barely made a sound when she came to the dining room for some of her meals.

"It's not our problem," Nana reminded him. "Lights out," she added as she turned their living room lights off. "Tomorrow will arrive before we know it."

"Yes, ma'am." Latrell headed to his bedroom on the left side of the wide hall which led to the kitchen, laundry room, and eventually, the rest of the east wing of Swamp Oak Manor as Nana closed her bedroom's door on the right side.

Sleep didn't come for Latrell for what seemed like hours. As the night sounds of the bayou poured through his bedroom window's screen, his mind churned with thoughts of Miss Coralee and what hold her husband had over the woman to keep her in this rotting mansion. If it wasn't love, what could it be? Threats of violence? A family money debt? A promise made by their parents? The possibilities seemed endless. The last thought Latrell had before finally falling asleep was of a terrible secret that Mr. Judson knew and threatened to reveal.

When he woke in the morning to the sounds of Nana getting pans out to cook breakfast, Latrell was soaked with sweat. The night had been balmy so, while he couldn't remember dreaming, his sleep must have been filled with nightmares. He dressed quickly, then hurried to the kitchen where Nana was almost finished plating scrambled eggs, fried ham, and grits for Mr. Judson and Miss Coralee.

"Please take these plates into the dining room. I'll carry in the coffee, tea, sugar, and creamer," said his grandmother as she handed the plates heaped with a steaming hot breakfast to him.

He could hear the concern in Nana's voice. Mr. Judson demanded mealtime punctuality. If they served any meal a minute late, he'd be sitting at the table looking at his watch with a scowl on his face. Though a scowl was Mr. Judson's most common expression.

In the nick of time, Nana and he carried breakfast into the dining room. Mr. Judson sat straight-backed at one end of the long, mahogany table, while Miss Coralee sat at the other end. Though it was summer, the dining room was dim. The huge windows on one end of the room, like all the windows in the manor house, were covered with drapes to keep the sun from fading the upholstery fabric. Upholstery fabric which, according to his grandmother, hadn't been replaced in all the years Pappy and Nana worked for the Beauregards.

Two silver candelabras on the table, plus four wall-mounted candle holders provided limited lighting. Enough, supposed Latrell that the silent couple could see what was on the plates he was placing before them, but unlikely enough for them to clearly discern each other's facial expressions.

"Ma'am," he said as he put Miss Coralee's plate before her.

"Thank you, Latrell," she said, then fell quiet as the statues on either side of the brick walk leading to the mansion's front door.

He walked to the other end of the table, set Mr. Judson's plate before him, and said, "Sir," before taking two steps back, then turning and exiting the dining room.

Nana did the same with the bone china tea and coffee pots, sugar bowl, and cream pitcher. Then, they ate their breakfast in the kitchen and waited for the owner of Swamp Oak Manor to ring a bell for them to clear the table.

"That poor woman," said Nana as she cut two slices of pecan pie, then placed them onto dessert plates. "Pale as mashed potatoes."

Latrell smiled. Nana always thought of everything through the lens of a cook.

"Well, she never goes outside in the sunlight." At least she hadn't since he'd moved in three weeks ago.

"That's because *he* won't let her." There was an edge to his grandmother's voice. "He brought her here before you were born. Back then, she had hope, and a sparkle in her eye. She'd jabber with Pappy, me, and your mom."

"Where'd she come from?" Latrell tried to picture the sad woman garbed in filmy dresses who spent most of her day in her room on the swampside corner of the house laughing. He couldn't.

"Don't know," replied Nana. "I suppose it's far away, because none of her kin has ever come to visit."

"Does she get letters from anyone? Or a phone call?"

"No." There was a finality to the tone of his grandmother's response which squelched any further questions. "You take these pieces of pie out to the Beauregards," she ordered. "See if they need anything else, while I start to do the dishes."

Latrell did as he was told. Miss Coralee declined the pie. Mr. Judson took both pieces.

Before he could leave the dining room, Mr. Judson said, "You tell your grandmother I've got business in town today. I won't be back for lunch or dinner—so my wife will be eating those meals in her rooms."

"Yes, sir." Latrell glanced at Miss Coralee to see if she was happy about sitting in her room for the rest of the day, but her expression was hidden by the dimness of the dining room.

Focused on vacuuming the first two floors of the main section of Swamp Oak Manor—including the drapes—Latrell was surprised by the time when Nana called him to the kitchen for lunch.

"There must be rain coming, because my knees are aching bad," said his grandmother as she handed him a tray. "So I need you to carry Miss Coralee's lunch up to her rooms." Before he exited the kitchen, Nana touched his upper arm, and said, "And be careful when you're climbing the stairs not to spill the iced tea."

"No worries," he answered.

This was the first time Latrell had gotten to take Miss Coralee a meal or view her rooms on the third floor. Now, he could see for himself if she was chained. As he climbed the stairs to her rooms, he sensed a change in the air. Instead of the expected dryness, the third floor air was moist and had a slight swamp-vegetation smell. He breathed deeply. The word, *bayou,* popped into his mind.

"Miss Coralee," called Latrell as he walked past a living room furnished with heavy wooden furniture. Upon the walls, he noticed tapestries featuring forests, streams, fair maidens, and mythical creatures.

The Lady of Swamp Oak Manor didn't answer him, so he went down the hall to the first door on the right. He stuck his head in, and saw the walls of the room were lined with bookshelves filled to capacity with old, leather-bound books. "Miss Coralee?" he said.

No response.

Mindful of the tall glass filled with iced tea balanced on the lunch tray, Latrell proceeded to the next doorway. "Ma'am?" he said before taking one step into the room.

"In here, Latrell," called a woman's voice.

He took a couple more steps into what appeared to be a sitting room with a small dining table. He saw Miss Coralee seated by a pair of open French doors. She was painting.

Those must lead to the balcony I saw her on last night, he mused.

"Come, have a look," said Coralee Beauregard. She stood and gestured toward the canvas she was working on.

Hesitating for a moment, Latrell thought, *What's the harm?,* before moving closer to the easel and studying Miss Coralee's painting. The image was so realistic, it appeared to be a photo of the bayou. A full moon hung like ball lightning from the clouds and will o' wisps flickered between loblolly pines, black willows, and river birches. Wads of Spanish moss draped over some of the tree branches, and hidden among the undergrowth were snakes, lizards, and alligators. The most curious part of the image was a pair of golden eyes peering from the depths of the bayou.

"Wow," gasped Latrell as he placed the lunch tray on the eating table. "That's amazing."

"Thank you." The corners of Miss Coralee's mouth curled up. "I love painting my home."

"Maybe you should paint Swamp Oak Manor?" suggested Latrell as he waited for her to dismiss him or tell him to fetch something else for lunch.

She laughed—not a fun laugh, but a bitter one. "The manor house isn't my home." The woman pointed at the canvas. "*That* is my home."

"You mean the bayou?" Latrell frowned. Maybe that's why no family visited Miss Coralee. If her people were poor folk who lived deep in the bayou, they might be uncomfortable visiting a mansion—even if it was a dilapidated one.

She nodded. "The bayou is where I was born and raised. Where I lived happily with my sisters until Judson Beauregard decided to wreak his revenge on me."

"Revenge? For what?"

Miss Coralee tilted her head and looked at him from beneath her partially lowered eyelids, "I felt your compassion yesterday with the copperhead, then again last night. Therefore, I'll share with you what binds me to Swamp Oak Manor and its owner. But if I tell you, you cannot speak about it to my husband. To do so would mean punishment for me, and dismissal for you and your grandmother."

"I won't say anything," whispered Latrell. He knew there was a secret about to be shared. One which might answer the questions in his mind concerning the Beauregards and their relationship.

"Judson's grandfather, Homer Beauregard, bought this ground and brought his new wife, Sarah Ann, here. They welcomed a son, Willis, shortly thereafter. Homer had barely finished the main house when the first Lady of Swamp Oak Manor was snatched by an alligator, because she wandered too close to the swamp. So Willis was raised by a bitter father angry at the bayou and its inhabitants."

"Did they ever get her body back?" asked Latrell. He didn't want to think about how the gator probably drowned Sarah Ann then stashed her under the roots of a cypress to ripen before eating her flesh.

"No," answered Miss Coralee. She sighed, then continued, "Willis married late. Then, he and his wife, Nettie Mae, moved into Swamp Oak Manor with Homer. It looked like good times had returned to the mansion after they had a little boy whom they named Judson. Even though both Homer and Willis loved little Judson, they weren't affectionate men, so Nettie Mae gave the child most of the hugs, kisses, and kindness he received. It would've been enough, had she not been bitten by a coral snake when Judson was five. Nettie Mae died a few hours later. Poor Judson was left to be raised by a strict, unfeeling father and bitter grandfather. Both of whom were angry at the bayou and her reptiles."

"I can't blame them," said Latrell. He thought how he'd feel if a gator killed Nana. "I'd be mad, too, if the bayou took someone I loved."

"But I don't think you'd be cruel," observed Miss Coralee.

"No," he agreed.

"Sadly, Homer Beauregard died a year later of swamp fever. Which left Judson working and living with Willis until eighteen years ago when his father died, and he married me." She patted down a few of her hairs which were frizzing due to high humidity. "But it could never have been a normal marriage. You see, Judson blames his unhappy childhood, the decline of this manor house, even his nasty temperament on reptiles. To satisfy his need for vengeance, he kills snakes, alligators, even turtles whenever he gets a chance to do so."

Confused, Latrell continued to stare at the Lady of Swamp

Oak Manor. There had to be more to the story. She was leaving something out.

Miss Coralee remained silent. She stared at the open space between the French doors and out at the bayou, then turned her golden-brown eyes on Latrell. "Eighteen years ago, Judson spotted me sitting on a log by the edge of the swamp. He saw me remove my scaly skin and assume a womanly form. But rather than be enamored with a shape-changer, he was filled with hate and stole my skin. Thereafter, I was under his control, and will remain that way until I can regain my skin."

If she wasn't so serious, Latrell would've laughed. "So you're a..." He searched for the correct word. *Mermaid* was a half-fish woman who could take human form. *Werewolves* were humans who could take wolf-shape. "...a were-snake?"

She shook her head. "No, Latrell. Though that's a good guess." Miss Coralee smoothed the front of her dress with her palms, then studied him with those golden eyes. "I'm a very rare bayou creature—a swamp dragon."

"Seriously?" The question slipped out before Latrell could stop it. He knew he'd said it in a mocking tone. *Way to lose both Nana's job and yours,* he thought.

"Deadly serious," responded Miss Coralee. "The only way I can leave Judson Beauregard is to find my skin, put it on, and return to dragon shape."

"Find your skin?"

"Yes," said the Lady of Swamp Oak Manor. "Judson took my skin and hid it. I fear time is running out. For years, my sisters returned every full moon to this part of the bayou in the hope I could join them. They'd call from the bayou, and I'd answer. Now, only one sister comes looking for me. You heard me calling to her last night."

"She didn't answer?"

"No. But I have hope she might answer tonight." Miss

Coralee lifted her chin, glanced once more at the bayou before continuing. "Unfortunately, if I don't return to the swamp soon, I'll never see my family again. Or worse, Judson will burn my skin, and I'll die screaming in agony in this woman-shape. Which is why I need your help."

"My help!" He should walk—no *run* away from the woman. But the image of her screeching with pain and crumbling to the floor in agony was more powerful than his fear of Mr. Judson.

"I beg you, please find my skin and return it to me before tonight's full moon." Coralee fell to her knees and clasped her hands in front of her.

"Get up Miss Coralee," urged Latrell as he helped the woman to her feet. "I'll help you, just eat your lunch before Nana has *my* hide."

The reed-thin woman smiled, sat on a ladder-backed chair pulled up to the table, and picked up the chicken salad sandwich Nana had prepared. "I knew you were the one to save me when I observed that you've spared three poisonous snakes since you arrived. Then, last night I felt your compassion for me. Which was why I spoke to you—"

"—in my dreams," finished Latrell. Suddenly, he could remember bits and pieces of his dreams. Dreams of sliding through the bayou, smelling waterlilies floating on the swamp's surface, feeling tiny fishes swim by, seeing egrets standing on stilt legs, and watching alligators bow their wide heads in reverence.

"What does this skin look like?" he asked.

"Much like a very large snakeskin," replied Miss Coralee. "Not the thin, colorless skin shed by snakes, but the thicker, patterned skin removed from a living snake after it's killed. Mine will be mottled green with flecks of gold, yellow, and turquoise."

"I suppose you've hunted for it before?" Latrell wanted to eliminate the places which had already been scoured.

"Many times," said the Lady of Swamp Oaks Manor. "The third floor has been thoroughly checked from floor to ceiling. As to the second floor, Judson's bedroom, office, and bathroom have been meticulously scrutinized. The other second floor rooms have also been examined—though with less intensity. The wing to the west of the main house was used for parties and balls. I've gone over that area with a fine-toothed comb as well as the second floor storage area in the east wing."

"So parts of the second floor, the manor house's first floor, and the first floor of the east wing needed to be searched?"

"Yes," said Miss Coralee, "and today."

Latrell scratched his head. This was going to be tricky. If he told Nana what he was doing, she'd likely put a stop to his quest to free Miss Coralee. If he didn't tell Nana, she'd wonder what on earth had gotten into him.

"Cleaning!" he exclaimed. "I'll tell Nana since we don't have to serve dinner in the dining room tonight, I'll do some extra cleaning for her."

"Thank you for lunch," said Miss Coralee as she pushed the tray towards him. "Tell your grandmother it was delicious." She reached out, placed her hand on top of his, "And thank you, Latrell, for trying to rescue a trapped swamp dragon."

He nodded, picked up the tray, clamored down two flights of stairs, and took the dirty dishes to the kitchen.

After drinking a glass of sweet tea and eating two chicken sandwiches, Latrell began his quest for a large snakeskin secreted somewhere on the first floor of the main house. Disguised as additional cleaning, dust cloth and furniture polish in hand, he went from room to room feeling under love seats, sofas, and chairs. With a keen eye he scanned drapes and sheers and looked in drawers and cupboards. Not deterred by the enormity of his task, Latrell reached behind highboys, bookshelves, and china cabinets. Dust was his only reward.

It was late afternoon when he began his search of the lower level of the east wing where he and Nana lived. First, he checked the laundry room, then the kitchen. Both rooms were his grandmother's domain and had been so since she began working for the Beauregard family. So as he'd anticipated, he found no snakeskin. Before he rummaged through his bedroom then Nana's, Latrell went into the spare bedroom which had belonged to his mother when she was younger.

The room still smelled like his mom. The closet had some of her old clothes hanging from pegs. A pair of her shoes rested beneath the bed as if she were going to climb out from under its quilt and slip them on in the morning. Her books lined the bookshelf. Her brush and comb lay before the dresser mirror. Of course, the curtains in the window weren't the cheerful gingham the rest of the room seemed to demand. They were the same heavy drapes which hung below painted wooden cornices that served as fancy, yet practical window dressings throughout the mansion.

As he had done with every window checked this afternoon, Latrell climbed up on a small ladder he'd lugged from room to room and ran his hand across the top of the cornice. But this time, instead of dust, he touched something leathery.

"Snakeskin!" he exclaimed as he pulled a carefully-folded bundle of shimmering emerald skin down from its hiding place. "Or more correctly, dragon-skin."

"Latrell."

He climbed down the ladder nearly dropping the precious skin.

"Latrell, where are you?" hollered Nana. "I need you to carry Miss Coralee's supper up to her."

"Coming," he shouted. He slipped the folded reptile skin inside his shirt. It felt like chilly, textured silk. Where it touched him, his flesh tingled.

When he hurried into the kitchen, Nana pursed her lips, put her hands on her hips, and asked. "What's gotten into you, Latrell? You've been cleaning like a crazy man."

"I wanted to get ahead of things, so maybe we can take a break this weekend." He smiled at Nana.

"You don't fool me," said his grandmother as she handed Latrell Miss Coralee's supper tray. "You're up to no good. I just haven't figured out what it has to do with yet."

"Relax, I haven't done anything you wouldn't do."

Nana replied with a shake of her head and a loud, "Harrumph!"

When Latrell entered Miss Coralee's sitting room where she'd been painting earlier, she looked at him with lips parted, ready to ask about the skin Mr. Judson stole from her eighteen years earlier.

"I've got it," said Latrell as he pulled the reptile skin from beneath his shirt.

Fingers trembling, the Lady of Swamp Oak Manor reached for her skin. Once she clutched the bundle to her chest, a tear trickled down her high-boned cheek. "Thank you, Latrell. Now, you must go. And tonight, no matter what you hear, you and your grandmother must stay in your rooms."

He nodded, then said, "After Nana takes out her hearing aids, she doesn't hear anything. As for me, I'll stay in my room, though I might take a peek out the window."

"Look if you must, but don't come near," warned Miss Coralee. "I hope to retain all my human memories when I return to dragon shape, but I can't be certain I won't harm you. Because I assure you, I *will* repay Judson Beauregard for eighteen years of imprisonment. Eighteen years of proudly showing me every reptile he killed. Eighteen years of snarling nasty words at me. Eighteen years of slaps and shoves."

She gently rubbed the dragon-skin given to her by Latrell, then regarded him with a gaze more piercing than a water moccasin's fang. "Dragons *always* settle their debts. Tonight, I plan to settle mine."

Pulse racing, Latrell nodded, backed out of the room, fled downstairs, and hurried into the east wing of the mansion.

~

A full moon had risen and flooded the bayou with silver light by the time Mr. Judson returned from town. When they saw his car's headlights swing into the driveway, Nana suggested it was time for bed, as tomorrow would be a long day. Eager to be safely in his room, Latrell offered no argument.

Rather than go to bed, Latrell sat in a chair by his window and listened to the rhythm of the bayou. The swamp's peacefulness was disrupted as through the open third floor French doors, he heard shouts and curses from Mr. Judson directed at Miss Coralee.

"Look what I killed on the front walkway," bragged Mr. Judson in a harsh voice. "One of your belly-crawling relatives."

"Judson, don't." He heard Miss Coralee say.

Then, the sound of a loud slap.

"I'm warning you, Judson," said Miss Coralee in a tone darker than the muddy waters of the swamp.

"Warning me of what?" snarled Mr. Judson. "You're mine to do with as I will. And one of these nights, I *will* toss your skin into a lit fireplace. Then, as you shriek in agony, I'll feel to some small degree the bayou and I are even."

What Latrell heard and saw next was bound to haunt his dreams for the rest of his life:

First, the sound of furniture being knocked over. *She must be transforming into a dragon,* thought Latrell.

Second, a terrible scream from Mr. Judson, then the word *no* shouted again and again. Latrell's imagination conjured images of the owner of Swamp Oak Manor being torn to shreds and eaten.

Finally, the sound of Miss Coralee keening from her balcony —but tonight, the timbre of her voice was different. He ventured a peek out his window. He couldn't see what was going on, so he removed the screen, then leaned as far out of the window as possible. Illumined by the moon, he witnessed a beautiful serpentine dragon crawl from Coralee's balcony, down the side of the crumbling mansion to the veranda's roof, and onto the grassy lawn. The beast which was the former Lady of Swamp Oak Manor swiveled its fierce head and gaped at Latrell with gleaming gold eyes.

"Latrell," he heard whispered on the wind. "Fear not, I remember you."

Truth be told, if the lady dragon had *not* assured him of his safety, Latrell wasn't certain he'd have had the wherewithal to get back inside and close the window. He was dumbstruck by the creature's size, power, and terrifying face. He'd thought Miss Coralee's reptile head would be more serpent-like, but with a lizard's snout, frilled crest, and wide mouth brimming with teeth, there was no doubt she was a dragon.

"Miss Coralee, is Mr. Judson dead?" It was a silly question he knew, but Latrell wanted to hear of the man's fate before he found what was left of the body in the morning.

"Not yet," she replied with a flick of her tail, "but he's suffered a fatal reptile bite." The dragon smiled. "It will appear the rattlesnake he flung at me this evening bit him prior to its death."

"But it was you, wasn't it, Miss Coralee?"

The dragon nodded.

Latrell watched as her forked tongue slid out and appeared to moisten her lips. Then, the swamp dragon tilted back her fearsome head, opened her mouth, and called to the bayou with so much bottled-up pain and longing that Latrell felt his throat tighten and tears fall unbidden from his eyes.

"My name is not Coralee. It's Coranth, Lady of the Bayou," said the dragon as she studied him with such intensity, he began to chew on his fingernail. "I cannot reward you with possessions, Latrell."

"I wasn't expecting a reward," he managed to say.

"But good luck will be yours, and you never need fear any reptile," promised the swamp dragon.

Before he could respond, the creature exhaled a cloud of greenish smoke which surrounded Latrell. In the blink of an eye, he felt the fumes pouring into his ears, nose, and mouth. Even the pores on his exposed skin felt like they opened and absorbed the dragon's breath.

Suddenly, a keening came from the depths of the bayou.

"My sister!" cried the dragon. Latrell would've sworn the creature's intricately patterned skin shimmered with joy. She didn't acknowledge him again. Instead, she slithered toward the wharf.

"Goodbye, Coranth, Lady of the Bayou," whispered Latrell as the swamp dragon disappeared into a thicket of scrub trees beside the bayou's edge. He heard a splash as she entered its shallow waters. Then, in a haunting duet, the sisters wailed a farewell to Swamp Oak Manor and the doomed Judson Beauregard.

Latrell stepped back, locked the screen in place, and sat on his bed staring into the bayou. With Mr. Judson dead, he and Nana would pack up their things, find a nice bungalow, and move back into town.

As for Swamp Oak Manor, it wouldn't take long before the bayou swallowed the buildings, reclaimed the land, and erased any memory of the cursed Beauregard family and the strangely beautiful Miss Coralee.

DRAGONSKIN

Taking pity on the woman crying in the royal gardens, Granny Elder, tree fairy of birth and death, decided to reveal to Queen Glynnis how to break the curse which kept her childless.

"Cease your weeping, dear. I, Granny Elder, can help you," whispered the ancient fairy as she stepped from behind a massive holly bush. "A spell was spoken by a jealous rival on the day of your betrothal. It is that spell—a curse, in truth—which prevents you from becoming pregnant."

The queen stood, then dabbed her eyes with a hankie. "You can remove this curse?"

Taking Glynnis's soft hand in her rough, gnarled hands, the elder tree fairy explained. "Tonight, by full moon's light, you must peel the skin from two onions. Next, you must eat every last bit of the onions—even if your mouth burns and your eyes water. Once they are consumed, you need to toss their crinkly, outer skins into the fire, then go to bed. If you do everything exactly as I have instructed, before midsummer's eve, you will give birth to a set of twins."

"Thank you, Granny," said the queen with a bow of her head. "Please, let me give you a reward."

"No," answered the fairy. "No reward is necessary. I only ask for your promise that you will always be kind to your children. And should you no longer want one or both of them—you will give them to me."

"Of course." The queen's words had barely left her lips when the old woman vanished into the growing darkness.

Face flushed with excitement, Queen Glynnis hurried back to the castle. She stopped by the kitchen on the way to her bedchambers to pick up two onions. Her fingers trembled as she peeled one of the onions. Anticipating its burning tang, she took a deep breath and bit into the root vegetable's white flesh. Though her tongue smarted, her nose dripped, and tears slid down her cheeks, the queen consumed the first onion as instructed.

Eager to break the curse, she didn't remove all of the dry exterior skin layers from the second onion before taking a bite— rather slipping off only the top layer. After consuming the second onion, she gathered all of the crumbling, brown skins together and tossed them into the fire.

"It is done," she told the moon as she scrubbed her hands again and again in a vain attempt to remove the oniony odor from her fingers. Next, she gargled with mint water a dozen times hoping to rinse the taste of onions from her mouth.

As luck would have it, her husband was delayed two days in a distant corner of the kingdom by floods—so the queen didn't have to reveal to him the source of her sour breath and onion-scented hands. By the time King Harold returned, the smell was gone. Therefore, only Granny Elder and she knew of the curse and its undoing. And Queen Glynnis was happy not to have to discuss magic with her husband.

~

By autumn, the castle, town, kingdom, and surrounding lands were abuzz with the news that Queen Glynnis and King Harold were to become parents in the new year.

Though no one said anything to the queen, many members of court, as well as commoners were relieved to hear of the upcoming birth of a royal heir. Male or female, a child would soon be born that would rule after its parents were dead. The promise of continuity gave more peace and security to the kingdom than a great army could ever have brought.

As the months slipped by, the royal parents-to-be grew increasingly excited about the coming prince or princess. Queen Glynnis had decided against revealing to the king Granny Elder's promise of two children—afraid she was wishing for too much. One healthy child was enough.

On the last day of March, shortly after King Harold had departed the castle on a hunting trip, Glynnis felt the first labor pains. At the same time the court physicians and midwife were summoned, the queen secretly sent one of her maidservants to the woodland home of Granny Elder. When the babies were born, the queen intended to finally reward the crone for her help with enough gold coin to last for years, and perhaps, for the woman's lifetime.

The maidservant quickly returned with Granny Elder. Then, the pair quietly stood in a corner of the queen's chambers while the midwife and her assistants took care of Queen Glynnis. When the first baby was born alive and healthy, there were smiles on everyone's faces as the girl child was swaddled in the softest cloth.

"Wait," exclaimed the midwife. "There is a second baby."

Moments later, another child was born.

"Everyone leave," screamed the midwife to her aides. She

then motioned for Granny Elder to come to the bed. "It is a demon," muttered the woman. "We must kill it before our queen sees the monstrosity she has birthed."

The tree fairy touched the midwife's arm. "Now, *you* must leave the room. Go tend to the first daughter. I will watch over Queen Glynnis and her second child."

Eyes wide with fright, the woman nodded and left the queen's chambers without a backward glance.

Swaddling the second girl child, then gathering the squalling infant into her arms, Granny Elder stood beside the queen. "Glynnis, you didn't follow my instructions exactly," she said as she pulled back the edge of the blanket to reveal a squirming dragon.

Exhausted from the birthing process, the queen could only gasp at the sight of the dragonet.

"You ate the skin of the second onion, so your second daughter is covered in dragon skin. A mistake while practicing magic is not something which can be changed easily."

"I cannot show her to the king," said Glynnis. "What should—"

"Hush, I will take care of her." The elder tree fairy stroked the dragon child's cheek. "When the time is right, she will return to the castle."

The queen nodded.

"I just need a name for her," said Granny Elder.

"Her sister's name will be Linnet—for she is flaxen-haired," said Glynnis. "As for my second daughter," she shook her head, wiped away tears, then continued, "her name shall be Kiera—for she is my little dark one."

"It's a lovely name." The crone, who was the fairy of beginnings and endings as well as elder trees, nuzzled the dragonet. "Do not worry, my queen. I will raise Kiera with love and kindness. She will learn all that I know, then one day, she'll return to her rightful place within these walls."

As Granny Elder started to leave, the queen called, "Wait!"

The old fairy woman stopped, then turned around.

"I know her appearance is my fault. Is there nothing that I can do to take away her dragon skin?"

"No," replied Granny Elder. "But one day, another will have the chance to return her to her human form." Without further comment, the crone vanished with Kiera Dragonskin.

Days became weeks, weeks became months, months became years. Then, for the eighteenth time since the birth of Princess Linnet and Kiera Dragonskin, spring greened the royal gardens and woodlands beyond.

On the first of April, Princess Linnet heard a strange clicking noise beyond the garden walls. Curious about the repetitive sound, she slipped away from her drowsy nursemaid and wandered into the forest at the edge of the castle's grounds. She'd gone only a short distance when she came upon a thatched-roofed cottage. An elderly woman sat in front of the structure knitting.

"I'm Granny Elder," said the crone as she laid aside her needles and yarn. "I've been waiting for you." She stood, opened her cottage's door. "And so has your twin sister."

"You're mistaken," answered Princess Linnet taking a step back. "I'm an only child."

The elder tree fairy smiled. "It might seem so to you, but I can assure you that Queen Glynnis birthed a second daughter on the last day of March eighteen years ago. But because of her appearance, she gave Kiera Dragonskin to me."

"Dragonskin!" Linnet frowned. "What sort of name is that?"

"Unfortunately, your sister has had to pay the price for failed magic. Nonetheless, she is bright, goodhearted, and kind. Are you willing to meet her?"

Linnet didn't answer Granny Elder immediately. For her whole life, she'd felt a part of her was missing. Therefore, a twin from whom she'd been separated at birth made sense.

"Yes," responded the princess.

The word was no sooner spoken, then a bronze-scaled dragon crept from the shadows of the forest cottage. "Linnet," said the creature in the voice of a young woman. "Oh, Linnet, you've come for me."

The princess stood still-as-stone gazing into the eyes of the dragon—eyes which were the same sky-blue as her own. "Kiera?"

"Yes," answered the dragon. Then, Kiera Dragonskin held up her right front foot, stared deep into Linnet's eyes, and whispered, "touch me, and you will know for certain we are bloodkin."

Without hesitation, Linnet placed her right hand against Kiera's foot.

As Granny Elder—the tree fairy of crossing thresholds—watched, a faint green shimmer surrounded Linnet and Kiera. Then, in unison they said, "I know you, sister," and embraced.

As she looked out her bedroom window, Queen Glynnis saw Linnet, Kiera, and Granny Elder approaching the castle gardens. "Kiera," she exclaimed as she rushed from her chambers, down the stairs, through the halls, and out the wood-and-hammered-metal door. She paused as she neared the trio.

"My queen," said Granny Elder, "may I present to you, Princess Kiera Dragonskin."

"Your eyes—" began Queen Glynnis.

"—Are the same as mine," said Princess Linnet.

Without further delay, Glynnis stepped forward and embraced both of her daughters.

Greetings exchanged, questions answered, and forgiveness asked for and received—the time finally arrived when the queen and her twins turned once more to the tree fairy.

"You hinted long ago that there was a way for Kiera to regain her human form," said Queen Glynnis. "Is that still possible?"

Granny Elder nodded. "She must find a prince willing to marry her without being forced, threatened, drugged, or bribed. A prince willing to not only kiss her at the ceremony but spend the wedding night with his new bride."

"Impossible!" The queen pressed her hand to her forehead. "Where will we ever find such a man?"

"You cannot find what you do not search for," said the fairy. "But I suggest a double wedding. Send notices to every kingdom, no matter how small, that the two daughters of King Harold and Queen Glynnis are ready for marriage. Many men are sure to arrive eager to marry a princess."

"Linnet will have many suitors to select from," said Kiera, "but when they see me in dragon shape—they will turn away."

"Then, they must fall in love with you *before* they see you," responded Granny Elder, the fairy of transformation.

"First," said the queen with a heavy sigh, "I must tell the king about the night of our daughters' birth—and also, about how I muddled the magic nine months earlier."

After his initial shock at the magical origins of his daughter and Kiera's appearance, the king embraced Kiera Dragonskin as his daughter—but agreed that her dragon form must remain a carefully-guarded secret until after the wedding ceremony.

Hoping to wed a princess, suitors came by the hundreds to woo the daughters of King Harold and Queen Glynnis. Linnet sat on the podium beside her parents as men brought gifts for the royal family and proclaimed their worthiness to marry Princess Linnet. Kiera sat on the podium, too. But she was hidden behind a curtain which surrounded her on all four sides, so no one could see she was a dragon.

Most of the eligible men focused their efforts on winning the hand of the beautiful Linnet. After meeting the suitors, she told her parents which of them she'd like to meet in a more personal manner at a royal dinner to be held two days hence. Thirteen gallant princes received invites to what was certain to be an elaborate feast.

A few brave souls approached the curtained gazebo where Princess Kiera waited. Three were obviously from poor kingdoms and unable to provide lavish gifts for a potential mate. Two others were elderly—needing a nurse for their last years more than a wife. One was clearly weak in the mind. Unable to talk, he had a manservant speak for him. The last, while well-dressed, apparently sound of mind, and handsome of face—had a pronounced limp.

Though the seven suitors could not see Kiera Dragonskin, she could see them through a small sheer fabric panel. She quickly dismissed the two old men and the weak-minded lad as unsuitable husband material. Another prince was not only poor, but filthy. She also declined his attentions. Which left three potential mates to invite to dinner.

For the next two days, the castle was bustling with preparations for the elaborate dinner party. Finally, the evening of the royal event arrived.

Floral arrangements and sprays of fragrant tree boughs

decorated the reception area, dining room, ballroom, halls, and outdoor pavilion. Fresh fruit and sweets were spread on several tables in tempting displays. Breads and baked goods filled huge baskets beside generous bowls of fresh-churned butter and berry jams. Dozens of meat and vegetable platters were placed in the center of long, candle-lit tables.

When the doors to the castle opened to welcome the guests, a parade of princes and invited nobles streamed into the reception area. With soft music playing in the background, King Harold, Queen Glynnis, and Princess Linnet greeted the throng. Kiera Dragonskin peered through the translucent panel of fabric in her curtained nook but could neither curtsy to nor shake hands with the fabulously garbed guests. She could but observe the festivities. The only people to wander over to her corner were her three princes and several curious nobles.

The first penniless prince soon made it clear that he could not marry her unless she allowed him to see her face. Should she prove unsightly, he said he wouldn't marry her.

"Thank you for your honesty," said Kiera. "But I am sworn not to reveal my face to my groom until after we're married."

"Then, I must bid you farewell," said the prince before he strode away.

The second modestly-dressed prince admitted he'd only pursued Kiera so he would be invited to dinner. He explained, "In truth, I am more interested in Linnet, but I felt without abundant wealth, she wouldn't ask me to the suitors' dinner."

"You are probably correct," agreed Kiera Dragonskin. "Linnet would likely have skipped over a poorer royal house for a more well-to-do one."

"Thank you for your understanding," responded the prince as he turned and walked toward the crowd of handsome, wealthy royals courting Princess Linnet.

Kiera sat in her curtained corner feeling hope slip away like starlight at sunrise. She was about to escape the humiliating event via a secret passageway behind her when the lame prince spoke.

"Princess Kiera, I have been standing nearby listening to the other two princes whom I thought were also vying for your hand. They were unkind to you—and for that I apologize."

"Thank you." Kiera Dragonskin wondered what sort of man would be so concerned about her feelings. "But it is I who must apologize—for I have forgotten your name."

Through the filmy fabric panel before her eyes, Kiera saw the prince bow before saying, "I am Prince Eamonn. My homeland is a fair island across the sea where the rains are frequent, the sunshine is dazzling, and rainbows are plentiful."

"It sounds beautiful." Kiera laughed, then said, "But there must be some parts of it that are not so perfect."

"No place and no one is perfect," answered Eamonn. "There are evil creatures and sorcerers scattered here and there. But on the whole, it is a land of good folk and pleasant things."

"It sounds like a place I'd like to visit." Kiera Dragonskin felt herself relaxing as she chatted with Eamonn. "But is it a long journey?"

"Journeys are only long when the weather, traveling companions, horse you are riding, or all three are terrible. So my journey was interesting."

"What made it interesting? Surely not your horse," replied the dragon princess.

Now, it was the prince's turn to laugh. "The horse was a hearty animal with agreeable gaits, but he was no more or less interesting than most horses. No, it was the stunning landscape which made it interesting. But certainly, you know the uniqueness of your country."

"Actually," said Kiera, "I have seen little of my country."

The prince nodded. "King Harold is wise to guard his

daughters. There is no telling when raiders might swoop in and try to abduct a royal heir."

"Before we talk further, I must tell you, though we are twins, Linnet was born a few minutes before me. I am not the first heir —it is *she* who will likely be named queen."

"I am looking for *my* queen. I do not want the queen of a different kingdom," replied Eamonn. "I don't care that you won't inherit your country's throne—only if you are willing to return with me to *my* country to sit beside me in *my* throne room."

Kiera paused a moment before responding. This decent king-to-be deserved better than a dragon who may or may not transform back to human shape. "I cannot reveal myself to my groom until after we are married," she said. "But I must warn you, I do not look like my sister."

"I don't expect you to." Eamonn sighed, then slapped the thigh of his lame leg. "But I must be honest, too." He pulled up one leg of his trousers to reveal a misshapen foot—where a booted man's foot should be, instead there was a hoof.

"When I was a child, I was cursed by one of those sorcerers I mentioned. I was chasing a rabbit when I stumbled into his lair causing him to drop a vial of irreplaceable potion. Furious, the sorcerer gave me this." The prince stomped his hoof twice before letting his trouser leg drop back down.

Had she been able to do so, Kiera would have embraced the prince and told him it didn't matter to her that he had a misshapen leg. Instead, she whispered, "If you will take a chance on an unseen princess, then Prince Eamonn of Fair Isle, I will agree to marry you."

~

The suitors' feast proved a success. Princess Linnet agreed to marry Prince Agoston, heir to the throne of a nearby, wealthy kingdom. Princess Kiera agreed to marry Prince Eamonn of Fair Isle.

Just a week later, a double wedding, the likes of which had never been seen, was held at the castle of King Harold and Queen Glynnis. Hundreds of guests from both of the grooms' families were easily accommodated in their vast castle. All of their assorted servants and assistants were housed in both the less grand areas of the castle and in the town's plentiful taverns. Though the royal stables were near overflowing, all of the fine horses which carried the guests to the wedding were also housed.

While Princess Linnet walked down the aisle with her mother on one side of her and her father on the other, Princess Kiera waited in front of the spectators in a lovely, white-draped gazebo. Vows spoken, promises made, the royal couples were pronounced man and wife. Linnet and Agoston kissed, and cheers rang out. Then, Eamonn kissed Kiera, though a filmy piece of fabric separated their lips.

After the ceremony, there was a banquet of untold splendor. It was followed by dancing and fireworks. Through it all, Kiera Dragonskin remained secreted in her tent of white fabric. Finally, it was time for the princesses to retreat to their bridal chambers to be followed a few minutes later by their grooms.

Kiera stood by the fireplace of her room. The blazing fire warmed her and caused her scales to shine like molten metal. Granny Elder had been waiting for her when she first entered her bedchamber. The tree fairy of beginnings and endings kissed her, stroked her scaly cheek like she had done so many times over the years, and promised all would be well. Still, Kiera Dragonskin was afraid of her husband's reaction when he saw her true form.

When Granny Elder left, Kiera found herself trembling as she waited for Eamonn.

∾

A s soon as she left Kiera, Granny Elder, the fairy of what to keep and what to cast away, hurried to find Eamonn.

"Good sir," she said when she spotted the lame prince. "I am Granny Elder, Princess Kiera's nursemaid."

"Then, it is to you I must say, thank you." The prince grasped her hand and squeezed it gently. "For Kiera seems a decent woman who is willing to accept an imperfect husband." He stomped his lame foot for emphasis.

"Enough pleasantries. We need to prepare you to unravel a twisted spell."

Eamonn's face had a puzzled look upon it. "What are you talking about?"

"Your wife," explained the elder tree fairy, "is called Kiera Dragonskin for a good reason. But you can help her regain her human form, if you are willing to do as I say."

"A dragon! So that is what she was hiding." The prince rubbed his chin. "It makes sense now. Why else would such a wonderful woman not show her face?"

"There is no time to explain how the spell went awry—but in order to break the spell, you must put on several more layers of clothing. Then, strike a bargain with Princess Kiera when you enter the bridal chamber. And most importantly, do not recoil when you see her covered in dragon skin."

Eamonn listen carefully to Granny Elder's instructions as he pulled on additional clothes and took a vial from the fairy. He coughed at the foul odor emanating from the container. Barely able to walk with the extra layers of clothing, he made his way to

Kiera Dragonskin's bedchamber, knocked on the door, then entered her room.

Kiera turned to face Eamonn.

His eyes widened slightly, then softened. "You are beautiful in the firelight."

She took a step toward her husband.

"Kiera Dragonskin, for every layer of clothing I remove, you must sip this tincture, then remove a layer of your skin," said Prince Eamonn.

"I will try to do as you ask," she answered.

Eamonn took off a heavy jacket.

Kiera took a swallow of bitter-tasting liquid from the vial. Afterwards, though it hurt to do so, she was able to peel off a layer of dragon skin.

Eamonn removed a vest and one set of trousers.

Kiera gazed into her husband's eyes as she drank more of the acrid tincture. Then, steeling her mind against the pain, she tore off another layer of scaly skin.

Eamonn removed his shoes, socks, and a shirt.

Kiera sipped more of the sour-smelling brew provided by the elder fairy. And though tears fell from her sky-blue eyes as she did so, she ripped off a third layer of reptilian skin.

And so it went, until Prince Eamonn stood in his underthings and an exhausted Kiera in her final layer of dragon skin.

Now, it was easy for Kiera to see that the horse leg extended to above her husband's knee. She was amazed he was able to walk as well as he did.

Eamonn glanced down at his malformed limb. "Is it too much for you to bear?" he asked.

"No," replied Kiera. "I see a good man before me—one who wanted me when all others shunned a dragon princess."

Then, the prince removed the last bit of his clothing, and Kiera shed her final layer of dragon skin. In a shimmer of green light, she transformed into a young woman—identical to her sister in appearance, except her hair was dark as night.

As Eamonn and Kiera embraced and kissed with a passion born not just of desire, but of trust, understanding, and shared suffering—another spell was broken. For when Kiera murmured, "I love you," a malformed horse's leg and hoof morphed into a man's leg and foot.

Outside the bridal chamber, Granny Elder sighed. Spells untangled and wishes fulfilled, the world was right—at least for the moment. Then, the elder tree fairy pulled up the green hood of her cloak, exited the castle on foot, as silent as moonlight, and returned to her forest.

VEIL

On June twenty-first, a dragon appeared behind Dylan Goodwin's grave marker.

Vision limited by the dark veil she wore, Leanna didn't notice the creature until it tapped the top of Dylan's tombstone with a wickedly-curved claw and said, "It's a shame he was executed. He was, as you know, innocent of murder."

Too shocked to respond, Leanna stood, took several steps away from the dragon, tripped over an urn, and landed with a *whompf* on the soft cemetery grass.

"Sorry to startle you," apologized the beast. "I've witnessed you visiting this spot for a year and decided to offer you a chance to right this wrong." The dragon tilted his head. "You can stop Dylan Goodwin's hanging." He scratched an eye ridge, then continued, "but only if you have the courage to cross time and tell the truth."

"If I do so, my husband will likely kill me." She drew the fabric of her veil through her fingers. "Still, I'd give up this last year for a chance to save Dylan," answered Leanna. "Though it seems, no one but you knows what I did, or what I *failed* to do, on the day of his hanging."

"What of your husband?" inquired the dragon as he rested a front paw on the next tombstone over.

"What of him?" Leanna stood, brushed the dirt off her skirt, and even though her heart threatened to burst from her chest with its pounding, looked the dragon in the eye. "I thought Dylan and Garret Goodwin to be much the same until I married Garret. Only then, did his true nature became apparent."

"I think Garret wore his nature on his sleeve, but you were blinded by his charm," said the beast as it traced Garret Goodwin's birth and death dates with a claw. "Then, only two days after Dylan's hanging, Garret was knifed. So, when Garret's widow wanders these hills in her black veil and lingers in the graveyard, no one questions why she's here. Or which Goodwin brother she mourns."

"You're right," responded Leanna before putting her palms to her face and moaning softly. Even after removing her hands, her head hung down. "The people of Old Fort think I'm a dutiful widow. In truth, I'm grieving for a man I only held in my arms one evening."

"But a most eventful evening," the dragon reminded Leanna

"It's all my fault, isn't it?" She looked at the reptile, hoping he could somehow offer her absolution.

"Not all of it," replied the dragon, "even though a portion of the blame rests on your shoulders. But that's not the question you need to answer tonight."

She frowned. "What do you mean?"

"I offer you a chance to go back to whatever moment in the past you'd like to change. Perhaps, we can alter the course of this tragedy." Cocking his head at an angle like a curious hound, the beast continued, "Will you cross time to right a wrong?"

"Yes," whispered Leanna as she dropped her veil to the ground. "Yes."

The dragon smiled. "Very well, but there's a price to be paid."

"Name it. I'll pay," answered Leanna

"Don't be too quick to agree to a fee which I've yet to set," warned the dragon as he studied her. The creature narrowed his eyes, licked his lips, then said, "The cost of traveling to the past is the hearing in your right ear."

Leanna remained silent for a few seconds. After pressing her fingertips lightly to her ears, she said, "I agree."

Quick as lightning, the dragon reached forward with his left paw, brushed aside her fingers, cupped her right ear, and with a sharp pain that felt like it pierced her brain, he took her hearing.

For a few moments, Leanna felt off-kilter. She turned her head and realized she could no longer hear the tree frogs' songs with her right ear. Suppressing her desire to weep, she said, "An instant of discomfort and less noise is a small price to pay for a man's life."

"True. But before I send you off, you'll need to know my name." The reptile touched a paw to his chest then swung it to the side while lowering his head in strange dragonish bow.

"I am Tionil the Ageless. I can travel to Before, Now, Yet-to-be, Never-was, and Never-will-be. Remember my name, repeat my name, and tonight, you'll return to yesteryear."

"Tionil the Ageless," repeated Leanna. At first, she said it quietly to herself to commit the name to memory. Soon, she spoke the dragon's name louder.

"Very good," said Tionil. "Next, you must continue to repeat my name while spinning around and thinking of the exact moment to which you want to return."

Leanna nodded, then resumed chanting, "Tionil the Ageless. Tionil the Ageless." She pictured the hanging platform as Old Fort's executioner, sheriff, judge, and priest escorted Dylan to the noose. Then, she spun around as fast as she could. She'd closed her eyes to avoid becoming dizzy, so the last thing Leanna remembered about the dragon was his warm, smoky breath surrounding her like a cloud and his voice wishing her good luck.

"What's wrong with you, Leanna?" asked Garret as he grabbed her shoulder. "You're twisting around like a top."

"Nothing," she answered. "I was just trying to see better."

"Not much to see." Garret yawned. "They don't even have the rope around Dylan's neck yet."

"He's your brother—aren't you upset he's about to hang?"

"Better him than me," answered Garret Goodwin.

As her husband spoke these words, even though she only heard them with her left ear, Leanna realized Garret's voice sounded much like Dylan's voice. She glanced at Garret's face and noticed how similar the brothers looked.

"Then, I'm not too late."

Leanna pushed through the crowd toward the gallows. Even deaf in one ear, her head rang with the cries of people gathered in the square. They smelled death coming, and wanted to watch the murderer, Dylan Goodwin, dance on air. Except, she knew he wasn't the man who'd shot Perce Dundee outside the Old Fort Town Hall—because he'd been with Leanna that evening.

Finally, she shoved her way to the edge of the hanging platform. Leanna waved her arms and hollered at the judge, executioner, sheriff, and priest, "He's innocent. He was with me that night. He couldn't have shot Perce. He was with me."

But no one heard her above the screams of the people cheering on the hanging. No one but the man standing beside Leanna—her husband, Garret Goodwin.

Just like the first time, Dylan was hung by the neck until dead. And just like the first time, Garret Goodwin was stabbed to death outside The Dapple Pony two days later—but not before he beat Leanna for admitting she'd been with his brother on the night Perce Dundee was shot.

A s she'd done on each full moon for the last year since Dylan and Garret Goodwin's deaths, Leanna stood at the foot of Dylan's grave quietly repeating, "Tionil the Ageless, take pity on me again."

But tonight, like so many before, only the calls of owls and the flickering of lightning bugs answered her. She wiped her tears on her veil, dropped a daisy on Dylan's grave, and turned to leave Old Fort Cemetery.

"If I give you another chance to change the past, what will you do differently?" asked a deep voice.

Leanna whirled around. "Tionil!" She ran towards the towering reptile. Paused, then took the last few steps slowly. Tionil hadn't shown any ill-intent on their first meeting, but that had been a year earlier. Perhaps, the dragon's disposition toward her had changed.

As if he could read her thoughts, Tionil said, "There's nothing to fear, child. I gave up eating women and children eons ago."

"Of that, I'm glad," replied Leanna with a smile. She tucked several wayward strands of her dark hair beneath her veil. She took a deep breath, exhaled slowly, then took a step forward and gazed intently into the dragon's sapphire eyes. "Will you help me?"

"Yes, but again, there's a price to be paid."

"Name it. I'll pay," answered Leanna

"Caution, child. The price is steeper this time," warned

Tionil. The dragon reached out a paw, tilted her chin up with one claw and stared into her amber-colored eyes. "The cost of traveling to the past a second time is the sight in your right eye," he said.

Leanna felt tears slide down her cheeks. She looked beyond Tionil at the treetops twinkling with fireflies, the summer moon, and the ocean of stars covering the heavens. Despite the fact the night wind seemed to whisper, "*No*," Leanna said, "I agree."

Swift as rattlesnake's strike, Tionil reached forward with his left paw, covered her right eye, and with pain like a hundred bee stings, the dragon took her sight.

For several seconds, Leanna shook with fear. She turned her head from side to side trying to see everything that surrounded her. With only one functioning eye, she knew a bear or cougar could easily attack her from the right. Digging her fingernails into the palms of her hands to stop herself from crying, Leanna said, "A moment of discomfort and seeing less ugliness in this world is a tiny price to pay for a man's life."

"True."

The dragon continued to observe her, and had she not been taught otherwise, Leanna would've sworn Tionil cared for her. Lest she let her guard down, she reminded herself that dragons are cold-blooded creatures who only do what pleases them.

If Tionil read her thoughts, the dragon didn't acknowledge them. Instead, the creature warned, "This time, choose more carefully when to arrive in the past. A hanging is a bit late to proclaim someone's innocence."

"Agreed." Leanna took a deep breath and smoothed her skirt before asking, "Is the process the same?"

"It is," replied Tionil. "You may start to chant as soon as you've focused your thoughts on the exact moment to which you'd like to return."

"Dylan's trial," she said. "Surely, my voice will be heard there."

"Perhaps," said Tionil the Ageless before exhaling a cloud of smoke. Leanna coughed, then began to repeat his name and spin.

The courtroom was filled to capacity. As the defendant's brother and sister-in-law, Garret and Leanna were given seats near the front. When he was brought in, Leanna saw Dylan brush aside his shaggy hair and scan the room until his eyes found hers. With her one good eye, she spotted no fear on his smooth, clean-shaven face—just resignation.

"All rise," proclaimed the clerk as Judge Dittimus entered.

Leanna stood. As she did so, she glanced at her husband. Garret's hair was clipped so short, people might think he was in the military. After she sat down, Leanna continued to think about Garret's appearance. The day after the shooting outside Old Fort Town Hall, Garret had visited the barber for a buzz-cut and he'd stopped shaving his beard. Whereas before the shooting, Dylan and Garret had looked alike, now it was difficult to tell they were brothers.

During the opening statements, Leanna stared at the back of Dylan's head. How had she been so blind? If Dylan hadn't murdered Perce Dundee, the person who looked like his doppelganger must have. She turned her head, gazed at her husband, and knew sure as rain that Garret had killed Perce and intended to let his brother hang rather than tell the truth.

Farnel Tifton was the first witness. He swore when he exited The Dapple Pony on that fateful night, he saw a man who looked like Dylan Goodwin shoot Perce Dundee. Dylan's lawyer got Farnel to admit he'd been drinking, the lighting was poor, and he was a fair distance from the site of the murder. Nonetheless, his testimony was compelling.

Farnel's half-brother, Butchie Tifton testified next. His story seemed to corroborate Farnel's account of the murder. Though the defense attorney did his best to challenge the accuracy of Butchie's version of events, again the testimony was damning.

The final eyewitness was Janie Sue Whitsun. Janie Sue had worked as a waitress at The Dapple Pony since she was eighteen. Most everyone in Old Fort knew who she was, because she also picked up day shift hours at the Battlecry Diner, Mondays through Fridays. One of Leanna's few friends, she knew Janie Sue would tell the truth.

"Miss Whitsun, what did you see and hear the night Perce Dundee was killed," said the prosecutor.

"I came out for a smoke," explained Janie Sue, "saw them Tifton boys staggering down the steps, and just about the time they hollered a goodbye to me, I heard a pop sound."

"Did you see where the sound came from?" asked the prosecutor.

"I did," answered the waitress. "I looked over to the town hall and saw a man standing over Perce Dundee."

"Is that man in the courtroom?" inquired the prosecutor.

"He is," replied Janie Sue as she pointed toward Dylan Goodwin. "The man who shot Perce is sitting right over there."

She's right, thought Leanna. Because sitting directly behind Dylan, right where the waitress's finger pointed, was her husband, Garret Goodwin.

At the end of the first day of the trial, the sheriff took Dylan back to jail, but not before Leanna caught his eye and smiled at her brother-in-law. He managed to respond with a half-hearted smile before being led away.

The next morning, Leanna got up early and dressed for court. As she watched the minutes tick by, she thought about what she had to do today. First, she needed to tell the defense lawyer she was Dylan's alibi. Second, she had to get on the stand in front of her husband, the minister, and the rest of the town and reveal that she'd been with her husband's brother at the time of Perce's murder. She knew they would all be leaning forward focused on her every word. Next, the prosecuting lawyer would try to punch holes in her story. Last, once she was finished testifying, she'd have to face an angry husband and admit she didn't love him.

I married the wrong brother. And after I testify, Garret will kill me, she thought. *But I need to set things right by telling the truth.* Of course, that would mean the sheriff would be looking for another suspect. Even though he'd done everything possible to change his appearance, it wouldn't be long before someone figured out who looked a lot like Dylan. Someone who was known to always be in a bit of trouble. Someone Leanna couldn't be made to testify against, because he was her spouse. She was so deep in thought that she didn't notice her husband stroll into the living room.

"What are you sitting here for?" asked Garret as he grabbed her upper arm. "I've decided we're not going to the courthouse today."

"We've got to go."

"We don't *have* to do anything," replied her husband shaking her by her arm. "I didn't like the way people were looking at us like we were guilty, too."

"Are you?" asked Leanna. "Are you guilty?"

If Garret answered her question, she never heard his response. He hit her on the jaw, she saw stars, then crumpled to the linoleum.

That evening, Janie Sue stopped by on her way home from work and told Leanna that Dylan was convicted of murder and that Judge Dittimus sentenced him to hang on Friday. "Shame he's to die," said the waitress. "Dylan seemed to be a nice fellow."

"He didn't do it," whispered Leanna.

"That's not what the court says." Janie Sue patted the back of Leanna's hand, then gently touched her bruised upper arm. "Honey, what happened to your arm and face?

"She fell," said Garret from behind Janie Sue. "And she needs her rest, so kindly leave."

"She no more fell than I did," snapped Leanna's friend as she got up, walked to the door, and turned around. "And I better not see evidence of any more falls, or I'm talking to the sheriff."

"Leave," growled Garret before switching on the charm and adding in a pleasant tone, "Please."

"Later," said Janie Sue as she waved to Leanna then slammed the screen door.

Garret wouldn't let Leanna out of the house until Friday. Then, just like the first and second times, Dylan was hung by the neck until dead. And just like the times before, her husband was stabbed to death outside The Dapple Pony a couple of days later for his womanizing ways.

She'd given up half of her hearing and sight and failed to change a thing.

∾

On the twelfth full moon since Dylan and Garret Goodwin's deaths, Leanna knelt at the foot of Dylan's grave repeating, "Tionil the Ageless, take pity on me once more."

The whirl of cicadas was the only response.

"I now know the moment to which I need to return," said Leanna as she pulled back her long, black veil. "Isn't three the magic number? The third time *will* be the charm, if only you'll give me that chance."

"Three *is* a magic number," agreed the dragon as he stepped from the shadows of the white pines which edged Old Fort Cemetery.

"Tionil!" She ran to the dragon, spread her arms wide, and did her best to hug the beast. "It's so good to see you—to know you still watch over me."

"Child," said the dragon, "I'm no guardian angel. We've bartered for time. Nothing more."

Leanna stared up at the huge, scaly muzzle above her. Maybe her dealings with Tionil *were* nothing but business. Still, she was certain the creature felt more toward her than he let on.

"Then, let us make one more deal," she said. "I want to return to the moment when I walked into the Old Fort Mercantile and saw two brothers stacking sacks of feed."

The dragon nodded. "So you want to return to the beginning?"

"Yes."

"Do you think you'll be able to resist Garret's teasing, grins, and devil-may-care charm? Will you instead choose the quiet, shy brother this time?" asked Tionil the Ageless.

"Yes. Please, let me go back in time once more and change the past."

"The price this time is higher," warned Tionil.

"Name it."

"I claim bone," replied the dragon.

"Bone!" Leanna bit her lip. Maybe the price *was* too high this time.

"I claim half an inch of your leg bone," said Tionil. "You will still be able to walk, but you'll have a limp."

"The partial loss of hearing and sight were explained by a serious fall I suffered as a child. Will the limp be the result of that same fall which I cannot remember?"

"It will," answered the dragon, "and though you can't

recollect the fall from your neighbor's tree fort, others will remember it."

"How are you able to accomplish this?" asked Leanna as she crushed her veil between her hands.

"Did you forget I'm able to travel to Before, Now, Yet-to-be, Never-was, and Never-will-be? I went back to Never-was and changed it to Before," explained Tionil the Ageless. "I'll do it again to explain your limp, if you agree to pay me in bone for your third attempt at changing the past."

Leanna relished her long walks beneath the towering trees, along stream banks, across wildflower-filled meadows, and through snowy drifts—but a man's life was worth more than a few hikes.

"I agree," she said, then steeled herself for the expected pain.

This time, her leg felt as if it was being torn asunder. With a sob, Leanna fell to the ground.

"You must stand, repeat my name, and spin around whilst thinking of the moment in the past where you want to arrive," said the dragon in a solemn voice. "And this, child, is the last chance I will give you."

Unable to stand on her own, Leanna reached for the dragon. Tionil allowed her to grasp his black-scaled leg and pull herself upright. "I'm not sure I can spin," she gasped.

"Focus," urged the beast. "Once you begin, I will exhale and surround you with dragon's breath. It will help ease the pain as it floats you back through time."

Leanna nodded and began to chant, "Tionil the Ageless," as she thought about her first encounter with the Goodwin brothers. Lastly, pushing through the pain, she began to spin.

~

Old Fort Mercantile looked exactly as Leanna remembered it on the crisp October Tuesday that she'd arrived in town for the first time. With Father away at sea most of the year, after Momma passed away, Leanna had been sent to live with Beatrix, her mother's first cousin. An unclaimed blessing, Momma's term for a spinster, Beatrix was a seamstress who lived alone in a stone house just off Main Street.

"Leanna!" exclaimed a short, gray-haired woman with wire-rimmed spectacles perched on her nose as she hurried toward Leanna.

Resisting the urge to say, "Nice to see you again," Leanna reminded herself that in the past reality, she'd never met Beatrix prior to today. She'd relied on a photo Momma had kept on her bureau to identify her mother's cousin.

"Cousin Beatrix?" Leanna raised her eyebrows in a quizzical expression.

"You look like your mother," said Cousin Beatrix as she swooped in and gave Leanna a hug. "Let's head home and get you settled in."

"That sounds wonderful." Leanna enjoyed seeing Beatrix once more. With information from the future, she knew Beatrix would have a heart attack in three months' time. She'd linger for a day, then die holding Leanna's hand. Leanna would inherit her stone cottage, its contents, and a tidy sum in her bank account. Thus, making her a "catch" for whichever local man she married.

"Dylan. Garret. Would you boys please carry Leanna's suitcases and other belongings to my house?" said Beatrix as she held Leanna's hand and headed toward the Mercantile's front door.

That's when Leanna spotted the Goodwin brothers stacking bags of feed. Just like the first time she'd met them, Dylan smiled, gazed at her briefly, nodded, and said, "Yes, Miss Beatrix. I'd be happy to carry Leanna's things."

Whereas Garret stepped forward, bowed grandly, grinned, winked at Leanna, and announced, "I'm Garret Goodwin. Welcome to Old Fort, pretty lady."

This time, Leanna didn't blush and lower her eyelashes. Instead, she looked directly into Garret's eyes and replied, "Thank you for the welcome. I'm glad to be here."

While leaving the Mercantile and on the short stroll to Beatrix's home, her cousin chatted about the town of Old Fort and its history. Pretending to listen to information she was already familiar with, Leanna instead studied the Goodwin brothers.

As they exited the store, Garret pocketed some penny candy and winked at a young woman standing near the cash register. Leanna knew he'd never drop a few cents into the register to cover the candy he'd stolen. And single or married, she was sure he'd try to court the young woman.

Meanwhile, Dylan set down the suitcases he was carrying, opened the door for Beatrix and Leanna, then called over his shoulder to the store owner, "I'll be back shortly, sir."

They'd only gone a short distance when Dylan said, "I noticed you're limping. Are you okay or do you need a doctor?"

"I'm fine. It's an injury from childhood," she replied, suddenly aware of his honest concern.

"Why don't you let me carry that, too," offered Dylan as he reached for a small parcel she held.

As Leanna started to hand it to him, Garret grabbed the package from her.

"Let me carry that for you, little lady," said Garret as he leaned close to her. "And is that enticing scent filling the air rosewater or lavender?"

Not a wide-eyed innocent this time, Leanna caught the

practiced nature of his flirting. As she relinquished the parcel to Garret, she answered, "Neither. It's Lily-of-the-Valley."

"Makes sense," he replied. "A beautiful flower for a beautiful woman." Then, Garret smiled in his most charming manner and brushed his long hair out of his eyes.

"Is May your birth month?" asked Dylan as they reached Beatrix's house.

"Actually, it is." Leanna tried to remember if he'd asked her this question the first time she arrived at Beatrix's home. *He did ask me,* she recalled, *but I was so busy flirting with Garret I don't believe I even answered him.*

"There's a dance tonight in the Mercantile's warehouse if you're interested," said Dylan. "Unless you're too tired from traveling."

"Are you asking me to go *with* you?"

"Why should she go with you when she can go on the arm of the most eligible bachelor in Old Fort?" Garret stepped in front of his brother, took Leanna's right hand and kissed the back of it.

"I'd like to go with you, Dylan," said Leanna, as she firmly removed her hand from Garret's grasp. "I'd like to go with you very much."

The first full moon after Garret Goodwin's hanging for the murder of Perce Dundee, Dylan and Leanna stood at the foot of his grave.

"I wish there was something I could've done to save him," said Dylan as he wiped his eyes with the back of his hand.

"He was fun-loving, but flawed," Leanna reminded her husband. "There wasn't anything anyone could have done."

"I know he wasn't perfect, but I loved him." Dylan reached for her hand, squeezed it.

"We'll get through this," replied Leanna. "Now, you go on back to the house. I want to visit Beatrix's grave for a few minutes."

"I can come with you."

"No. I'm fine," she assured her husband. "But a hot cup of tea when I get home would be nice."

"Done," he replied before kissing her forehead and striding toward the cemetery's gate.

"Tionil the Ageless," called Leanna as she pulled her black veil away from her face. "Are you here? Tionil?"

"I am here, child." The dragon rose up from the shadows until he loomed above her.

"Thank you for letting me save a decent man—the man I love —from a wrongful hanging." Voice quavering, she continued, "What I couldn't have guessed, is that, in saving him, I saved myself."

Tionil was silent. His stare seemed to penetrate flesh and bone and see directly into Leanna's heart. "You don't regret the loss of hearing, sight, and mobility?"

"No," Leanna assured him. "They're nothing compared to what I've gained. And though you claim our relationship is nothing but bartering, I'll always be grateful to you."

"In that case, I will tell you a secret," said the dragon. "I've offered countless people the chance to go back to the past to right a wrong. Most decline when they hear the price. A few cross time once. Several have crossed time twice. But you, Leanna, are the only one who's been willing to endure the pain and pay the price three times."

"I didn't know that."

"How could you know?" Tionil the Ageless's sapphire eyes glinted as moonlight struck them. "But I never said the price was non-refundable."

Leanna frowned. "I don't understand."

The dragon exhaled. As the cloud of dragon breath surrounded her, she felt her right eye burning, heard a ringing in her right ear, and felt a pinch in her right leg.

When the mist cleared, Leanna gasped. "I'm healed. How is this possible?"

"I am Tionil the Ageless. I can travel to Before, Now, Yet-to-be, Never-was, and Never-will-be. I've been to Before, changed a thing or two, and returned to Now before you knew I was gone."

"The fall..."

"Never happened," finished the dragon. "As to this veil," Tionil snagged the length of lace with a dangerously-curved claw, "it should be white." He closed his eyes and drew the veil though his paw. "Then, it can serve as a christening wrap for your children." He handed the now white-as-bone veil back to Leanna.

Before she could ask, "What children?" Tionil the Ageless melted into the shadows.

The snowdrops had just begun to bloom when Dylan and Leanna Goodwin welcomed their first born and named her Beatrix. When Dylan and the doctor left the room for a few minutes, Leanna held her daughter close and breathed in her sweet scent. Happier than she'd ever been, she adjusted little Bea's receiving blanket and noticed a small birthmark on her daughter's right arm.

"Tionil," whispered Leanna, "Thank you."

For the birthmark was shaped like a dragon.

WHAT LIES BELOW

To view the town beneath the man-made lake, Ambereen was willing to hike alone if need be. But wandering deep into the 1,600-acre woods around Loch Raven Reservoir, especially in the middle of a weekday, seemed an unsafe thing for a single woman to do. The woods in that section of the reservoir were far from traffic and bike trails. She remembered hearing about a man shot there three years ago. No one had ever been arrested for the murder. So she asked a friend to come with her.

As long as he got to fish for a while, she knew Vernon Dotson would agree to keep her company and help her locate the underwater town of Warren. She was right.

After Vern parked his beat-up sedan alongside Warren Road, he and Ambereen pulled on their knapsacks. Vern grabbed his fishing gear as well as a small cooler. Then, they entered the forest at the Warren Road Bridge Trail Head.

"Beautiful day," commented Vern as he navigated the path ahead of Ambereen. "But it looks like there haven't been many hikers on this trail since hunting season."

"Makes sense," she replied. "On this side of the reservoir, the map marks the lands: *Hunting*. On the other side, it says: *Safe*. I expect most hikers choose the trails to the east of Loch Raven. But it's not hunting season, so we are probably safe from being mistaken for a deer."

On cue, a doe and two fawns bolted across the path in front of them in a whirl of last autumn's leaves. Without so much as a glance in their direction, the graceful trio dashed down the hill toward the lake.

"I didn't even see them until they moved," said Vern as he took off his baseball cap, wiped his forehead, then replaced the cap. "Makes you wonder what else is watching us."

"We probably don't want to know." Then, unable to resist a chance to tease her co-worker, she added, "Wood elves, maybe? Or trolls?"

Vern rolled his eyes, then started down the path again.

While her companion trudged in front of her, Ambereen noticed the late spring woods around them. Wide awake now, the forest was teeming with life: mosses had greened, fiddle-heads had unfurled into fern fronds, tree branches were filled out with new leaves, mushrooms had sprouted in the rich soil, and insects scurried across debris. The sunlight streaming through the canopy highlighted spiderwebs strung from saplings to tree trunks to sticker bushes. It also revealed the clouds of insects buzzing nearby.

Vern slapped the back of his neck. "Gnats, mosquitoes, and other biting bugs are out today," he observed. "We should have put on some insecticide."

"I did," answered Ambereen. Though she did not mention it was an all-natural, herbal bug-repellent. Friend or not, Vern was sure to snicker at her attention to not harming nature.

"Nice. So only one of us will be a smorgasbord for biters," Vern said as he swatted the air in front of his face.

Before she could respond, the tap-tap-tap of a woodpecker echoed through the woods. "Look," Ambereen said while pointing to a deadwood tree to their right. "About twenty-five feet up. Can you see it?"

"Yeah. It's a woodpecker." Vern barely glanced at the large bird drilling into the wood.

"It's a pileated woodpecker. You can tell by its size and by the oval holes it is pecking in the tree trunk."

"Come on," said Vern. "It's just a bird."

Ambereen followed in silence—a silence which allowed her to hear the various bird calls filling the June air. She recognized blue jays, cardinals, robins, and of course, sparrows. Suddenly, the chatter of squirrels drowned out the birds' twittering.

"Well, somebody doesn't want us here," laughed Vern. Even he couldn't resist the antics of the half dozen gray squirrels positioned overhead who seemed determined to let every creature within miles know a couple of humans were wandering the forest.

"I think you are right," answered Ambereen as one of the noisy squirrels looked her in the eye before leaping to a branch farther up the tulip poplar tree on which he perched.

"You know, they filmed some of the scenes of *The Blair Witch Project* in these woods," said Vern as he adjusted one of his backpack's straps.

"Really?" She looked around. The woods was certainly remote enough to inspire fear in those not used to being outdoors. "Just the forest or some of the ruins, too?"

"I don't know," answered Vern. He pointed to a crumbling stone house. "I guess it could have been either—or maybe both."

The ruined building was not the first they had passed on their way to a finger of land jutting into the waters of Loch Raven. Ambereen hoped the last scary scene of the movie had not been filmed here—even though it was all imagined evil.

"Finally," said Vern as they reached a nice fishing spot with a clear view of the town lying somewhere beneath the viridian waters. "Warren should be here—though I don't know if you will be able to see it." He gestured at the lake. "I'm going to find a nice spot a little farther down the trail to relax and toss a line in. Maybe I'll catch a sunfish or bluegill."

"Maybe a catfish," added Ambereen with a grin. She knew he was not a fan of catfish. If he caught one, it was sure to get tossed back into the water rather than into the cooler he had lugged along. Which was just fine with her.

"Don't jinx me." Still holding the fishing pole, he crossed his forefingers in a warding sign. "I'll be over there," said Vern as he pointed to another finger of land past a tumble of rocks. "Yell, if you need me."

"Okay," answered Ambereen as she made her way to the edge of the lake.

Though no botanist, she spotted a few plants she recognized: wood sorrel with its little yellow blossoms, May apple umbrellas, the purple flowers and heart-shaped leaves of sweet violets, and gill-over-the-ground. Of course, there were plenty of other plants she didn't know the names of—though she was sure she had seen them before.

Once she reached the water, she scanned the surface for signs of the drowned town of Warren. Though Warren was not the only town swallowed by the waters of the reservoir when the City of Baltimore decided to build a second dam on the Gunpowder River, it was the one she wanted to find. Hoping a slightly different view of daylight striking the water might better illuminate what was secreted beneath the surface, Ambereen moved several meters to her left.

"I can see something down there," she whispered. Only the birds perched in the chestnut oaks and Osage orange trees above her head answered.

Then, she heard it—a church bell ringing from deep in the lake. *I suppose it is possible,* she thought. *If the current is moving the bell's tongue enough and forcing it to strike the cup. I guess it could still ring.*

As abruptly as it had started, the muffled ringing stopped. The birds and insects quieted. Even the rustling of the leaves silenced. All Ambereen could hear was the lapping of the water at her feet.

The hairs on the back of her neck prickled as she felt the eyes of an unseen someone or some*thing* studying her. Rather than shout for Vern, Ambereen whispered, "Hello. Who is there?"

She was answered by a splash in the nearby water as a great blue heron flapped skyward, its long legs dangling below its beautifully feathered body.

"Oh, my gosh." Legs feeling like jelly, Ambereen sat down on a rock to wait until her heart stopped racing. Not usually skittish when in the woods, she hoped the insects would feast upon Vern for mentioning that a horror movie had been filmed here.

Expecting relief to soon wash away the prickly neck sensation and fear of a stalking *something* gawking at her, Ambereen rubbed her eyes with shaky fingers and studied the water at her feet. From below the surface, large eyes stared up at her.

Perhaps it is my reflection, distorted by the lake's wavelets, she told herself. But the face moved sideways, then a long-clawed paw broke the surface of Loch Raven.

Ambereen gasped and moved spider-like away from the water. Before she could call out for Vernon, the creature reached forth its scaly front foot and touched her lips. Ambereen found herself unable to speak.

"Hush, child," said the beast. At least Ambereen thought it spoke aloud, though it could have been talking only in her mind. "I am not here to harm, only to enlighten an inquisitive young woman."

The creature crawled farther out of the lake, exposing the front half of an enormous, sinuous body covered in iridescent scales. It stretched its snaky neck and tilted its head to get a better look at Ambereen. "You have come to my lake seeking to understand what lies below. Have you not?"

Still unable to speak, Ambereen nodded.

"I can tell you over a hundred years ago, men stopped the flow of a river. The river backed up and began to swallow the land and all of her creatures. Barns, homes, roads, even mills were flooded by the rising water. At first, the lake was too shallow for my kind, but as the months passed, the water level rose. Deeper, deeper, even deeper Loch Raven became until it was perfect for dragons."

The reptile smiled—a most terrifying sight. "But I waste words when I can show you more clearly the wonders of Warren and the other towns hidden beneath the lake," said the creature as he wrapped his neck around Ambereen.

"Now, you must grasp my neck, climb onto my back, and hold on like your life depended on it."

Too scared to disobey, she climbed onto the dragon's back, holding fast with her hands and legs.

"Do not let go. No matter *what* you see," warned the beast as it twisted lakeward and dove beneath the water.

Afraid she would drown, Ambereen held her breath as the dragon plunged into Loch Raven. When she thought her lungs would burst, she finally gave up and opened her mouth. She fully expected to drown. She did not. Instead, she found herself in a bubble of air, surely of the dragon's making.

I'm safe, she thought. *Though I have no idea how the dragon is creating this air bubble.*

Must you know the "how" of everything? came the response.

This time, Ambereen was sure the reptile spoke to her via thought.

How long were you listening in on my words and thoughts? she asked.

Today, since your feet touched the ground at the beginning of the trail, responded the dragon.

That is creepy, thought Ambereen. *You are like a stalker—spying on unsuspecting hikers.*

You suspected something was watching you from the first. So my appearance could not have been a surprise, answered the reptile.

Seeing a dragon is always a surprise.

The creature seemed to consider that statement as it swam to the bottom of the deepest part of the lake.

But further comment was not required, as before Ambereen stretched not only the stone ruins of the town of Warren, but additional structures built by non-humans. The otherworldly architecture had wide, round-arched doors. Many of the buildings were little more than sleeping quarters. Some were occupied.

Dragons! thought Ambereen. *There is a colony of dragons in Loch Raven.*

More than one, answered the dragon on whose back she rode.

Considering the lake was over 2,400-acres in size, she supposed there was room for several dragon colonies. It occurred to Ambereen that she didn't know what to call *her* dragon to distinguish him or her from the others. *What is your name?*

The dragon paused before answering. *I am female. My true name is a secret, since to share it would give you a bit of power over me.*

Well, you looked greenish to me so...

I altered my color to match the water. I appear whatever color, pattern, and texture will help me blend into the background, explained the dragon.

So you use camouflage like a chameleon. I can call you Chameleon if you'd like, suggested Ambereen.

Chameleon will do, answered the dragon as another of her kind swam nearby.

Who is this? asked the other dragon. *And why have you brought her below?*

She is the girl I have talked about for years, said Ambereen's dragon. *She finally came to find me.*

The other dragon twisted its neck so its face was inches away from Ambereen and studied her with its huge silver eyes. *She looks no different than all of the other female humans I have seen. Though I suppose you would know if she were yours.* Then, quicker than a lizard darting away from a child's hand, the other dragon swam into the dark waters closer to the upper dam.

What did you mean when you said that you have talked about me for years? I only met you today, said Ambereen.

You have known about me since you were a child, replied Chameleon. *Every time you rode in a car over the Warren Road Bridge what did you think?*

That I heard a dragon roar, but it was only the sound of the car wheels on a rough metal bridge, answered Ambereen.

No, I did roar when a car carrying you drove across, because I heard you thinking about me.

She considered what Chameleon had said. It had a ring of truth to it.

What did you call that bridge then? And even now, as a woman, you still use your pet name for it, thought the dragon.

The Dragon Bridge, answered Ambereen.

So I have been waiting for you to come find me all these years. And now, you are finally here! Chameleon did a little twirl in the water to emphasize her happiness.

But I cannot stay, thought Ambereen. *I guess I can visit you once in a while, but a reservoir is no place for a human.*

But we must stay together. You are meant to be my... Whatever Chameleon meant to think next was swallowed in Ambereen's scream.

Swimming parallel to them, just a couple of arm-lengths away, were the skeletal remains of men, women, and children. Ambereen looked from side to side. Dozens of animated corpses were closing in on them.

Who are these people? she asked. She supposed even her thoughts must sound panicked because Ambereen not only felt her heart racing, but her throat tightening like it did just before she cried.

The long-dead, thought the dragon.

Why are they chasing us? The finger bones trying to claw her and the chomping teeth in the closest skulls seemed more personal than anonymous restless spirits.

They do not tolerate living humans very well. I thought because you were with me, the dead would leave you alone, mused the dragon.

That's why there are "No Swimming" signs posted everywhere around Loch Raven. And why anyone who swims away from the public areas ends up drowning. Though their bodies are not usually found for months. The ghosts or haunted skeletons or undead remains or whatever you call them —drag the living to the bottom, thought Ambereen.

They will not get you, Chameleon assured her.

I don't know, they look determined. I'm not sure you can out-swim them.

Then, we will go ashore. They cannot leave the water, yet, answered the dragon as she paddled to the shallows, then climbed up onto a weedy embankment at the edge of the lake. *We are far from the populated areas here, so no one will spot us.*

"Look at the dead," whispered Ambereen as dozens of skinless hands dug into the dirt at the bottom of the embankment. In silence, she observed several skulls pop up from the water, appear to look at her, then duck below the surface.

"It seems I have underestimated the bitterness of the undead who reside beneath the surface of Loch Raven," conceded the dragon in a voice like wind singing between branches.

Chameleon sighed, then switched to mindspeak. *You see, there were graveyards in Warren and the other towns flooded by the construction of the Gunpowder River's second dam. When Loch Raven started to fill, there was barely time for the people who had lingered to get out of their homes safely. No one thought to exhume the graves and move the dead. Instead, the gravestones, graves, and bodies they contained now lie at the bottom of the lake.*

"That's awful." Ambereen frowned. "But you and I had nothing to do with the flooding of their graves."

"True, but the land below the lake was their resting place before it became home to my kind. And before your birth. They *do* have prior claim."

"I don't think there are any laws or legal rulings in any court hereabouts concerning land-usage and water rights between uneasy ghosts and dragons," joked Ambereen. Though she knew the situation was far from funny.

Even as she spoke, Ambereen noticed Chameleon's actual size and current coloration. Though winged and shaped somewhat differently, the dragon's body was the size of a large work horse —like a Belgium Draft or Clydesdale. Of course, when the long tail and neck were added, Chameleon was much longer than a draft horse. As to color, while resting on a weedy bank beside Loch Raven, Chameleon's skin now looked like a mishmash of green and brown weeds with a few darker thin sapling-like vertical stripes crawling up her sides.

"Do you have to tell your skin what to look like, or does it change on its own to match its surroundings?" Ambereen inquired.

"It just happens," responded the dragon in her melodious voice. "Therefore, I never have to think about it." Chameleon's eye ridges lowered into a dragonish frown. "But my skin isn't our problem—what to do about the undead and the necromancer is."

"Necromancer!"

"Of course," said the dragon as she examined the claws on her front feet. "A necromancer is required to reanimate the dead. A simple haunting would not include bodies which, even if you tear them apart with your teeth, come back together and continue wreaking havoc."

Chameleon sighed before speaking again. "I must be honest with you, Ambereen-who-believes-in-dragons. We need a human to destroy this human who calls forth the dead before things get any worse."

"So you brought me here under false pretenses?" She stood and brushed leaves and twigs from her jeans. "All that stuff about the Dragon Bridge and you waiting for me was..."

"True," said the dragon. "I believe you and I are destined to rid Loch Raven of a necromancer who has taken up residence near the shoreline on the east side of the lake. But before we do, we need to visit my colony's home. So, climb aboard."

"But the undead," began Ambereen as she crawled onto Chameleon's back and grabbed her neck, "will surely..." The dragon dashed into the reservoir, then dove beneath the surface faster than Ambereen could finish her question.

Once again, she held her breath until it felt her lungs would burst, then in desperation, Ambereen gulped whatever oxygen the dragon provided. As before, there was a bubble of breathable air surrounding her. Of the undead, Ambereen saw little more than a few flailing bones and fluttering bits of graveclothes. Chameleon's notched-up speed was more than the animated corpses could keep up with. So, faster than an arrow, she and the dragon shot through the water, through a deep water tunnel, then into the lowest level of an underground complex.

This is the nest of my colony, thought the dragon. *Here, we will use mind-speak, so all who want to listen to our conversations may do so.*

I see, responded Ambereen. She was happy Chameleon had warned her of the many minds who could—and probably would—listen to their exchanges.

As she slid down from the dragon's back, Ambereen studied the abode of one of the colonies of the Dragons of Loch Raven. Though not directed at Chameleon, Ambereen assumed her thoughts screamed, *Wow!*, to any dragon listening—because that was what her brain was thinking. The ramp which Chameleon had used to climb from the water was constructed of carefully fitted and polished rocks. The rock pavement continued into an enormous central gathering area and several hallways which branched off toward what Ambereen assumed were rooms for sleep, eating, and other dragonish activities.

A glance at Chameleon's front feet convinced her that, while the dragons might have aided in the excavation of their cave, someone else was responsible for the mosaic-like paving below her feet. As for the fabulous murals which decorated the walls—perhaps a dragon could hold a paintbrush and render the scenes of dragon lore she beheld, but she suspected someone else had a hand in those, too. Before she could ask Chameleon about the art, several dragons who had apparently been discussing something at the far end of the gathering area strode forward to greet them.

Is this the human you have been waiting for? asked a deep voice.

Yes, this is Ambereen, replied Chameleon.

She is young—perhaps too young for the task, suggested a high, nasally voice.

Age is not an important part of the equation—intelligence, a good heart, and pure soul are the deciding factors, the deep voice assured all who were listening.

He must be the head dragon, Ambereen surmised.

The largest of the dragons lowered his head slightly, studied Ambereen's face, then said, *I am. Were you told of the necromancer who calls forth the dead to attack your people?* he asked in his deep voice.

Yes, Ambereen thought. *Though I'm not sure I can do much to help. I know no magic.*

None? inquired the largest dragon.

Well, I do know some folklore. And I read lots of dark fantasy books. Plus, I guess I know a little about herbs, stated Ambereen as several of the dragons, including Chameleon and the head dragon chuckled.

She will do, said the deep voice. Then, the chief dragon lifted his head, looked at Chameleon, and ordered, *Come up with a plan. Get the girl whatever she needs to eliminate the necromancer. We have endured this foulness for too long.* With a final nod in her direction, the chief dragon, followed by his entourage, walked away.

That went well, thought Chameleon as she smiled down at Ambereen.

I'm not sure if you know it, she responded, *but when you smile, it looks like you are ready to eat me.*

Chameleon chuckled. *We do not usually eat humans. Instead, we try to protect your kind. Which brings us back to the necromancer. Any idea how to eliminate him?*

Relaxing in Chameleon's room on a jewel-toned rug with the dragon's tail curled around her, Ambereen and the dragon came up with a plan—not an elaborate, magic-filled assault—rather a common-sense approach to a necromancer who was human.

How long do you think we need to leave the mirror and knife in salt? asked Chameleon as she stirred the white mineral covering a lovely, antique, hand-held mirror and a fabulously-jeweled dagger —which until recently had rested on top of the dragon's personal hoard.

At least an hour, replied Ambereen as she snuffed out the white candle she had circled over the salt pile while singing hymns. She had no idea whether the hymns she'd selected were the correct ones to sanctify an object, but she imagined any holy vibes she could attach to the mirror and blade would help. She knew necromancers were condemned in the Bible and other holy writings, so it seemed natural to her that the man who was manipulating the long-dead of Warren and nearby towns would be weakened by adding the messages of hymns to any object used against him.

At the mention of time, she suddenly remembered the companion she had left fishing on the banks of Loch Raven. *Vernon! I need to let him know I'm okay.* Then, Ambereen frowned, and solemnly thought, *How long have I been with you? Minutes? Hours?*

Chameleon shook her head.

Days?

The dragon shook her head again. *Dragon-time moves differently than human-time,* explained Chameleon. *You have been gone for months of your time. By now, your cousins have collected your things, and someone else has been hired to work at the store where you framed art.*

Rather than question Chameleon about how the dragon knew so much about her life, Ambereen said, *You should have told me when we first met. I should have been able to make my own choice whether or not I wanted to give up so much of my life.* Another thought came to her, *Can I return to my old life when this business with the necromancer is finished?*

Chameleon shook her head. *You are part of our world now. Rather than stay here, you and I will set out to find a new place to reside. Once there, you can resume a human life if you desire.*

Though it had been a quiet life, Ambereen was sad to think her life in Maryland was over. Truth be told, she worked at a low-paying job and had little family and few friends. The idea of traveling to new places and discovering unimaginable wonders *was* appealing. She wondered if Chameleon felt the same.

Must you leave, too? Don't you want to remain with the Dragons of Loch Raven?

The dragon reached over, grabbed a golden arm cuff, and turned it around and around with her claws. *When I appeared to you, I made my choice. I must go where you go until one of us is no more.*

No more?

Lowering her scaly muzzle, Chameleon stared into Ambereen's eyes with an intensity that seemed to burn a hole in her retinas. *We are bonded until one of us dies. With any luck, that will not happen later today when we take on the necromancer.*

I hope you're right, replied Ambereen, suddenly aware of the reality of the danger they were about to face.

As do we all, said the deep voice of the leader of the colony. This served as a reminder to Ambereen that Chameleon and she were not alone in their conversation or the mission to kill a necromancer. For the necromancer's death seemed to be the only solution to the problem.

While we wait, began Ambereen, *would you tell me who built this dragon lair, who painted the murals, and who wove this stunning rug on which we rest?*

Chameleon scratched the side of her face, sighed, then started to explain how the colony's home was created. *First, I need to explain about the dwarves who live under the earth...*

M ore relaxed as she rode Chameleon now, Ambereen mentally went over their plan and checked off the items they had brought with them. The outcome would be more certain if she were a magic-wielder, but even a salesclerk from an arts and crafts store could hold a mirror. As for the necromancer's undead minions, the dragon promised to hold them off until Ambereen had thwarted their master. She smiled. She liked the word, *thwarted*. It sounded far less final than *eliminated*.

The undead have joined us, warned Chameleon. *I expect even more will gather and try to stop us. But a change in speed will give you more time to confront the necromancer.*

Ambereen pressed against the dragon's back and held more firmly onto her neck spikes.

There, thought the dragon, *near the entrance to that old building is the necromancer.*

Lifting her head, Ambereen saw a balding, middle-aged man dressed in black clothing standing before a rundown house. Both of his hands were raised slightly, and he was chanting loudly. Had the situation not been so serious, she would have laughed because he looked less like a threat and more like a bad actor in an amateur video. That is, until the undead started to crawl onto the shore and surround their master.

Can you get me safely to him? Ambereen asked as the animated skeletons, facing outward, encircled the necromancer. She noted that some of their number held weapons in their fleshless hands.

I will handle the undead. You be ready to deal with the necromancer, replied Chameleon. *Remember, by the laws of my colony, I cannot kill or harm a human. So the man must be stopped by you. But do not fear—if you fail, I am allowed to rescue you.*

Let's hope it doesn't come to that, replied Ambereen as she drew the salt-purified, hymn-blessed mirror from the bag slung across her shoulder. Next, she pulled the jewel-encrusted dagger which they had also purified and blessed from her satchel. She placed the knife between her teeth. Lastly, the moment the dragon and she burst from the water, she grabbed a handful of salt mixed with sage, rosemary, and other smudging herbs and tossed it into the eyes of the necromancer.

The man howled an unearthly howl which chilled Ambereen to the bone and sent his minions into a frenzied attack on the dragon. This man was truly evil. The grain of pity she'd had for the necromancer vanished when she saw the soulless being who stared out of his eyes. The creature before her made no attempt to hide the fact he demanded the death of the dragon, Ambereen, and anyone else who dared to cross him.

He closed his eyes, raised both hands, and shouted a garbled string of syllables. Though Ambereen understood none of what the necromancer said, the waters of Loch Raven did. They bubbled like a pot left to boil.

After glancing at the churning lake surface, the man clapped three times and uttered another string of words. The wind responded. It whipped Ambereen's hair across her face and shoved her toward the water's edge.

Tossing salt again will be difficult. She pressed her lips together. She knew salt was an important part of their plan.

Make a new plan, thought Chameleon.

As Ambereen re-evaluated their strategy, the necromancer mumbled another jumble of sounds. Lip curled in a distorted smile, he pointed at the ground.

The rocky shore heaved as if a small earthquake were directly below them. Ambereen struggled to keep upright. She wondered if the dragon was having trouble standing, too.

The changes in the environment agitated the undead. They attacked Chameleon with even greater ferocity. Some of them glowered at Ambereen. Clacking their remaining teeth, they pointed at her then flexed their fingers.

The necromancer chuckled at her distress. Satisfied the undead would deal with Chameleon, he raised his hands once more and turned his full attention to Ambereen. Heart beating faster than the wings of a songbird, she held up the mirror. In fairy tales and fantasy stories alike, a mirror reflected the curses and spells of a sorceress or wizard back upon the spellcaster. Chameleon and she hoped it worked on necromancers, too.

Behind her, Ambereen heard the crunch of bones as the dragon did her best to hold off the throngs of undead. But she also heard the scrape of blades against scales.

Are you okay? she asked.

For now, but you must hurry, came the reply. *The undead are many. As soon as I tear them apart, they reassemble and attack again. They will overcome me eventually.*

Frightened for Chameleon, Ambereen dared a quick peek at the necromancer. Face distorted with rage, the man continued to screech the darkest, most foul curses imaginable.

A sizzling sound made her glance down. She saw the scruffy grass which had been growing on the shore at her feet wither, then burst into flames. The scent of burnt hair hung in the air. She dared not turn the mirror around to check, but Ambereen was sure the ends of her hair had also been singed.

It is only hair. It will grow back, Chameleon assured her. *But your hair won't matter if the necromancer wins.*

Suddenly, a swarm of beetles surrounded Ambereen. Clicking their mandibles, they crept up her shoes and onto her pants. She longed to use both hands to brush the insects off before they crawled any higher.

Ignore them. Focus on holding the mirror steady.

She couldn't be certain, but Ambereen thought she heard worry in the dragon's voice.

Locking her hands together on the mirror's handle, she pushed it closer to the necromancer.

He wailed. Then, the man screeched another series of spells. But the mirror reflected the magic: *His* skin and lips cracked. *His* eyes wept blood. *His* tongue blackened.

When the chanting paused, Ambereen lowered the mirror slightly. It was clear the necromancer had been weakened by his own curses.

This is my chance, she thought. She stepped close enough that the wind couldn't snatch the herb-laced salt and misdirect it. Grabbing a handful, she tossed the salt into the necromancer's eyes.

Wailing like a madman, he grabbed his face.

With his eyes momentarily covered and his curses silent for a split-second, Ambereen took the dagger from between her teeth and plunged it into the necromancer's chest about where she thought his heart might be.

She screamed as a jolt of pain shot up her arm. Ambereen's fingers tingled as if she'd touched an electric fence.

He dropped his hands. Mouth gaping, the man tilted his head to look at her. Whatever he meant to say next stayed in his throat. Ambereen watched as the gleam behind his eyes dimmed, then darkened, and the necromancer crumbled to the ground. She dumped the last of the blessed salt onto the body of the dead necromancer. Finally, she withdrew the dragon's dagger from his chest.

Then, Ambereen wheeled around as behind her, she heard the bones of the undead clattering to the rock-strewn shore. Without their master to give them life, the skeletons instantly became heaps of jumbled bones.

"Chameleon!" she exclaimed when she saw the dragon was barely able to stand. Her scales were marred with blood and upon her muzzle there was a gaping wound. Without being told, she knew her dragon couldn't swim back to her kind for help.

We have rid Loch Raven of the necromancer, thought Ambereen. *But we need help. Chameleon...wait, that's not her real name. Your dragon, my friend, cannot make it back to the colony without...*

Hush, young one, a deep voice spoke in her mind. *We will be there soon.*

As they waited for rescue, Ambereen wrapped her arms around Chameleon's neck and cried—her tears falling upon the scales of the dragon. By the time she realized much of the colony stood beside them on the shore of Loch Raven, the dragon colony had witnessed the bond between Ambereen and her dragon.

Carry the bones of the humans back to the graveyards beneath the lake where they came from, ordered the head dragon. *As for the necromancer, his remains must be burned, then scattered below the second dam.*

I will see to the necromancer, said a high, nasally voice.

Child, climb onto my back, said the chief dragon to Ambereen in his lovely bass voice. *I will take both you and your dragon back to our cave. And weep no more. She will heal in time. Then, both of you will sail to a new home and new adventures.*

Wait, said Chameleon as she pressed her cheek to Ambereen's, *let me tell you my true name.* And there on the bone-littered shore of Loch Raven, the injured dragon whispered the most precious gift she could give to a human into Ambereen's ear.

SALAMANDER

"**D**emon-spawn," said Widow Esenwine as she pointed at a salamander crawling from a Daghini Manor fireplace. "Born of fire and poisonous to boot."

"It looks harmless," said Kenway.

"Slaughter the slimy beast, then get its body out of here," snapped the cook, "or I'll take a switch to you." Assuming the kitchen boy would obey her orders, she stalked out of the kitchen.

But Kenway had not the heart for killing. He picked up two pieces of bark which had fallen from the logs stacked next to the hearth. Making shushing sounds, he gently scooped the soft-skinned creature up and carried it outside. If the cook found out what he'd done, he would be beaten. But he would willingly chance a hickory stick, rather than kill an innocent.

"If you know what's good for you, you'll stay away from the cook," he told the amphibian as he placed it in the leaf-litter beneath a thorn bush at the edge of the Manor's woodlands.

The salamander turned its tiny face, looked up at him, and opened its mouth as if to speak. Then, apparently reconsidering its decision to converse with a kitchen boy, it shook its head and crept under the leaves.

"Boy! Where are you?" called a shrill voice.

"Be well," Kenway told the salamander before he ran toward the Manor's kitchen.

The remainder of his day was filled with hard work. Kenway thought little of the salamander. As sundown neared, he was grateful all his tasks save one were completed. For tonight, he planned to visit his parents' graves. It was the anniversary of their deaths.

"Don't dawdle with the logs, boy," growled Widow Esenwine as he stacked the last load of firewood beside the kitchen hearth. "Lord and Lady Kasley are expecting last-minute dinner guests. I've got much to do—which means you have even more to do. I hope you didn't have plans, because you'll be working until the wee hours."

"I was supposed to go to my parents' graves to..."

The cook slapped his face, knocking him to the ground. "Stop complaining. Remember, you're supposed to obey me without backtalk. Show me disrespect again, and I'll have the Kasleys toss you out into the streets. Your parents are dead and gone. Now, you only answer to me."

Cheek stinging, Kenway stood and nodded.

"Take those buckets and fetch water," said Widow Esenwine. "Then, carry the meat platter to the dining room. And I'd better not catch you pilfering a slice. For your disobedience, I've decided you'll not receive supper."

Kenway did as he was told. Stomach already growling, he knew it would be a long night with an empty gullet. He also knew he had no choice but to accept the cook's cruel ways. The pallet in the Manor's barn was his bed, the scraps Widow Esenwine gave him were his vittles, and opportunities to change his circumstances were nil.

When Kenway returned to the kitchen, the cook was still in bad humor.

"Boy, get another ham from the smokehouse," she snarled with a smack to the back of his head. "Then, start scrubbing the pans."

Kenway hurried outside. The cook would be counting the minutes until he returned. He knew no matter how quickly he retrieved the cured meat, Widow Esenwine would be displeased. He rubbed his throbbing head and thought of his parents, victims of the fire that swept through the poorer area of Daghini last summer. "I wish I had a full belly and a place to live where someone cared about me," he whispered.

"That can be arranged," said a voice from the forest behind the smokehouse.

"Who's there?" Kenway suspected a thief or worse had crept up to Daghini Manor. He considered reaching for the dagger he kept secreted in his boot.

"I'm a distant cousin of the salamander you saved this morning," came the reply as a dragon stepped from between two trees.

Unable to speak, he studied the towering beast. Like the salamander, golden stars were scattered across its black as soot body. Unlike the dull-eyed salamander, no whitish fluid oozed from the dragon's skin. Instead, the last rays of the sun glinted off its obsidian scales and flickered in its eyes like flames.

"You showed mercy to the salamander," explained the dragon, "so I will repay your kindness with—"

Before the beast could finish speaking, Widow Esenwine said, "There you are, kitchen boy," as she slapped Kenway from behind.

"Enough!" roared the dragon.

"Stay out of this devil-beast," answered the cook, "and return to your den." She spat at the dragon before raising her butcher knife like a sword. "Or Daghini Manor will have dragon for dinner."

"Move, Kenway," said the dragon in a voice as calm as stacked kindling before a torch sets it aflame.

Kenway ran from the cook who screamed, "Get your things. There's no home for you here any more, boy."

As he watched, Widow Esenwine turned toward the dragon. Brandishing her knife with deadly skill, the burly woman lunged forward. "As for you, beast—"

The dragon exhaled a cloud of fire.

Unable to tear his eyes away from the conflagration which had been the cook, Kenway pitied the widow. *Perhaps*, he thought, *she had a hard life and knew no kindness, so she could show none to others.*

"It is a generous thought on your part," rumbled the dragon as he kicked the ashes at his feet, "but that woman incinerated dozens of salamanders for the joy of it. Widow Esenwine assumed I belonged to the Cave Dwellers clan. Unfortunately for her, I am a member of the Fire Breathers."

"Still, I'm sorry," said Kenway.

"It is not your fault or concern," replied the dragon. "Now, you must do as she ordered—retrieve your possessions. Then, I will take you to an elderly magic-wielder who needs a lad like yourself for an assistant."

With thoughts of wizards, dragons, and salamanders burning through his mind like shooting stars on a summer's night, Kenway did as the dragon asked. When he raced back to the tree line carrying the few things which were truly his, he asked, "Is there any way we can stop by my parents' graves, so I may say goodbye?"

The dragon grinned. "Who's to stop us?" he asked. Swift as a wildfire, he scooped up Kenway, set him upon his back, and with a flap of his wings, soared into the sunset-reddened sky.

MAGIC

Trees had spirits. As did waterfalls, fjords, and even the land itself.

Which was why Oddvar was told to be careful when selecting wood for carving the dragon heads and tails to be mounted on the stems and sterns of his village's longboats. One *had* to be careful. Humans weren't the only beings living in the forests, waterways, and caverns.

Tomorrow, he'd be going into the wilds alone to find the wood for the next dragon head to be carved. His thoughts jumped from one otherworld creature to the next, wondering if he'd encounter any of them on his wanderings.

"Where are you, Oddvar?" asked Farfar Tor as he nudged his grandson with his elbow.

"I'm here," answered Oddvar with a smile. He paused a second to clear the cobwebs from his mind before continuing. "I was thinking about the soul of the ship we're working on. Wondering where the gnome who guards this longboat hides when we're onboard."

"One doesn't need to see the otherworld folk to know they're here," replied his grandfather. "When the tree used for the keel was cut, the ship-spirit emerged from the tree. Then, he came with the timber to the shipyard. Now, he's somewhere on the boat keeping the timbers clear of rot and woodworms. But if we should fail to properly construct and attach the figurehead, I dare say he'll make an angry appearance."

Farfar Tor raised his bushy brows, pulled his lips down, and glanced sideways at Oddvar.

Oddvar laughed at his grandfather's grimace before rubbing the last of the oil into the carving of a fearsome drake which graced the bow of the boat. When whittled from a blessed tree and well-shaped, the carving would scare away enemies and ward off evil spirits on both land and sea.

No other local woodcarvers could guarantee this protection. Only Oddvar's family, because Farfar Tor like his father and grandfather before him, knew how to imbue timber with the magic of dragons. The trick, which their family kept secret, was to boil a dragon scale in the oil used for polishing figureheads.

"I think the iron curls we inserted into the wood add a regalness to the drake," said Farfar Tor as he caressed the arched neck of the dragon.

"And they provide protection for ship and crew from sea serpents, merrow, and kraken when they journey across the waters," added Oddvar. "Just like our trollkors." He touched the iron troll cross hanging from a leather cord around his neck.

"Iron works most of the time," agreed his grandfather, "but be cautious nevertheless when wandering in the forest. Some creatures of the otherworld won't be detered by a trollkor alone."

"You don't have to worry, Farfar Tor," he boasted as they climbed off the longboat, "I'm always careful."

His grandfather answered him with a shake of his head as they hiked back to their house.

~

After feeding and watering the livestock, Oddvar and Farfar Tor locked the barn then entered their stone, wood, and wattle-and-daub home. The fire crackling in the central hearth took the bite off the evening air. Though the days were still bright, the nighttime chill indicated autumn's first frost was near.

Oddvar sighed. It was always comforting to return home at the end of the day. He felt the tension in his shoulders vanish when he saw his grandmother's loomwork hanging at one end of the room and her preparing a meal at the other.

I'm lucky to live with Farfar Tor and Farmor Britt, he thought as the aromas of one of his grandmother's savory stews bubbling in a pot and fresh bread made his mouth water. When his mother died in childbirth and his father was killed in a raid across the sea a year later, Oddvar could have been given to another family, sold into servitude, or even left out for trolls to find. Instead, he was cherished by his grandparents.

"Another boat outfitted with a dragon head and tail," announced his grandfather as he stretched his arms above his head, yawned, then sat on one of the wooden beds running the length of each side of their home.

"I'm sure it looks fearsome indeed," said Farmor Britt before handing her husband a bowl of stew and a hunk of bread.

Oddvar's grandmother smiled at him. "Are you ready to whittle and mount the carvings by yourself yet?" she asked as she gave him his supper.

"I think so," he answered. "I'm going out tomorrow morning to look for a piece of wood from which to carve the next *dreki.*"

"But not alone!" exclaimed Farmor Britt.

"Yes, alone. If Oddvar is to someday run the business, he must do more on his own," insisted Farfar Tor. "Now, sit, woman. You need to eat, too."

~

The sun had not yet risen when Oddvar woke. His grandmother was already up preparing porridge, while his grandfather was carefully placing items into Oddvar's travel bag.

"I can do that," he said as he pulled on his boots.

"I know," replied his grandfather. "But now that packing is done, except for the ax, you'll have time to help me with the animals before you depart."

Oddvar grinned, slipped on his outerwear, and followed Farfar Tor to the barn. They filled the hay bins, milked the goats, collected a few eggs, then turned the livestock out in their pen—except for their horse, Stig. They left Stig in his stall with extra feed. Then, they attached the harness to the cart. By the time they returned to the house, Farmor Britt had sliced what remained of last night's bread and ladled steaming porridge into three bowls.

"You're wearing your trollkor and carrying a knife?" his grandmother asked after breakfast when Oddvar slipped his leather travel bag over his shoulder.

"Yes, Farmor Britt." He kissed his grandmother on the cheek. "We even tied a small trollkor onto Stig's halter and nailed one to the cart."

"Remember, mark your path as you hike so you can easily find your way home," said his grandfather. "And once you locate your tree, thank the guardian spirit before chopping it down and loading it onto the cart."

"I will."

"Stig won't wander, so free him from the harness and let him graze while you chop." His grandfather scratched his chin, then cleared his throat. "And make sure you're back before dusk. There's no sense tempting the otherworld folk."

"Tor," snapped his grandmother. "Don't frighten the boy."

"There are gasts, ghosts, and dark elves of all sorts out by dark. I'm just reminding him to be mindful of the time," replied his grandfather.

"I'll be back long before sundown," Oddvar assured his grandparents as he exited the door.

Stig raised his head and whinnied when Oddvar entered the barn. An even-tempered work horse, the gelding stood still while Oddvar secured him in the harness and attached a lead to his halter. After placing the ax and his travel bag in the cart, he gave a slight tug on the lead and Stig began walking beside him. They hiked north along the fjord's edge into more densely forested land.

To keep his spirits up and settle his racing pulse, Oddvar talked to Stig.

"We're sure to quickly find the perfect tree, and be home long before dark."

The work horse twitched his ears.

"I bet I won't even need my lunch."

Stig snorted.

"Still, I'm glad we are wearing trollkors." Oddvar touched the troll cross dangling on a cord around his neck. He smiled when he saw the talismans attached to Stig's halter and the cart.

The gelding nickered.

As they walked the flat lands near the water, Oddvar marked trees with his knife. The notches he cut were big enough he'd be able to see them on their return journey, but not large enough to damage the trunks. There was no sense in angering the Huldra.

Even thinking about the Wood Wife caused him to stare into the thickets on either side of the path. The Huldra could take the shape of a woman, tree, animal, moss-covered rock—even an old troll woman.

While scanning the forest, he spotted a stump about fifteen steps into the tangled vegetation.

"Whoa," said Oddvar. He went back to the sledge, rummaged around in his sack, and tore a piece of bread and a bite of cheese from his lunch. After again scanning the wildwood pressing close to the trail, he left the relative safety of horse and cart, and headed for the remnents of a felled tree.

"A small offering to the Huldra," he said as he placed the food upon the stump. "Thank you for allowing us to pass through your domain."

Rather than wait beside the stump, Oddvar backed away, grabbed Stig's lead, and resumed hiking. He'd only gone a few steps when he heard a branch snap behind them. Oddvar stopped and looked back at the stump. The food was gone. He swallowed the fear which rose up in his throat and resumed treading the forest path.

A half an hour later, as if the Huldra had read his mind and knew his purpose, Oddvar saw a sunbeam slice through the forest canopy and spotlight an oak tree. The oak had storm damage to its upper branches, but a perfect, undamaged, disease-free trunk of the circumference and length Oddvar was searching for.

"Perfect!" he exclaimed. "It's already been gifted by the Wood Wife and blessed by Thor—even before we carve protection runes into the oakwood."

As if agreeing with him, Stig nodded his head and stomped his right front hoof.

Oddvar released Stig from his harness,thus allowing the gelding to nibble on the underbrush. Next, he retrieved the ax, went to the spotlighted oak, and thanked its spirit. After chopping a deep notch on one side of the trunk, he began to chop vigorously on the other side of the oak. When the tree was ready to fall, he checked to make sure Stig was out of the way, then pushed against the trunk. With a series of snaps and groans the oak fell.

"Whew!" Oddvar wiped his brow with the back of his sleeve. Then, noticing Stig was wandering farther down the path, he carried the ax to the cart, grabbed his leather sack, and ran after the work horse.

Stig picked up his pace.

By the time Oddvar was able to catch up with the work horse, Stig had reached a small pond fed by a spring bubbling from between a pile of boulders. The gelding had lowered his head, and was drinking from the pool.

Suddenly wary, Oddvar held onto his trollkar with his left hand, pulled his knife from his belt with his right, and plunged the blade into the soil at the edge of the water to bind the Neck should he be near. He doubted the Neck would be looking to drown the careless in such a small body of water, but one could never be sure until they were dragged to the bottom. Rather, Oddvar thought this was just the sort of place inhabited by a spring guardian.

As if to confirm his guess, he spotted a large frog half-submerged in the middle of the pool.

"Thank you for allowing us to drink of your water," he told the frog before breaking off a bit of cheese and bread and placing them on a mossy spot by the edge of the water.

"A kind and wise gesture," said a voice from the shadows on the far side of the pool. "Do you have anything in your bag for me?"

Oddvar retrieved his dagger, then stepped back until he was pressed against Stig. He felt the horse quivering behind him.

"Who are you?" he called. He squinted his eyes. "I can't see you."

"Is this better?" said the voice as an enormous snake-like beast crawled out from the shaded roots of an oak tree.

Oddvar gasped. The lindwyrm, who must have been watching since Stig arrived, was now clearly visible as it slithered its huge body over stone, grass, and fallen trees. The beast's crown-like mane of white spines sprouted from its head, then ran down the length of its sinuous body. As Oddvar's eyes traced the path of the wyrm's pale, spiky mane, he noted it slowly grayed to nearly black by the time it reached the creature's tail. Having no wings and only two front legs, wyrms were thought of as lesser cousins of drakes and sea serpents. But now, standing before it, the lindwyrm was quite impressive.

"Yes," he managed to say to the wyrm, "I see you now."

"And what do you think, boy?" asked the reptile.

Oddvar chose his words carefully. "I think you're amazing. The green-gray pattern on your upper scales is more intricate than the finest dragon carvings my grandfather whittles. Your diamond-shaped scales shine like polished silver. Your eyes are redder than the sun as it slips below the horizon at dusk. I am honored to meet you."

The wyrm clacked its dangerously sharp claws upon the boulder on which its belly rested and seemed to consider Oddvar's response.

"I could swallow you both whole," stated the lindwyrm.

"I'd rather you didn't."

There must be a way out of this, thought Oddvar. *What can I offer the beast to save our lives? Or is there a way to kill it before the wyrm consumes Stig and me?*

"Unfortunately for you, boy," began the lindwyrm, "I haven't had a meal in days. So as much as I've enjoyed our conversation, I must eat you and your horse."

"Wait!"

The wyrm lowered its snakish head and gazed at Oddvar and Stig with burning eyes.

"We would both be more tender and taste better if we're smoked."

"Smoked?"

"Yes," responded Oddvar, trying to retrieve the details of killing a wyrm from his long-ago memories. He'd heard Farfar Tor tell the men working on a longboat with them when he was a child that there was a way to kill a lindwyrm. Of course, when questioned, his grandfather admitted no one he knew had ever tried, much less suceeded in, such a feat.

"Tell me about this smoking," said the wyrm leaning his bearded chin upon a paw.

"It's quite simple," explained Oddvar. "I'll build three bonfires beside the pond. Then, my horse and I will dash through them. By the time we've run through the third bonfire, we'll be smoked, flavorful, and tender."

"I suspect you'll try to run away." The lindwyrm ran its forked tongue around the rim of its mouth.

"Which is why you must follow directly behind us," he explained. "Then, it will be impossible for this boy and his work horse to escape your jaws."

The lindwyrm yawned, then scratched its belly. "I've never had smoked meat before, so I'm willing to give it a try." It yawned again. "But hurry, my stomach is grumbling."

Oddvar nodded. Certain the horse would bolt the first chance he got, he tied Stig to a tree. Next, he gathered three piles of wood being careful to pile sufficient kindling and tinder for lighting in the center of each pile.

"How much longer," asked the wyrm as poisonous drool dribbled out of its mouth and splattered the nearby vegetation.

Oddvar cringed as the affected plant life wilted, then shriveled to a pile of brownish mush.

"Not long," he answered as he took a piece of flint from his belt and knelt by the first heap of wood. He struck the flint with his knife until a spark caught. Then, he babied the flame. Soon, the bonfire was crackling. Once the first wood pile was burning brightly, he took a flaming stick from the fire and used it to light the two remaining heaps of wood.

He glanced at the lindwyrm. Its head still rested on a paw. It appeared to be mesmerized by the flames.

This just might work, Oddvar thought as he untied Stig, tossed the lead over his neck and knotted it to the other side of the horse's halter. Makeshift reins in place, he used a nearby rock to climb onto the gelding's back.

"Ready?" he asked the wyrm.

"Yes," it hissed—once again dribbling poison onto the ground.

"Come on, Stig," Oddvar urged the work horse as he gave Stig a nudge in the ribs. "I know you can do it."

The horse tossed his head back and forth, backed away from the first fire, and seemed to dance in place. Suddenly, perhaps because he saw the lindwyrm winding its way closer, Stig snorted and lunged forward. Unwilling to run through the bonfire, the gelding gathered his legs beneath him and jumped over the blaze.

"Run!" hollered Oddvar. He gave Stig another nudge in his ribs, but it was unnecessary. The work horse didn't slow his canter. Rather, he'd increased his pace. Without further encouragement, Stig raced to, then leapt over the remaining bonfires.

Oddvar tugged the reins, slowed Stig, and turned him around to face the oncoming lindwyrm. He was careful to keep his horse well back from the final fire.

Eyes blazing and jaws hanging open ready to consume Stig and him, the beast crept through the first two fires. Protected by thick scales, Oddvar doubted the wyrm felt the heat. Then, staring at its smoked dinner, the lindwyrm squirmed into the final bonfire. When the creature had crawled halfway through, it stopped—caught in the magic of which Farfar Tor had spoken.

Clear as the dragonish wail pouring from the lindwyrm's throat as it turned to ash, in his mind Oddvar heard his grandfather's words, "To kill a lindwyrm, you must trick it into crawling through three bonfires. But stay back—or the wyrm will drag you into the third fire as it dies."

Hungry and exhausted, Oddvar slipped from Stig's back. He patted the work horse on his neck.

"I need what's left of my lunch, and I expect you need more water and to graze," he told the gelding.

Stig leaned down and pushed gently against him before trotting over to the pond. Oddvar followed, sat on a rock, and unwrapped bread, cheese, and a pouch full of dried berries. As he ate, he studied the surface of the pool. The frog was nowhere to be found and the food offering he'd left before the lindwyrm showed up was gone.

Maybe a wood mouse took it, he mused. But in his heart, he knew the spring's guardian had taken the bread and cheese.

When he was finished eating, Oddvar walked to the first bonfire, took a piece of blazing kindling, and went in search of the wyrm's home. Not twenty steps from the pond, there was a burrow beneath the roots of a gigantic oak. Knife in his right hand and torch in his left, he climbed into the lindwyrm's lair.

"Thank the gods," he whispered as the torchlight revealed a heap of gold. Coins, goblets, wrist cuffs, necklaces, and other items gleamed like sunlight on water. But even more valuable than the precious metal items were the piles of shed skin.

Long had Farfar Tor's family used dragon scales to imbue figureheads with magic. But his grandfather had warned Oddvar there were only three scales remaining from the hundreds his great-great-grandfather had collected when he'd stumbled on a treasure hoard near the edge of a fjord. Ignoring the gold, he'd gathered as many scales as he could before the drake returned to its nest. For magic is worth more than gold.

With magic a priority, Oddvar cut three huge swatches of lindwyrm skin with his knife, folded them up as compactly as possible, and stuffed them in his satchel. Only then did he grab handfuls of coins and drop them into the bag. When the bag was near overflowing, he picked out a beautiful necklace for Farmor Britt and slipped it in the top. After tying the satchel closed, he filled his pockets with additional gold coins and stepped out of the burrow.

Stig waited for him a short distance away. The gelding, who'd been munching on grass and swishing his tail, lifted his head and took several steps toward him when he spotted Oddvar. But the sky behind the horse was already darkening.

"We're never going to make it home before nightfall," he told the work horse.

Stig seemed unconcerned.

"I'm going to need to ride you again," he said. Using a rock for added height, he climbed onto Stig's back. He made a clucking sound, and the horse trotted back to the site where the cart and cut oak waited.

In the dimming light, Oddvar used his ax to chop off branches and shorten the length of the oak trunk until it was perfect for carving a figurehead. The only thing left to do was to load the oak onto the cart and secure it. He re-harnessed Stig, making sure the gelding's trollkor was still attached to his halter. Next, he had the horse pull the cart into position beside the oak log. Then, he contemplated the best way to maneuver the log onto the cart. So focused was he on the task at hand, Oddvar didn't hear the trolls until one of them spoke.

"We could lift that for you," offered someone behind Oddvar.

He spun around and found himself face to face with three trolls. Two were males. Both of them were bald with low foreheads, tiny eyes, and over-sized mouths, ears, and noses. The third was an ancient troll woman. Slightly humpbacked, she had stringy hair and carried a walking stick.

"My sons could lift that log onto the cart for you," said the troll woman.

As she spoke, Oddvar recognized her voice. He realized she'd been the one to offer assistance initially.

"I'd be grateful for your help," he responded. "I can offer you payment, or if it is more acceptable, gift you with valuables for your help."

Her sons, standing like two hulking bears on either side of her, the troll woman wrapped all eight of her thick fingers around her walking stick and took a few steps forward. She studied him with her black eyes. Moments later, a gap-toothed smile spread across her face.

"What can a youngling like you offer us?' she asked.

"The location of a lindwyrm's nest filled with gold and shed skin," he replied.

"We've no intention of tangling with a wyrm. Their poison is deadly."

"You don't have to," responded Oddvar. "I killed the wyrm. Its treasure trove is there for the taking."

"What proof do you have that you killed a lindwyrm?" asked the troll woman.

Again, he thought before responding. *If I show them what's in my bag, they'll likely take it all. If I empty a pocket, they'll believe me, but I'll still have something to take home.*

"I grabbed what I could, but I was afraid to linger in the forest any longer," said Oddvar pulling a handful of coins from his pocket.

The trolls leaned forward.

"He's telling the truth," mumbled one of the troll brothers.

"Mm-hmm," agreed his sibling.

"We're not hoarders of gold, but it would be useful for

trading," said the troll woman. "As for the lindwyrm skin, that *does* have value in trolldom."

When she'd finished speaking, she pointed at the oak log, then snapped her fingers. Obedient as hounds, her sons each grasped an end of the log and placed it on the cart.

"It's nearly dusk. Night creatures will be out soon. You'll never make it home in one piece," warned the troll woman. She tilted her head, then added, "But for the gold you have in your pockets, we'll escort you home."

"I'd be grateful for your company," responded Oddvar with a bow. "I'll give you the coins in my pockets when we're in front of my grandparents' house."

"While we walk," said the troll woman, "you must tell me how you killed the lindwyrm. It seems a task too great for a youngling."

Knowing better than to argue with a troll, Oddvar didn't challenge her classifying him as a *youngling*. Instead, he told her in great detail, with embellishments here and there, about his defeat of the wyrm as they followed the tree notches he'd made earlier in the day southward.

Her sons soon tired of the slow pace.

"Can't we unhitch the beast and pull the cart ourselves?" asked one brother.

"We'll be back at the human settlement three times faster," said his sibling.

"As you wish." Their mother waved her large trollish hand. Then, she stopped walking and stared at Oddvar. "Get on your pony, so you can keep up."

"If you think that's best," he replied.

Before he could find a rock or stump to help him climb onto Stig, the troll woman picked Oddvar up and placed him on the work horse's back.

"Now, I can look you in the eye while we're speaking without bending down, youngling," she said. All three trolls laughed.

Again, rather than argue with her about his age or lack of trollish height, Oddvar forced a pleasant expression and tolerated the trolls' humor. When the trio stopped their laughter, he asked, "Would you tell me about trolls?"

The troll woman pushed her hair behind her pointed ears, nodded, then began, "Trolls have been here longer than humans..."

Though he heard occasional moans and growls on either side of the trail on the rest of the trip home, Oddvar felt no fear. Instead, he listened to the troll woman tell of trolls, giants, elves, and more otherworldly creatures. When she finally stopped speaking, he glanced around and found he was home.

"Slip down from the pony and hitch him to the cart," said the troll woman. "We're not going any closer to your house and grandparents."

After doing as she asked, Oddvar emptied his pockets of coins by giving them, a handful at a time, to the troll brothers.

"Go back to the lindwyrm's lair. Gather the treasure and wyrm skins," the troll woman directed her sons. "I'll join you shortly."

Once the brothers had lumbered away, she turned to Oddvar.

"Before you leave," she began, "you should know your troll cross only stops us from stealing you or any of your possessions which also bear trollkors. We can still harm you."

"But I thought—"

She held up a four-fingered hand to stop his objections, then continued, "The iron from which your trollkors are made will protect you from some magical folk and creatures, but not all."

"Like the lindwyrm," said Oddvar. He shivered, recalling how close he'd come to being the dragonish creature's dinner.

The troll woman nodded. "Dragons and their kin aren't held

at bay by iron. But used correctly, the wyrm skin hidden in your bag will prove quite useful in protection."

He gaped at her. Suddenly afraid she'd take the lindwyrm's skin and remaining treasure from him, he stepped away from her.

"Not to worry, youngling," the troll woman assured him. "Your honesty and good nature have served you well. We were watching you before you'd even killed the wyrm and witnessed your efforts to honor the nature spirits. You'll be allowed to keep your part of the plunder."

"Thank you." He felt his heartbeats return to a more normal pace.

"But do not share the details of our encounter with anyone— including your grandparents," the troll woman warned. "Most magical folk prefer to keep interactions with humans private, and become quite annoyed if their privacy is not honored."

"No one shall know of our meeting," promised Oddvar. He'd share the rest of the day's experiences with Farfar Tor and Farmor Britt but leave out the trolls.

"As to the magic of the wyrm skin..." The troll stared into his eyes with such intensity, he felt like she was looking into his soul. "Before you do anything else, cut a small piece from the skin, then boil it in water. Next, drink the water. Once it's gone, do your best to consume the now softened lindwyrm skin. You'll be blessed with future-seeing skills, good health, long life, and most importantly, no dragon or any other creature of magic will harm you."

"Will it work for my grandfather and grandmother as well?"

She shook her head. "This magic is yours to claim, not theirs, for they didn't kill the beast."

Then, the troll glanced at the nearly forgotten oak log. "Whittle a marvelous dragon head, use the wyrm skin to give it magic, and mount the figurehead upon the bow of one of your village's longboats." She reached out, touched Oddvar's brow with her forefinger, then continued, "But I've seen your future. You're not destined to carve dragon heads for the rest of your life, or sail on a dragonship. Instead, you're destined to sail with dragons."

Before he could question the troll woman about her prediction, she turned and strode away.

With thoughts of dragon wings thrumming in his head, Oddvar took Stig's lead and walked beside the tired horse up the path toward his grandparents' barn.

"You hear that? I'm going to meet a dragon," he whispered.

The work horse stopped, turned his head, and gazed down at Oddvar. As if the gelding understood the implications of every action taken and word uttered today, Stig winked then nudged Oddvar with his velvety nose.

"I should give you a sip of lindwyrm water and a bite of its flesh," said Oddvar as he laid the palm of his hand on the horse's shoulder. "You've earned a swallow of magic, too."

The work horse whinnied and nodded his head.

As Oddvar, Stig, and the cart carrying the wood for the next dragon head neared the barn, Farfar Tor and Farmor Britt ran out of the house.

All of a sudden, an icy gust whistled through the evergreens. The cold wind scattered needles, whipped Stig's mane, tugged at Oddvar's hair, and murmured in a voice no louder than a sigh, "Magic."

"We were so worried," called Farmor Britt as she neared Oddvar. She stretched her arms out.

Farfar Tor put a hand on his wife's shoulder. "Today, he's proved himself a man. Perhaps, he's too old for grandmotherly embraces."

"Never," said Oddvar. He stepped to his grandmother and gave her a hug. "I'm not sure if I am a man yet, or still a youngling." He paused and thought of the trolls. "In either case, I found more than a blessed oak tree in the forest."

Oddvar retrieved his bag from the cart and opened it. First, he handed Farmor Britt the necklace from the lindwyrm's lair. Then, he placed one of the wyrm skins into his grandfather's hands.

"Now, we will never run out of dragon magic."

"How did you come by this?" asked Farfar Tor. His bushy eyebrows came together as he examined the skin.

"There's much to tell," replied Oddvar, "but Stig needs food and water. As do I."

"Oh, my. I'll warm up your dinner, while you put the horse away," said Farmor Britt. Still clutching the finely-wrought necklace in her hand, she hurried toward the house.

He turned to his grandfather. "It was your stories that saved us."

Farfar Tor patted Oddvar's shoulder. "I suspect it was you, not my tales that did the saving. Let's tend to Stig. Then, you must share today's adventure with your grandmother and me."

His grandfather released the work horse from his harness, grabbed Stig's halter, and led the gelding toward the barn.

Again, the wind slipped from the forest. This time, it whispered, "Dragons."

Oddvar surveyed a stand of trees to the north before following Farfar Tor. He saw no one.

Just before he strode into the barn, the wind spoke for the third time, "Magic and dragons await you."

First, the troll woman's words. Next, the wind. Oddvar didn't need additional confirmation. No matter how improbable sailing with dragons seemed, he was certain it would happen.

DRAGON RAIN

S*afety,* thought Voruntil, Beloved of Nyzenth, as she
spotted a cave opening at the base of a rocky outcrop.
She scanned the horizon. The stars had already faded and
the pale apricot of sunrise tinted the edge of the sky. She and her
wyrmlings needed to find shelter before daylight revealed their
presence to humankind.

"You've had a drink, now it's time for sleep," she told her
brood as she corralled them into the cavern which would serve as
today's sleeping quarters.

"Supper?" asked several wyrmlings.

"Not this morning." Voruntil stroked the necks of her
offspring. "But tonight after sunset, I'll find breakfast."

This seemed to satisfy her brood. With scraping of belly
plates, scritching of claws, and rustling of wings, the ten
juveniles settled into a scaly heap around Voruntil.

"Tell us a bedtime story," asked Nukai, the runt of the clutch.
"One about the Long Ago."

"I will tell a story, if *everyone* promises to go to sleep when I'm
done," said Voruntil.

A chorus of "Yes, we promise," erupted from her wyrmlings.

Voruntil reviewed the distance they'd covered last night. Even on fresh mounts, the men who'd slain her beloved Nyzenth wouldn't catch up with them until late tonight. Voruntil smiled. There was ample time for sleep and story. Leaning her muzzle down, she started retelling the history of dragonkind.

"In the Long Ago, dragons ruled the world," began Voruntil. "Our reign began two-hundred-and-forty million years ago. Maybe more."

Her wyrmlings snuggled close, lifted their scaly chins, and with eyes fixed on Voruntil's face, listened to their mother's storytelling.

"The Earth was wetter in the Long Ago, with shallow oceans where deserts and plains are today. The world was newer, less spoiled, as warm as summer sun on your belly, and filled with dragons."

"Tell us about the different kinds," urged Ombin. He pushed closer to Voruntil. *He's the spitting image of his father,* she mused. She sighed. Even a passing thought of Nyzenth brought back the pain of his recent death.

"As you wish, son." Voruntil patted Ombin's crested head with her paw. "There were dragons who rode the air currents on great leathery wings. They filled the skies with their lovely shrieks and dove down to the ground faster than the wind to catch their prey. Dinner in foot, they'd flap to their nests far up on the cliff tops where they surveyed the dragon empire spreading out to the horizon. There, they'd thank Gralba, the Great Mother, for this blessed planet, and the prey creatures for their gift of life."

She studied each wyrmling's face before adding, "The wings of the flying dragons were wider than the wings of any of today's birds. When the dragons moved them up and down to soar from one place to another, it sounded like thunder. In the Long Ago, lesser creatures would scurry to their hiding places and peek out to admire the kings and queens of the heavens."

"Tell about the water dragons," said Nukai. Not one to be outdone by her clutch-mates, she stretched her neck above the rest of the wyrmlings and fluttered her undersized wings.

"Patience, Nukai," said Voruntil. She itched her daughter's forehead between her ears with an obsidian claw. Smallest of the clutch, Nukai often demanded notice.

But she's strong for her size, mused Voruntil before continuing.

"In the Long Ago, the oceans were brimming with shellfish, a wonderful assortment of fishes, and other good things to eat. With food so plentiful, the oceans were also filled with dragons. The sea dragons were enormous. Even so, their huge, muscular bodies floated easily in the oceans of two-hundred million years ago. Wingless, the water dragons propelled themselves through the waters with strong tails and mighty feet. And in today's world, there still exist miniature versions of those Long Ago water dragons."

"But there are no flying dragons anymore," said Ombin sadly.

"No, son, not like the sky dragons of the Long Ago," agreed Voruntil. "But little ones, once your wings have grown, you *will* be able to fly short distances."

Her statement was met with growls and snorts of excitement.

"Lastly, there were land dragons," said Voruntil.

"Like us," added Ombin.

"Like us," agreed Voruntil.

The wyrmlings gleefully yelped and flapped their tiny wings.

"In the Long Ago, there were plant-eating dragons with necks long enough to reach the leaves on the treetops," Voruntil told her clutch.

"They never ate prey?" said Nukai.

"Never," replied Voruntil.

She let the strangeness of plant-eating dragons sink in. The brows of her children were furrowed like windblown sand. She knew they craved fresh meat, not vegetation.

"Alas, their dependence on plants would lead to their demise," stated Voruntil. "But I'm getting ahead of myself. Where was I?"

"You were telling us about the land dragons," said Ombin.

"So I was." Again, Voruntil scratched each wyrmling's neck.

"Dragons with armored collars walked the lands as well as dragons with bony heads hard as rock." She rapped a stalactite hanging down from the cave's ceiling for emphasis.

Her children grinned.

"There were dragons with one, two, or three horns sprouting from their heads who wandered the great plains and sweltering swamps of the Long Ago." Voruntil noticed several wyrmling's eyelids were partially lowered. Her lips curled upward.

"There were dragons covered in armor and dragons with spikes marching down their spines like great, wide teeth." She pulled her lips back to reveal her teeth.

Two of her children didn't see her toothy storytelling antics. They were already asleep.

She continued, "Some of the land dragons walked on two feet and some on four. Some laid eggs in nests, while other dragons gave birth to live wyrmlings. And all of them honored Gralba, the Great Mother, and the prey creatures."

"Just like we do every day and when we take life," said Nukai. Her clutch-mates that were still awake nodded their muzzles in agreement.

"Yes. It is important to honor Gralba, as well as those whose lives we must end in order to live." Voruntil scratched the eye ridges of each of her ten offspring, even the three who were sleeping, before continuing.

"Thus, as rulers of Earth, the blessed children of Gralba thrived for eons until The Darkness arrived."

The wyrmlings who were still awake pressed closer. She could see fear in their bright, sun-illumined eyes as they listened to the details of the turning point in the history of dragonkind.

"Heavy with evil, sixty-six million years ago The Darkness rushed between stars. It raced past the moon and crashed into Earth sending dust, dirt, and tiny rocks into the atmosphere. The strength of its impact wounded the planet, so Earth's scorching blood burst from her skin with loud rumbles and explosions beyond imagining."

The wyrmlings gasped.

Voruntil lowered her voice. "The steam and ash from those explosions added to The Darkness until most of the planet's life succumbed to foul air, sunless days, food-less nights, and bitter temperatures. Without enough sunshine and warmth, the plants soon withered and died. The first dragons to perish were those who survived on plant life. Then, the dragons who consumed plant-eaters could find no food, and they died. The dragons who remained consumed one another rather than starve, but there was still insufficient food."

She opened her wings and spread them like a leathery blanket over her brood. "It was then the dragons died—except for a few who took refuge in the oceans and deep caves in the still tepid parts of the world. But all was not lost. Our smaller cousins lucky enough to live in those warmer climes survived as well. In this way, the reign of dragonkind ended. The Age of Dragons lasted more than one-hundred-and-eighty million years. And though we are Gralba, the Great Mother's chosen ones, even she couldn't save us from The Darkness."

Now, only Nukai and Ombin weren't asleep. They gazed at her from beneath half-lowered eyelids.

"Now, humankind gathers the bones of dragons from where they were buried beneath the ash, mud, and pebbles of the Long Ago. They gather the dragon bones, raise them up in awe, store them in sacred places, and tell stories of the fantastic dragons of the Long Ago."

"Then, why do they hunt and kill us?" asked Ombin.

"Because humans, who've only been here for three-hundred thousand years, fear that which they don't understand. It is a flaw in their nature," observed Voruntil as first Nukai, then Ombin finally closed their eyes.

Silence filled the grotto where Voruntil and her children hid. As she gazed down on her wyrmlings, her heart ached. With her mate murdered, Voruntil would produce no more eggs unless she found a new partner. Her throat tightened. She realized this was likely her final clutch. And there was no doubting her mate, Nyzenth's death. She'd seen his wounded body decapitated.

Beheaded so a human king can hang a trophy in his throne room, she thought bitterly.

As for Nyzenth, like all the dragons before him, at his death he'd risen as a vaporous spirit. Before fleeing from the soldiers with her children, Voruntil had witnessed Nyzenth's misty essence depart his corpse like smoke rising from a dying fire.

It gave her some comfort to know at this moment above the crawl-way in which her children and she sheltered, her beloved mate hovered over his family in the day sky. Like his forefathers and foremothers, when Voruntil and her children's mouths were parched, Nyzenth would shed tears. Then, dragon rain would save them from thirst.

But lack of water was the least of Voruntil's problems.

The familiar history of dragonkind told in Voruntil's soothing voice had sent her wyrmlings into dreamland. While her brood slept, she needed to carefully plot the remainder of their land journey. It was her duty to get her children to the safety of the waterways, then to the seas and oceans beyond.

On day one, she'd fled the Tantali Mountains with their clutch while Nyzenth fought the dozens of Roman soldiers who came to slay a dragon. For the past four days, Voruntil had managed to locate various caves and hidey-holes in which to take haven during the sunlit hours. According to her calculations, tonight would be their final night to travel by land. She prayed to Gralba they'd reach the shores of the Seihan River by moon-down. Then, they'd begin the long swim to the Mediterranean Sea.

But she knew soldiers didn't quickly give up a prize as desirable as a dragon. After slaying Nyzenth and searching their Tantali cave, the men would soon locate footprints left by Voruntil and her children. There was little doubt, the soldiers would follow Voruntil's family's trail with murder in their hearts.

Though it was not dragonkind's way, fame and fortune among humans seemed a goal many of them deemed worthy of pursuing. Therefore, Voruntil believed she and her clutch were in imminent danger of losing their heads.

~

Voruntil managed to grab a few hours of sleep before moonrise. The stirrings of her wyrmlings woke her as twilight dimmed the patch of sky visible through the grotto's entrance. She was certain her children would soon be asking for food.

"Wake up, my babies. Time to find breakfast," said Voruntil. She stood, stretched her wings, refolded them against her back, and walked out of the cave into the night with her wyrmlings following. She was grateful the usually noisy youngsters were silent. Even at their age, they knew sound warned prey of a hunt.

Voruntil's ears twitched as she scanned the surrounding terrain with her night vision. Her shoulders relaxed when she spotted a flock of goats to the east of their location.

A food source found in the direction of the Seihan—what could be better? Perhaps we will successfully make our escape, she thought.

"Stay here," she told her children. "I'll fly to that field," she pointed to the east with a black claw, "and kill eleven goats. You may begin walking in that direction after counting to three hundred."

"What if there are men watching over the herd?" asked Nukai in a quavering voice.

"Let's hope the herders know it's safer to run from a hungry dragon than to confront one."

The wyrmlings' heads bobbed up and down in agreement.

Sure that her children would comply with her instructions, Voruntil leaped into the air and winged her way to the goats. She'd already killed six of the animals when the bleating of the frightened herd woke the man assigned the task of watching for predators. He rushed to the field where the terrified goats were racing around, saw Voruntil standing over a fresh kill, and backed away.

Wise man, thought Voruntil. *He decided no prey animal was worth dying for. Thus, he will live to see another sunrise.*

As her clutch arrived, Voruntil grabbed the eleventh goat with her front claws and quickly broke its neck. She saw no reason to prolong the suffering of panicked prey. She embraced the rule of Instant Death taught to her by her mother when Voruntil was a wyrmling. She hoped her brood would follow this compassionate practice as well.

"Thank the prey for their sacrifice, then eat, children," said Voruntil. "We cannot linger. I'm sure soon the goat herder will return with friends."

"Will we reach the river tonight?" asked Ombin between bites.

"Yes, but only if we hurry." What she did not add, though it was in her thoughts, was they were likely still being pursued by soldiers. Frightening her wyrmlings seemed counterproductive. Their focus must be stealthiness and speed.

~

After traveling for six hours, the wyrmlings begged to take a break in the shelter of a cluster of heavily-leafed trees. Voruntil decided the oasis was suitable for a rest stop. In addition to cover, it had a pool of water in its center, so the young dragons could quench their thirst.

She surveyed the landscape and listened for approaching humans. She neither saw nor heard anything worrisome.

"We will rest here briefly," Voruntil told her children. "Then, we push to the Seihan. Think how wonderful its chilly water will feel on your feet."

"Will we swim all day before sleeping?" asked Ombin before laying his head on his front legs.

"No." Voruntil studied her exhausted wyrmlings. "We'll swim until I spot a suitable hollow or hideaway to spend the sun-bright hours. There, we'll rest until dusk."

"We will never see Father again—will we?" Nukai gave voice to the question Voruntil knew all her children wanted to ask.

"No, we won't see him again in this life." Voruntil lowered her head slightly. "But we'll feel his love for us every time it rains. He'll shed tears to wash away the dirt and dust of our journeys. He'll shed tears to fill the watering holes and cool our heated brows. He'll shed tears to swell the Seihan, so we can escape to the Mediterranean Sea."

"Just like all the dragons from the Long Ago until today," added Ombin. "They all watch over us."

"Yes." Voruntil was pleased with Ombin's understanding of the ways of dragonkind. She hoped it was an indicator of the thoughts of his clutch-mates.

Suddenly, she swung her head in a westerly direction. She smelled horses and humans.

"Soldiers are near," Voruntil told her wyrmlings. "We must race with the speed of the dragons of the Long Ago to the river."

Her children got to their feet. Silenced by fear, they awaited her instructions.

"I will lead the way," she told them with as much calm as she could muster, "but you must keep up. If you notice anyone falling behind, let me know." Voruntil studied each of her children's precious faces. "I will try to protect you from harm, but the soldiers are determined—and they might be riding fresh horses."

Her brood nodded.

"We're going to make it," said Ombin with certainty. "Gralba will protect us."

His clutch-mates chimed in with words of agreement.

"Let us hope so." Voruntil pointed her head in the direction of the river. "Off we go," she said, and trotted eastward at a speed she felt her clutch could match.

The wyrmlings ran behind her. She heard them calling words of encouragement whenever one their siblings fell behind.

Voruntil smelled the scent of river water at about the same time she heard a man shout, "There they are!"

She ventured a glance at the flatlands behind her wyrmlings.

Mounted on a white horse was the man she'd heard called *George* when the soldiers were attacking Nyzenth. He wore armor and carried a spear. She'd witnessed his heartlessness, so there was no doubt in her mind he'd gleefully impale all her children if he was given a chance.

"Faster," she urged her ten offspring. "Look deep in your minds. Feel the strength of the Long Ago ancestors. Though we be few, we are still dragonkind."

Inspired by her speech, her clutch moved more rapidly.

Voruntil looked back at the soldiers once more. They were closer.

She recognized a second soldier. The other dragon-killers had called him *Theodore Tiro*. He rode a horse as black as his soul must be to murder a dragon guilty of nothing more than protecting his family. Beneath his helmet, Voruntil saw his hate-filled eyes staring at her. She knew Theodore Tiro longed to behead her and her wyrmlings with the metal sword strapped to his side.

"The Seihan isn't far, my children," she shouted as she swung her head forward once more.

"I see the river," yelled several clutch-mates. "We're going to make it!"

A sense of relief washed over Voruntil. She was going to fulfill the promise made to her beloved Nyzenth before he sacrificed himself to guarantee his family's escape from the Tantali Mountains.

"I've done it, Nyzenth. Our clutch will live, grow, find mates, and keep alive dragonkind," whispered Voruntil as she, too, spotted the green waters of the Seihan River flowing between several low-rising hills.

She peered behind her wyrmlings one last time. The soldiers had drawn even nearer. She recognized a third man. His battle-mates had called him *Demetrius of Thessaloniki*. Mounted on a red horse, Demetrius was in the lead. He yelped a blood-curdling scream before kicking his horse. Voruntil noted the stallion jumped forward—his hooves a blur.

Her eyes moved to the location of her two slowest children.

Nukai had dropped behind her clutch-mates. Legs shorter than her siblings, she was having trouble maintaining the pace set by Voruntil. By choice, it appeared, Ombin had slowed his pace to run beside his sister.

Voruntil's heart told her to swing around and face George, Theodore Tiro, Demetrius of Thessaloniki, and the rest of the soldiers. Such an action on her part would give all of her children a chance to reach the river. But if she made that choice, the ten wyrmlings wouldn't know where to go or how to survive the arduous journey to the sea—much less how and where to locate more dragons. Because she realized if Nyzenth, with his greater fighting skill, hadn't been able to defeat these men, she'd surely be killed by them and her orphaned wyrmlings would all soon die.

As much as it pained her, Voruntil knew she must listen to her brain. The sacrifice of Nukai so nine of her children could survive was the only choice. She studied her daughter's face one last time. Nukai's skin was the green of juniper trees with orange flecks specking her muzzle. Her eyes were the color of garnets and full of curiosity. Even racing for her life, Nukai's mouth curved pleasantly upward.

Voruntil would grieve for her daughter for the rest of her life. But a wise mother chooses the action, no matter how painful, which results in the greatest good.

Ombin, she mindspoke.

Mother? he replied.

Nukai cannot keep up. She won't reach the river before the soldiers overtake her.

I know, responded Ombin.

You must leave her, said Voruntil in her son's mind, *and join the rest of the clutch.*

No, replied Ombin. *I am Ombin, son of Nyzenth, and like my father before me, I will sacrifice myself to save my family.*

Before Voruntil could argue with her son, Ombin slowed his pace.

In her mind, Voruntil heard Ombin speak to his sister. *Nukai, run like your life depends on it. I will drop behind and face the men.*

No, Ombin, answered Nukai. *Let them have me.*

No, Nukai. You can raise many clutches of wyrmlings. I am male, and therefore, more expendable.

Then, Ombin spoke with a force which sent his voice into the minds of Voruntil and all of his siblings. *I will face the men. The rest of you must get to the river, swim to the sea, find other dragons, and raise another generation of dragonkind. Please, remember me.*

Ignoring the protests of his clutch-mates and Voruntil's wail, Ombin stopped running and turned to face the humans and their weapons.

Instantaneously, the moon was swallowed by clouds and the sky changed from star-strewn to solid black as generation upon generation of dragons gathered above the soldiers George, Theodore Tiro, Demetrius of Thessaloniki, and their comrades.

As one by one her children splashed into the Seihan, Voruntil stood on the riverbank and watched Ombin.

Mimicking his father's stand of a few days before, Ombin flailed his tail, swung his neck, snapped his teeth, and slashed at the soldiers with his claws. But his small size and inexperience made his efforts less effective than Nyzenth's had been. Ombin had only managed to kill one of the soldiers before George charged forward on his white stallion and impaled the wyrmling.

Dragon tears poured from the sky as Theodore Tiro and Demetrius of Thessaloniki rushed forward and slashed at Ombin. Soon, the rest of the men crowded around Voruntil's child and stabbed his lifeless body with their knives and spears.

When the cruel George raised a blade to decapitate Ombin, the thousands of dragon spirits who'd gathered above the self-sacrificing wyrmling roared. Their roar echoed across the land. Voruntil witnessed the murderers fall to their knees with their bloody hands pressed to their ears.

Then, midst the torrent of tears falling from the heavens, she saw Ombin's spirit lift from his headless carcass. Next, with their spirits glowing soft as moonlight, she observed Nyzenth and hundreds of long-gone kin embrace Ombin.

Voruntil tried to push the carnage she'd just witnessed to the back of her mind, and instead focus on the wonder of the dragon spirits welcoming her child.

Tears of her own slid down her snout as a misty Nyzenth, arm still wrapped around their son stared at her. She felt his love cross the barrier between them.

Leave before they notice you, she heard in her mind as clearly as if Nyzenth stood beside her. *Nine wyrmlings paddle southward. You must catch up with them, protect them, guide them to the sea and beyond.*

Yes, Beloved, Voruntil answered Nyzenth's spirit. *As long as I live, I will watch over our children.* Then, in the torrential rain, she slipped into the Seihan River and swam away from the wyrmling Ombin's dying place.

Voruntil and her children traveled down the Seihan and into the Mediterranean Sea without further incident. They searched the Mediterranean's inlets, islands, and sea caves until they found other dragons. When her brood matured and they were able to fly, Voruntil and her last clutch traveled to the Atlantic.

As decades turned to centuries, one by one, her children found mates and began their own families, but not before they discovered accounts written and artwork created by humans of the dragon encounters in the Tantali Mountains and on the shores of the Seihan.

Always, Nyzenth and Ombin were wrongly described as vicious beasts who consumed human flesh and wreaked destruction. The settings of their slayings as well as the year of their killings were changed. The physical appearance of father and son were altered. Voruntil's family members were even cast as servants of a creature more evil than The Darkness which had ended the Age of Dragons.

Worse still, George, Theodore Tiro, and Demetrius of Thessaloniki were treated as heroes and given sainthood. Countries and towns placed the images of the dragonslayers slaughtering Nyzenth and Ombin on their shields, crests, and logos. Sometimes, they showed one dragon. Sometimes, two. And sometimes, though Voruntil never quite understood why, the dragon portrayed had two heads.

Perhaps the most heart-wrenching image was the one carved in red stone on the facade of Basel Cathedral in Basel, Switzerland. The statues of George and Ombin had been designed to show the true difference in size between man and wyrmling. One twilight, as Voruntil perched on the cathedral's roof watching the people who'd come to see the carvings, she listened to what members of the crowd said.

"That dragon looks like a baby," observed a fair-haired woman holding her child. "What sort of man was Saint George to kill a little dragon?'

What sort of man indeed, thought Voruntil as she took to the night sky, vowing never again to visit the cities of humankind.

"I cannot leave you alone," Nukai said one morning as she and Voruntil sunned on a rock jutting into the North Sea.

Voruntil studied her daughter. Nukai had turned down many opportunities to begin her own family, choosing instead to keep her mother company.

"But I grow lonely for a mate and children of my own," said her daughter wistfully.

Voruntil placed her paw on top of Nukai's. "But I am never alone," she said. "When I close my eyes, I see your father, Ombin, and my parents waiting for me in the clouds."

"Really?" Nukai's brows ridges were raised.

"Yes," said Voruntil. "Gralba, the Great Mother, blessed me with a life-mate who valued me above all others, and clutch after clutch of wyrmlings. I have contributed to the survival of dragonkind, and now, I wish to join those who bring dragon rain to their children and grandchildren and great-grandchildren to the millionth generation."

As she gave voice to her wish, a sudden, fast-moving storm rolled in from the sea. Voruntil spotted the spirits of hundreds, perhaps thousands, of dragons riding the clouds. The towering cumulonimbus formations opened and dragon rain poured down. As the deluge of dragon tears pelted her face, Voruntil saw a misty Nyzenth sailing toward her.

"Beloved," he said in a voice like thunder.

"Go find your future," Voruntil shouted to her daughter. "Gralba calls me. It's my time to join the dragons above."

Before Nukai could speak, a lightning bolt shot from the clouds and struck Voruntil. Then, Voruntil felt herself grow thin as dreams as the wind swept her heavenward and into the arms of her beloved.

ACKNOWLEDGMENTS

Thanks to Dawn Schiavone Crist and Patti Kinlock for their friendship and invaluable critiquing, Maya Preisler for a wonderful cover, Alexandra Christian for insightful editing, Rie Sheridan Rose for careful proofreading, and Nicole Givens Kurtz and Mocha Memoirs Press for taking a chance on a book of dragon stories. Thank you to my friends and family for supporting my creative endeavors and patiently listening to me spin tales about creatures both mundane and magical. Lastly, a special thanks to Ernie for always being there.

ABOUT VONNIE WINSLOW CRIST

Born in the Year of the Dragon, Vonnie Winslow Crist, MS Professional Writing, has had a life-long interest in reading, writing, art, science fiction, myth, fairy tales, folklore, and legends. An award-winning author and illustrator, she is a member of the Science Fiction & Fantasy Writers of America, Horror Writers Association, Society of Children's Book Writers & Illustrators, and National League of American Pen Women. Her speculative stories and poems have been published in Italy, Spain, Finland, Germany, India, Australia, Japan, Canada, the UK, and USA.

A cloverhand who believes the world is still filled with mystery, magic, and miracles, she loves to hear from fans at conventions, conferences, and online. Visit her website at http://vonniewinslowcrist.com or connect with her on Facebook: http://facebook.com/WriterVonnieWinslowCrist

Made in the USA
Middletown, DE
29 April 2022